"You're supposed to be asleep."

Charles stood at the threshold of Lucas's bedroom.

"Know a good story, Charlie?" Lucas asked as Charles tucked the blanket around him.

How would a bachelor know a kid's bedtime story? "Uh, not really." He grabbed a book off the nightstand and sat in the rocker. He inadvertently looked up then and nearly fell out of the chair as his eyes lit on a dramatic mural of his brother Dean on the far wall.

It was a youthful, happy Dean with a glitter in his eye. The artist had captured his late brother's strength and humor. Charles couldn't stop staring, admiring, *feeling*.

"That's my daddy's picture," Lucas said as he climbed into Charles's lap. "You cryin'?"

"No, just got something in my eye."

"That mean you can't read to me?" Lucas looked at him with the same expression in his eyes as Dean's in the picture, and instantly he realized how much Dean must have loved the boy. Charles knew, because he suddenly found himself thinking how wonderful it would be to be his daddy.

He opened the book. "I can do it," he said, hugging the boy to his chest. "All night long."

ABOUT THE AUTHOR

Leandra Logan simply loves to write! She made her debut with young-adult romances then turned to adult romance. Nominated for many awards, she won the *Romantic Times* Reviewers' Choice Award for Best Harlequin Temptation. In her free time, Leandra speaks on the craft of writing at local schools in Minnesota, where she lives with her husband and two children. When asked what other interests she had, she was, for the first time, at a loss for words!

Books by Leandra Logan

HARLEQUIN AMERICAN ROMANCE
559—SECRET AGENT DAD
601—THE LAST BRIDESMAID

HARLEQUIN TEMPTATION
420—CUPID CONNECTION
462—DILLON AFTER DARK
493—THE LAST HONEST MAN
533—THE MISSING HEIR
572—JOYRIDE
591—HER FAVORITE HUSBAND
619—HAPPY BIRTHDAY, BABY
635—BARGAIN BASEMENT BABY
664—ANGEL BABY
711—HEAVEN-SENT HUSBAND
750—HOLD THAT GROOM
763—MY JINGLE BELL BABY

Father Figure

LEANDRA LOGAN

HARLEQUIN®

TORONTO • NEW YORK • LONDON
AMSTERDAM • PARIS • SYDNEY • HAMBURG
STOCKHOLM • ATHENS • TOKYO • MILAN • MADRID
PRAGUE • WARSAW • BUDAPEST • AUCKLAND

For Lois Greiman
A true friend and a talented writer.
You go, girl.

ISBN 0-373-16732-6

FATHER FIGURE

Copyright © 1998 by Mary Schultz

This edition published by arrangement with Harlequin Books S.A.

® and TM are trademarks of the publisher. Trademarks indicated with
® are registered in the United States Patent and Trademark Office, the
Canadian Trade Marks Office and in other countries.

Printed in U.S.A.

Chapter One

Hilton was still awake at this hour?

Charles Fraser paused in the huge dark foyer of their Connecticut family mansion, frowning at the light streaming from the old man's study.

Seemed strange, as it was common knowledge that his father retired by eleven on weeknights, unless distracted by company business. Being that Charles himself had just left Fraser Advertising in Manhattan, tucked in all cozy and hassle free, there seemed no cause for any dramatics.

Hilton had to be waiting for him, with a personal ax to grind.

There was no avoiding the issue, of course. Committing to the agency fresh out of college, staying on part-time in the family mansion, Charles was undeniably beholdin' until Hilton's retirement. With a fortifying sigh he gave his rumpled gray silk suit a tug, ran a hand through his clipped black hair, and marched into the lion's den.

Hilton, positioned behind his mahogany desk like a emerald-robed sentinel, did indeed have an agenda. Presumably he'd heard his son's key in the lock, his footsteps on the polished Italian tiles, for he was setting aside his book and folding his hands over his ink blotter.

Like his heir, Hilton was a trim, fit, broad-shouldered man; still handsome at fifty-eight, with a full head of salt-and-pepper hair and a sturdy chin. The rosy hue from the brass desk lamp did much to buffer the signs of age on his face, but did nothing to fade the fire in his intense brown eyes.

Charles greeted him dubiously as he sauntered to the desk. His manner clearly inferred this confrontation could've waited until breakfast. The lift of Hilton's chin silently suggested otherwise.

"Father?"

"Son..."

Charles shifted from one hand-sewn loafer to another, growing more uncomfortable as Hilton's features began to crumple. He hadn't seen such a revelation since his older brother Dean's death. It was tough to watch this steely, driven parent attempt to process complex emotions so foreign to him. Thankfully, Hilton was rarely stricken with a strong attack of any kind of feeling.

Hilton cleared his throat after a drawn out moment and gazed down at his folded hands with a studied look. Charles unconsciously crossed his arms in a protective gesture. A chip off the old block, he too had little interest in deep exploration of self.

"Seems I'm to be a grandfather, after all," Hilton blurted out brusquely. "Just like that! I'm finally in the club."

Charles's heart slammed against his rib cage. Who? When? Suzette in Paris last autumn? Trish in the Hamptons at New Year's? It was late May now, and his mind raced ahead, doing the calculations. He hadn't been intimate with anyone since breaking off with Trish.

Charles's dark eyes centered on the answer man seated before him. Why wasn't Hilton spilling the facts? Why, dammit!

Blinking rapidly, Hilton refused to meet his gaze. With dismay, Charles realized he was fending off tears!

Déjà vu. So like the night Charles had been summoned to this very room to learn of Dean's accident. Hilton had done his best not to crack, washing it all away with a fifth of smooth Kentucky bourbon. But there was no need for booze tonight to numb the system. This was good news to the old man. The very best. An impossible dream come true.

Charles vibrated with anger. Who'd pulled this sneaky stunt? Gone crying to his father about something so deeply personal? No one he'd ever want to see again—much less marry, as Hilton would undoubtedly expect.

The older man waved a hand at him, his glistening eyes holding traces of amusement. "It's not what you think. Not you at all."

A miracle rescue! Relief surged through Charles's system, until reality struck. "Then what are you getting at here? I am, after all, an only child these days."

"Dean—" Hilton still found it difficult to say his late son's name, a problem in place long before the young man's death. "Dean and that...girl."

"His wife?" Charles asked mildly.

"Yes!" Hilton growled. "She gave birth to a grandchild right before Dean's accident. A son!" He pounded the desk with lamp-rattling force. "How dare she not inform me? *Me!*"

How not indeed? Charles wondered cynically. Didn't this woman know she was dealing with Hilton Fraser, creator of Fraser Advertising, who religiously swayed billions of dollars each day with his clever ad campaigns, and was the number-one guru to the free world?

"Our link to the next generation!" Hilton bellowed. "He already walks the earth, breathes the air."

And was probably told you're a creepy old tyrant who thinks his mother is dirt.

"Our earth! Our air!" Hilton boomed. "Fraser blood pouring through his veins. I can sense his presence even now."

Charles calmly glanced around the large antique-filled room as though expecting the child to pop out from behind a chair or bookcase.

"A genuine male heir." Hilton shuddered from the turbulent emotional roller-coaster ride over uneven patches of disbelief and elation.

His own heir, really, Charles mused, sucking in air as the idea took on full-blown proportion. A male to carry on the name, the estate. Perhaps the pressure would now be off him to marry and reproduce. *Perhaps.* Hilton's position with his daughter-in-law would best be described as beyond hostile, to just plain nonexistent. How Hilton would proceed was anybody's guess.

"So, Dad, are you sure of the facts? How did you ever—?"

"It's damn positive! In the bag!" He pushed a newspaper clipping across the desk. "This arrived here in the morning mail, and a call to the lawyers brought swift and efficient confirmation. It's been running in the *New York Times* for two days."

Charles picked up the square of newsprint and read an item circled in red in the Want Ad section.

Wanted: Father Figure
Widow in need of resilient male
mentor for five-year-old son.
Summer job. College student preferred.
Wages modest. Room and board an option.
Ask for Rose at 555-5276

Rose... Charles hadn't heard her name in such a long time. It was all he ever knew of her really, save for a faded photograph he'd found in Dean's dresser long after he'd gone off for good.

Fortunately, Charles was away at college when the whole marriage scandal occurred. Big brother Dean had eloped with a shop clerk five years his junior—Charles's own age. Hilton had been enraged. Apparently the girl, weeks out of high school, had met Dean at an art show in Soho, and had managed to capture his heart. They were married within months at a Vegas chapel and it was the beginning of the end for Dean and Hilton.

Hilton's abrupt and unshakable disapproval had always puzzled Charles, but when one was a kingpin, many mysteries were left unchallenged.

In any case, Hilton threatened to yank everything away from his eldest—the agency vice presidency, quarters in the mansion, his share of the wealth. All of this hinged on Dean coming to his senses and nullifying his marriage.

Dean called the old boy's bluff and walked away from the Fraser fortunes. They heard through intermediaries that the couple had settled on the West Coast, and were working in a Haight Ashbury art gallery.

Hilton unequivocally ignored Dean. Until news of his death in a plane crash over the desert nearly six years later. Tragically, even a burial was out of the question, as an incinerating explosion destroyed everyone aboard. Without any inquiry into Rose's position, Hilton had held his own memorial service.

In retrospect, Hilton's point of view at the time was rather narrow, amusing in a darkly comical way. He'd braced himself for the big sting, the assault Rose was sure to make on his bank account. When his daughter-in-law made no claim, initiated no contact whatsoever, Hilton had been satisfied and relieved, grateful to escape with assets intact.

How ironic that Rose held the real Fraser treasure in her hands for five long years—Hilton's grandson—the only thing Hilton perceived missing from his opulent life.

"So, Dad, who do you think sent this clipping?"

Hilton smoothed the satin lapels of his robe with a thoughtful frown. "A friend of the family probably spotted the ad in the paper and thought I should know. An old friend of Dean's maybe, one who didn't want to enter the fray firsthand. Dean was always so popular back in school."

Charles smiled faintly, thinking how big brother could string any number of girls along in his prime. "An old girlfriend with a grudge would especially see this as an opportunity to upset Rose."

Hilton sniffed. "I'm grateful under any circumstances. Catching Rose Weldon at her game is all that matters. Risky for her to return to my turf, though. Probably couldn't manage without her people. That's where she turned, of course, to the wild aunties who raised her." Hilton shuffled some papers out of a folder. "The attorney's office faxed me some preliminary stuff. She and the child are residing in White Plains with Daisy and Violet Weldon. Artist types named after flowers," he said disparagingly. "Raised Rose to be free and sensitive, all that hippie garbage. I remember it all too well."

"Sounds like you checked the family out pretty thoroughly back then," Charles noted with some surprise.

Hilton reared, disconcerted. "Naturally, I did. But they won in the end, anyway. Stripped the suit and tie off the most precious person in my life and made him some kind of beach bum." Rage deepened the creases in Hilton's whiskered face. "They're most likely in the process of turning my grandson into a ninny, too."

Charles winced, harshly reminded as to why he never dug too deeply into the semantics of their family history. Dean had always been the favorite son, Charles just a consolation prize. If Charles had been the one to kick over the traces with Rose, Hilton probably would've grumbled a little and thanked the Lord for sensible Dean. But losing Dean twice, first to an unsuitable bride, then to death, had nearly done the old man in. But now there was new hope, a second chance with this new heir. Already Charles sensed Hilton was ready to put it all on the line for him, sight unseen, simply because he was part of Dean.

Charles had thrown his whole life into the business, making an effort to be the best kind of executive and son. Hilton had seemed so satisfied, so proud. Until now, with this new discovery.

He cleared his throat, confirming that it was closing shut on him. "I think you should give Rose the benefit of the doubt. I mean, she is advertising for a male role model for the boy. She must care about his masculine side."

"The nerve, shopping around outside the family! What are we? Chopped liver?"

At this late hour, with his self-worth in question, Charles did feel like so much chopped liver! He closed his eyes, summoning his last vestige of strength and wisdom. "Dad, you instigated this crisis. You disowned Dean *because* of her. You even refuse to refer to her as a Fraser."

"But there's more at stake here now! She should know I'd— She should be bending over backward to be accommodating."

"What would you expect of her, to concede that she herself is an unworthy wretch, then graciously hand over her son to you?"

Hilton snorted. "Now you're talking ideals."

He was? "She has to hate your guts for the blanket rejection you dished out, has to figure you'd be the worst kind of influence on the kid."

The unvarnished truth hit home. Hilton clenched his fists on the blotter as though fighting off a sudden and sharp muscle cramp.

"I mean," Charles said in a milder tone, "it's only natural that she'd view any move from you as the most dangerous kind of threat."

"In a way, she'd be right. I don't want to cause her any deliberate damage, but I do want that boy."

"What do you mean, exactly?"

The old man's eyes glinted. "I'm speaking plainly."

Charles gasped. "You want *custody?*"

"Certainly. Sole custody. The boy deserves every opportunity."

"Naturally I'd want any nephew of mine getting the finest education, exploring all his options."

Hilton tapped the file. "A young lady with a high school education, hanging paintings all day in somebody's gallery, can hardly be honing a Fraser properly."

"Perhaps not—"

"Always a pleasure doing business with you, son."

"Meaning?" Charles asked suspiciously.

"That you've bottom-lined my position quite well. She wouldn't welcome me with open arms."

Charles nodded vigorously. "Any claim from you is bound to land us right smack in court."

Hilton tipped back in his chair with a groan, as though just finishing a delicious meal. "Oh, I expect to land there, eventually. But I need ammo to wage the war."

"And how would you acquire such *ammo?*" Charles's tongue curled around Hilton's term with sour amusement.

"The Trojan horse story ring any bells?"

The hairs on Charles's neck stiffened with his father's wily smile.

"All I need is someone to pass as a college student, infiltrate that magic mushroom they call home."

Charles's mouth hung open. "I'm too old to pass for—"

"You can be a graduate student. How does Columbia University sound?"

"I'm not cut out for a search-and-destroy mission like this!"

"I'm not drafting a soldier. All I require is an impartial observer, an explorer. Consider it an extension of your profession. Admen like us are always watching, calculating, collecting facts. 'Know your public' is Fraser Advertising's motto. All you'd be doing is homing in on one particular public."

"Trapped in a house of women, you mean."

"Like that poor innocent heir is right now. It's a tragic injustice."

After a sterile upbringing at the hands of servants and a

hands-off father, Charles nearly protested that such a trap might not be so bad. But he resisted, as family business was always a tense affair with Hilton and all his panic buttons were being pushed at once. The unsuitable daughter-in-law outfoxing him. The liberal family of creative muses holding his secret grandchild hostage, daring to hone a left brain, right wing Fraser! "Dad, I agree with you in principle. Dean was a fool to give up his birthright. But there has to be a more straightforward approach to this."

"She's set the sneaky standards, not me. Fight fire with fire, I say."

"I'm the one set to burn!"

"He is your nephew." Hilton punctuated each syllable with a pound to his desk. "You should deem it an honor to help. I'll probably have only one shot to get a man inside," he mused in a palm-rubbing trance, "and Rose is bound to be fussy in her father figure choice. This job will take strength and cunning. Any woman who could hold Dean's devotion against so much has to have some moxie to her."

The begrudging compliment to Rose amused Charles. Hilton was a huge fan of moxie. Seemed so unfortunate that there was no room in his tunnel vision for mercy here. "Naturally I want what's best for the boy."

"Good."

"But even if I thought the idea was sound...I'm not much of an liar. You must admit that this job would take some whoppers."

Hilton waved a dismissing hand. "Incidental misdirections at most."

"Not everybody can dissect the differences as easily as you can, or deceive with your talent."

"Don't try to flatter your way out of this."

Charles stared mutely. He wasn't being complimentary, was he? "You've also overlooked the fact that I know nothing of being a father."

"How tough can it be? I managed even after your mother's death."

He did, but to what result? Charles loved Hilton, but the first descriptive term that always came to mind was *difficult*. Charles didn't care to repeat the 'no guts, no glory' methods used on him, and knew no others.

"How bad can it be?" Hilton pressed. "What's the worst scenario?"

The worst scenario. How many times had he been forced to face his fears with those three sterile words? His defensive shields rose higher. Hilton wasn't the only one who could see to his own best interests. "Off the top of my head, I'd hate to be caught in the act."

"Whole thing should take only a few weeks at most," Hilton scoffed. "You'd be safe enough with the proper résumé, a different last name. As for looks, you barely resemble Dean—"

Charles jabbed a finger at him. "But I do resemble you!"

"I highly doubt they've kept an image of me in mind over the years."

They might have. Charles vaguely recalled reading of some old hippie sect that still used voodoo dolls with photos tacked to the faces. "We have so much work at the agency," he said, veering to another tactic. "The Calhoon Soup account is in motion. And I have so much invested in Jed Calhoon. That week on his dude ranch left me with saddle sores."

Hilton moved his lower lip in and out. "I suppose I could hire a private investigator for the job. Draper must know something of children. He's been married four times."

"Don't try to get a rivalry thing going here! You don't want anybody but a relative in that house and we both know it!"

"Dean would want his boy handled right."

Hilton's voice held a tremor strong enough to severely rattle him. Charles loved Dean, too. Very much, despite the age gap between them and Hilton's hero worship for the elder son. Those obstacles certainly weren't Dean's fault. Charles empathized with his father to some degree too, agreeing, at least in theory, that Dean had given up way too much for no sound reason. There was a touch of irony, now that Hilton was primed to send his last surviving son into the same den of madness.

Hilton watched his son's grimace give way some. "So, you in?"

"I would like to sleep on it."

"There isn't time!"

Charles sighed from the depths of his soul. "All right, Dad. Guess I'll give it a shot. Don't uncork the bubbly just yet, though. I may not get the position."

"Leave the details to me. You'll be irresistible when I'm through."

Charles turned to retreat, then paused with one last question. "Did you manage to find out what they named the boy, Dad?"

"Lucas. In honor of Hilton Lucas Fraser, I imagine." He stared off at a glass case full of Dean's football trophies and plaques, his voice a croak. "When it came down to it, he was still my kid. My pride."

Not caring to witness the saltwater flood on the rise, Charles turned on his heel and stalked out. He closed the door firmly after himself and stood quaking in the cool dark foyer.

How could one man be so pumped up with vanity? The boy was named after his own dad, Dean Lucas Fraser. In fact, everybody in the whole blasted Fraser family tree was named Lucas, including Charles Lucas Fraser. In a rush of spite, Charles hoped that Dean's precious Rose was doing a fine job with that kid. He'd sure hate to see little Lucas end up just another trophy in Hilton's study.

Chapter Two

"I cannot find my Magenta Sunset oil!" a matronly voice bellowed. "How can I be expected to give blush to Mr. Pennyfoot's attributes without a tube of number seventy-seven?"

"Daisy," a stronger young soprano objected. "I'm expecting another applicant and would appreciate it if you'd take your work, your paint—your subject, back to the attic!"

Charles's finger froze an inch from the Weldons' doorbell as the heated exchange drifted out to the canary yellow porch where he stood. Squinting behind his sunglasses, he stared through the screen door. The one named Daisy was a tall large-boned woman poised halfway down an open staircase, dressed in a black paint-speckled smock, her faded blond hair pulled back in a teenybopper ponytail. Her "subject" stood on the faded paisley carpet step above, looking mighty uncomfortable draped only in a sheet. His white fleshy shoulders probably could do with a dab of magenta, Charles decided.

The young blond in the foyer gripping the newel post had to be the Rose in the faded photograph: a small, shapely, soft-spoken bundle of nerves, obviously trying to play bully with little affect. Dean's precious Rosy.

He stepped back on the porch's plank flooring, not wanting to appear an eavesdropper at first glance, even though he was just that on the grandest scale. It was Friday afternoon, less than twenty-four hours since his nocturnal meeting with Hilton. Charles had been in their Manhattan headquarters a mere three hours this morning before Hilton charged into his office with a whole scam in motion. Before he knew it, Charles was calling Rose for an appointment, stripped of his navy suit, and jammed into some casual chinos, a cotton short-sleeved shirt and sports jacket. Phony résumé in hand, he was carted off to the Weldons' suburban White Plains home via limousine.

Charles pushed the doorbell then, taking in the details of the home's bright facade. Beware of Beast, said a sign tacked to the siding. *Ah,* thought Charles, *a gift idea for Hilton's own posh stoop. He'd never allow a dog in the house, but then he wouldn't need one to justify the sign.*

"Oh! Hello."

The soft breathless greeting got Charles's attention. A bona fide angel was propping open the wooden screen door. She had huge blue eyes set in a sweetheart-shaped face, a crown of pale golden hair that bounced on her shoulders, white jeans and a pink knit top hugging her petite form. *Oh, Deano, you had to be hypnotized pure and simple.* In fact, Charles would have to be careful he didn't sink like a rock himself.

"I'm Rose Fraser."

"I'm…Charles," he stammered, taking her small slender hand in his own. Since when did he have trouble schmoozing a woman? When she shimmered with a strange vulnerability, perhaps. Rose would be his first in that department. He was accustomed to the aggressive type who gleefully waged a worthy battle in Manhattan's boardrooms, the impetuous type who jetted the continents simply to party.

He pulled his best crooked smile, aware that he looked fairly appealing with his wraparound sunglasses slipping down his nose, his black hair windblown thanks to his walk from the shopping center where his limo was parked.

I need this job! I'm so unfit for this job! So waged his internal war of contradiction. He'd already spent one rest-less night over this charade and, though tempted to renege, he ultimately decided that he had a duty here. Hilton's ob-session aside, his own uncertainties aside, he was going to check things out for his own peace of mind. It was at this point that he realized he was still holding firm to Rose's hand. He gingerly released it.

She expelled a nervous breath. "Please, do come in."

Charles followed her into the house, conscious of the outer door's rickety condition, hoping the inside one had a decent lock. White Plains was a nice town, but things hap-pened here, just like everywhere else. He resisted giving the knob a test twist.

Rose was a couple steps ahead of him, leading the way to the dining room on the left. The square space was small and bright with a new coat of beige paint, its two windows raised to admit a breeze that tossed the olive green curtains. On an old round pedestal table she had a pitcher of lem-onade set out in welcome.

Charles was impressed with the homey atmosphere, the businesslike setup for the interview, until he looked up at the high ceiling. He nearly missed the seat of his chair as he stripped off his sunglasses for a better look at the chan-delier monstrosity, dripping with dusty egg-size crystals.

"Lemonade?"

"Uh, yes, thanks." He quickly recovered, instinctively taking hold of the heavy pitcher to serve. He hoped it wasn't too pushy of him, but her delicate wrist hardly looked as if it could handle the lead glass. Her collarbone looked just as fragile, draped with a slender silver chain that was holding an emerald stone between her rounded breasts.

"Quite a sight, isn't it?"

"Huh?" His gaze vaulted to her face.

"The chandelier. My aunts unearthed it in Venice, I be-lieve."

"Very unique." *Just like you.*

It took monumental effort to fight off the honeyed swell of desire rolling through him. Rose was so extraordinary in her simplicity, mild in manner and unadorned with makeup. How could Hilton have built up a protest to this gentle, earthy woman so quickly, so vehemently?

He took a sip of lemonade, hoping it was tart enough to force him to break out of the sugary web she spun around him in just a few minutes. Unfortunately, it was the sweetest he'd ever tasted, leaving him helplessly sinking in a sugary quicksand.

"I flavor this with my son Lucas in mind," she explained half-apologetically, tipping her glass at him before taking a sip.

He took another polite taste. "Understandable." He fidgeted when he realized she was intently surveying him.

"Sorry, I was just noting that you're about my age," she explained. "You said on the telephone you're a student."

"Both observations are true."

"So tell me all about yourself, Charles," she urged pleasantly.

He plucked the folded résumé from the lining pocket of his linen jacket and presented it to her. It was a deliberate move to keep her intelligent eyes busy while he launched into his bogus cover story. He went on to claim to be a graduate student at Columbia, studying communications and the humanities.

Her forehead wrinkled. "What brings you to us in particular?"

"I'm presently doing a study on children, how they relate to the world. One of my professors saw your ad—"

"My son is no experiment!" she gasped, coloring a shade darker than her pink V-neck top.

He raised his hands as though fanning flames. Just as he predicted—thrown directly into the fire! "No, of course not."

She calmed down again, though her color stayed high.

"To be honest, I was thinking of someone in his late teens, who still has some boyish spark—"

"I have some life left!"

A glint of appreciation flashed in her eyes, like an unexpected bolt of summer lightning in a cobalt sky. She quickly tightened her smile to cover up. "Are you willing to run and play? All the applicants I've seen so far have come in sweats and track shorts."

Charles's competitive hackles rose. How he hated to lose at anything! "Are you disqualifying me because of age and appearance?"

"Not at all. I'm being choosy, keeping an open mind. Though the job is a temporary one, I expect Lucas could become quite attached to the right guy. I would hope, out of the goodness of his heart, his father figure would keep in touch indefinitely."

"Good plan," he was quick to concede. "I do know my way around sports and I intend to stay planted here. I'm nearly finished with my studies and intend to work in the city." Resting an elbow on the table, he leaned closer, spoke intimately. "I will be around indefinitely, always a cell call away." He withdrew an inch as he gauged her breathing growing satisfactorily shallow. "Younger guys may be a bit more playful, but they're also unpredictable, easily distracted, uprooted. I can't see them as a better bet. I have staying power."

Charles shouldn't have said that, he knew. Busy with her job and parenting, Rose probably hadn't had much exposure over the last few years to sexual whimsy. But she was so ripe for the picking and he was a master at suggestive subtlety, of leaving a woman vaguely bothered, that he couldn't help himself. Besides, the way he figured it this might well be the biggest campaign pitch of his life, so he was drawing out every trick in the book.

As angry as his father made him sometimes, the child inside him wanted to please, to be the esteemed son. He knew if he blew this deal, Hilton would be next to impossible straight through to his deathbed scene.

Rose watched him curiously as she sought control of her own runaway blood pressure. How could she hope to judge Charles Johnson when she didn't recognize herself at this moment? Surely her reaction was understandable. He was incredibly attractive, and openly interested in…this position. She tried hard to set that fact firmly in the forefront of her mind. Charles wanted the job. Period. That her heart was skittering to new and dangerous places was beside the point and should not be considered. Was he right for Luke? That was the only issue to seriously consider.

To have a contemporary of hers in the house was a brand-new consideration. Her image of a father figure for Lucas had been so different a mere ten minutes ago—a safe young man who hadn't yet reached the age of legal consent.

Charles Johnson was legal way beyond the limit. *Illegal* in a sense. Incredibly handsome, with even, well-defined features, penetrating brown eyes, and sinfully long lashes like her son's. He knew all the ins and outs of consent, and had time enough under his belt for plenty of practice.

She shook her head, flustered as sensual images danced along the edges of her mind. Romance was such a thing of the past that she couldn't help indulging in the delicious feeling at his expense. All the more reason he wouldn't do, of course. But how to get rid of him? He looked so comfortable in his bow-backed chair. Too comfortable.

Perhaps this would be easier if she made leaving his own idea.

"There are things any applicant should know up front," she said evenly. "For starters, I can't pay much. The room and board mentioned in the ad are the biggest lures."

Her pretty face would be lure enough for the average man, he thought with some amusement. Did she never look in the mirror? "I'm not looking for income," he assured firmly. "I'd gladly accept the room and board as complete payment."

His generosity was astonishing. "The ad runs through the week," she hedged. "I thought I'd see what shakes out, make my decision then...." She trailed off, fingering his resume. "In the meantime, I'll call the referrals on your list. Anything I should know about them?"

Charles knew nothing much about them, being this whole scam had been so rushed. "Call them cold," he suggested lightly. "Form fresh opinions."

She smoothed the paper flat on the table. "Guess that should cover it," she said, dismissal in her tone.

"I'd give it my best, Rose!" He shifted in his chair like a petulant boy, then lifted a hand in quick repentance. "Sorry, I just want the job."

She laughed softly, drawing his puzzled scowl. "Sorry, you reminded me of my son just then. He's a charming scamp too, until things go amuck."

"We'd probably hit it off," he promptly reasoned.

"Probably..."

If only she didn't look so regretful about it. Charles leaned over the table again, aware that she wasn't meeting him halfway this time, but shrinking back in her chair. "I'm at loose ends right now," he claimed, digging into the artillery he and Hilton had stocked up. "I've been sharing a small apartment with another student near the campus. He just got married. Understandably, they want me out."

"Oh, I am sorry," she said with real concern. "Housing can be a problem in the city."

"They're on their honeymoon, so I've been scrambling for new digs."

"This place is a far cry from a bachelor lair for two. It can get really hectic around here at times," she cautioned, fingering the hem of the lacy tablecloth. "I'm sure you're accustomed to privacy."

"I'm sure Lucas is old enough to understand space."

Had she told him her son's name? She must have. "I'm thinking of my two aunts as well, Violet and Daisy. They're probably too old to understand, to change— Oh, what am

I saying? They've always been a couple of nomads who think nudity is an art form, rules are for suckers and snooping is all part of a person's education!'' Smelling his fear, she dared to lean closer, trumping him, in turn, with the intimacy card. ''They've been arrested fifteen times for various protests…this year alone!''

Charles's heart stopped cold. Good grief. Hilton just might be justified all the way. Rose was lovely, but how many of these wild notions did she aspire to? There was a twinkle in her eyes, but he wasn't sure if it was because she was deliberately harrassing him or simply preparing him.

Either way he had to stay the course. What was that last-ditch plea Hilton had come up with for him? Oh, yeah. *That.* Gripped in dismay, he'd either have to run or lay it on her. His finger stole to his throat, before he realized he was wearing no tie to loosen. ''You see, Rose, the studies, the apartment, the friend marrying, they're all part of the picture. Beneath it all, I'm a lonely man. Terribly lonely. This chance to hook up with Lucas, enjoy your family, seems like a fateful lifeline.''

She reached over the table and patted his large hand. ''It's okay. I figured that much out for myself.''

''You did?''

''Why, sure. No crime in it, Charles. I've been lonely on occasion myself. I recognize the signs, and I understand them only too well.''

''Why—? But—?'' He sputtered like a faulty helicopter. How could she have sensed something that wasn't really true? He was hoping to sell the tale with his cunning. Oh, how he wanted to cancel the ploy, tell her how very popular he was, erase that smug, sympathetic look from her face.

But even now she wasn't offering him the job. And there was no room for further pressure. He had to appear almost too desperate already, especially by offering his services free. It hardly seemed logical. But he'd blurted out the offer without thinking it through, because there was so little evidence of disposable income around here. The furniture was ancient, the rugs worn, Rose's clothes inexpensive. Charles wasn't the least bit uncomfortable with his family's wealth, but by all rights, Rose was a part of the fold and deserved a share, surely more than this.

"I'll let you know," she said in closing.

Charles rubbed his brows with a self-conscious grin. "I suppose I should go before you sic the Beast on me."

She gasped in surprise. "What?"

"The sign out front. Beware of Beast. I figure that's the threat of one impressive hound."

Rose hesitated with a wry grin. "Well, Beast is the name of our dog—"

A bark interrupted her. A semblance of a bark, anyway, Charles thought as he swiveled on his chair. There was a boy standing in the arched doorway, holding a small white puffy dog with black eyes and apricot ears.

It's Dean. Charles took one look at the boy's brilliant smile, dimpled left cheek, silky dark blond hair and saw his brother. He gripped the edge of the old table, his hip, smooth facade taking another hit with the onslaught of blurry flashbacks starring his brother, several years older than this boy, teaching him how to ride a bike, how to throw a baseball, how to sneak cookies out of the kitchen while the cook was having a cigarette break out by the pool. Their mother was already dead during those formative years and Hilton was hiding out in Manhattan, playing executive; Dean had been his everything.

In the presence of his brother's son Charles felt unfit and needed all at the same time.

"You're back already!" Rose gasped in dismay to the older woman entering the room, a stout and plump figure in a billowing pink blouse and white knee-length shorts, her sandaled feet slapping the hardwood.

"I'm sorry. The pet groomers had a cancellation and took Beast early."

Rose shifted attention to the boy. "Honey, I told you to stay clear of these interviews."

"But I heard you talking about Beastie Bichon..."

"Still, I told you."

He held the dog out. "But they done it again, put girl junk on him!"

Rose was at a loss. "Aunt Violet, I asked you not to let that happen."

"Don't know what the fuss is all about," Violet shrilled, her ample bosom quivering like mounds of gelatin.

It took Charles a moment to find his voice, another to find an opening. "So he's a bichon frise, is he?"

Lucas giggled as the pooch's tail tickled his nose. "Yup. He wants to know who you are."

Rose swiftly intervened, hoping to keep some control. "This is Charles."

"Are you a Charlie?" he asked excitedly. "My friend at kindergarten is a Charles and a Charlie."

"Sure, Charlie's fine." No matter that he'd once punched a classmate out for using that nickname on him, coming from Lucas it seemed to fit.

Encouraged, Lucas scampered closer. "You wanna pet Beast?" Without waiting for a reply, he thrust the dog into Charles's lap. "You wanna be my pretend daddy?" he asked in the same hurried, matter-of-fact way.

Rose blushed. This was the very reason she'd chosen to keep Lucas apart from the process, because he bonded so fast with adults. This was the first time he'd busted in on an interview, though. She'd spoken to four students already, all of whom hadn't quite clicked. One hadn't even made it into the house; she'd turned him away on the boulevard.

But it was tough to find valid fault with Charles Johnson on any front. Except for his disturbing sexuality. The air they shared was packed with a sizzling chemistry, steeped with new depths of emotion upon Lucas's presence. The dining room had never seemed smaller or stuffier or more inviting—including those times when the table held a Thanksgiving feast!

Livin' on lemonade with Charlie. Lemonade and fevered looks, and maybe some delicious kisses. Oh, the possibilities... But she didn't need the man—Lucas did! She didn't need anything anymore. Dean had been her world; he had given up so much to make her his own. Memories of their love would surely see her through her lifetime.

Still, it wasn't Charles's fault that she found him so attractive. Maybe he wasn't even trying to flirt. The fact that he seemed a bit unsure made him all the more appealing.

"C'mon, Charlie," Lucas chirped. "I want to show you my new swing set. It's not really new. It's old."

Charles's brows rose in perplexity.

"It's from a garage sale," Violet supplied.

"But it's refurbished," Rose was quick to add.

"It's transformed into a work of artistic glory!" All heads snapped to the doorway where Daisy stood, her black paint-dabbled smock ballooning as she raised her arms over her head.

Daisy speared Charles with an assessing gaze, and he stiffened a little defensively. Rose could only guess how her aunt would instantly size him up. But the only thing out of place about Charles was his age. His attire, like his manner, was unassuming, whereas Daisy tended to swoop in like a hurricane. She'd no doubt tell Rose he was too subdued for her, a far cry from the impetuous teenager they'd advertised for. But for some reason Rose was beginning not to care. It was a safe bet that Daisy ran things around here and it would be awful if she nixed Charles when he was doing so well with the others.

Rose laid a gentle hand on his shoulder. "Daisy's very proud of her works of art," she said. Leaning closer, she added in a whisper, "And a little defensive about our secondhand stuff."

"I heard that, Rosy," Daisy snapped. "There is too much waste in the world. Even the rich should not waste.

That swing set has plenty of life left, and now it's a work of art thanks to my psychedelic brush stroke.''

"I'd love to see it." Charles popped up from his chair, anxious to escape Daisy's penetrating eyes and Rose's tingling touch. This couldn't possibly work out. He'd be a wreck within hours. To his relief, Lucas took him in tow, leading him from the dining room, down the main hallway and out the rear door in the kitchen.

"Run, Charlie!" Lucas squealed as his small tennis shoes scrambled down the concrete steps and into the backyard. "They'll be watchin' ya run!"

It might have been a child's ploy, but it rang true in the circumstances. He begrudgingly picked up the pace. Halfway across the lawn he glanced back at the house, certain he saw three figures hovering behind the sun-drenched pane. He should be grateful for the live audition. But somehow he'd have preferred Rose spoke to his referrals first, formed a rock-solid opinion of him before he was put to this kind of test.

The brightly painted aluminum play set, complete with slide, glider and two swings, was positioned at the rear of the property, against some medium-size pines. Lucas had already popped onto one of the two bench swings, curling his fingers around the supportive chains, pumping his small bare legs for all he was worth. Unfortunately Charles couldn't close his eyes and imagine Dean in his place just then. Hilton had considered such play equipment too scrubby for their upscale neighborhood.

And dandelions like theirs? Forget it! The mansion's hybrid lawn appeared near artificial in its perfection. Charles impulsively picked up one of the flowers, and it put him in mind of Rose's flowing hair. Both were soft, yellow and inviting.

"Look how high I go, Charlie!"

Charles tossed away the flower, not caring for the way the swing set shook as Lucas swung to and fro. "Take it easy," he called to the boy.

"It's easy. You try it."

"No, I think I'll just have a look." Charles began to inspect the tubular structure at its joints, frowning at all the loosening screws. The play set wasn't about to collapse, but it definitely needed some work.

"I go to kindergarten," Lucas called down proudly at the apex of his swing.

"Oh, yeah?"

"All morning. You like my mommy? She works at a store. Puts frames on pictures. And Aunt Daisy paints pictures," he added excitedly.

"And Aunt Violet?"

"She cooks me food and cleans my room." Lucas batted his long lashes, slowing his swing. "If you go down the slide with me, Mommy will like you a lot and ask you to stay."

Charles squinted at him in the bright sunlight. "It's not that simple in your mother's mind. She has to be careful."

Lucas extended his lower lip. "Nobody's been good enough."

Disappointment weighed heavy in the air. Charles felt compelled to ask the obvious, what Hilton would want to know first and foremost. "Are you all right, Lucas? I mean, are you happy?"

The question was too big for him, so he blurted out his biggest complaint of the moment. "After school's out I won't have anybody to play with!"

Unlike the swing, that dilemma triggered memories. With great empathy, Charles looked at the houses on the right and the left. "Don't any kids live on this street?"

"Nobody next door. Except a *girl*."

Charles hid a trace of a smile. "Oh, yeah. That would be rough."

"That's why Mommy's hiring a big boy for me."

Charles couldn't find fault with Rose's explanation to the child. It certainly beat telling him that he didn't have any decent relatives to fill the male void. "Well, I tell you what,

Lucas," he finally said. "I have the feeling your mom's going to solve your problem one way or the other."

THE SLAM OF THE kitchen screen door had indeed sent the women into action. They scurried to the window facing the rear, pushing back the green curtain. Daisy was the tallest and peered out the pane over Violet and Rose. The trio had a clear view of man and boy.

"He sees us watching!" Rose gasped self-consciously.

"Something he'll have to learn to like," Daisy crowed.

"He's picking a dandelion," Violet murmured. "He likes them. I can tell by the way he ponders it. Must be sensitive."

They watched Lucas hop onto one of the swings and Charles test the structure. Rose would've been more impressed if he'd fallen behind Lucas to give him a push, but safety measures were important, too.

"Sensitive and good-looking," Violet observed. "But uptight."

"Fine tight buttocks," Daisy declared with the objectivity of a physician. "I wonder…" She trailed off, pressing a finger to her lips.

"I am not hiring Charles simply so you can do his portrait, Daisy," Rose admonished the surprised woman. "That's right, I'm a leap ahead of you this time. I caught you admiring him like Zeus come to life. Modeling is not part of this particular job description."

Daisy grew wistful. "You can't expect to teach a sixty-year-old new tricks, m'dear. Naturally I'm interested. And I do so tire of models like Mr. Pennyfoot. A charming man to be sure, but a body as mushy as a beanbag." Her eyes never left Charles. "I would have to invest my emergency funds in some bronze oils, but I think I could capture Charles's lean masculine planes in splendid justice—to your liking."

"You aren't listening, Daisy!"

Daisy smiled serenely at her enraged niece. "Of course I am. I just don't like what I'm hearing."

"Lucas is the one who needs a man most right now."

"So hire him."

"Just like that?"

"I hardly think we'll get a better qualified applicant," Violet stated, putting in her two cents. "I must confess, too that the younger boys made me awfully nervous, galloping round here like horses in those big heavy shoes."

Rose leaned against the sill, feeling the sway of their opinions. "I do like Charles—"

"Course you do, Rose," Daisy declared smugly. "It's plain that you do. Plant a cigarette in your mouth and you'd be me thirty-five years ago after hot sex."

"What!"

"Afterglow, girl. How easy a time you have reaching it."

Rose clapped her hands to her cheeks. "You're awful, simply awful!"

Daisy preened. "Lighten up. The exercise is good for your circulation. Vessels opening up everyplace." She inhaled, doing a deep knee bend.

"Now *I* don't like what I'm hearing," Rose protested shrilly.

Violet stroked Rose's fair hair with a plump hand. "Don't be upset, sweetie. Sensuality is all in keeping with nature's harmony. The mating call is a tricky and sometimes spontaneous happening. Can't let a pleasant father figure get away just because he turns you on, dear."

"Well said, Violet." Daisy fluffed her graying ponytail. "An especially good point taken about the teens. I myself never liked that idea."

Rose jabbed a finger at her. "Yes, you did! You nearly cracked a brush or two when I showed you the ad I placed. Nineteen seemed mighty fine back then."

"I like this Charlie best in any case," Daisy said airily. "He's at that perfectly delicious age. Has those lean hard hips of youth, with the added bonus of knowing how to use them.''

"You two are impossible!" Rose threw her hands up and stalked away.

"If you really don't approve of him, you shouldn't have allowed Lucas to take him outside," Violet said in gentle reprimand.

Rose balked. "I asked you to keep Lucas away from home altogether."

"You said your appointment was at noon."

"The original one was," Rose stated. "Charles called later. I warned you someone might. I told you to check in before you returned."

"Never mind," Daisy squawked. "No sense going on about spilled milk. Exactly what's keeping you from hiring Charles on the spot anyway?"

Rose picked up his résumé and waved it. "I haven't even checked out his references yet. I can't consider hiring him without doing so."

Daisy pulled a large smug smile. "So do it."

"Just like that?"

"It's why we pay the phone bill."

Rose wasn't at all sure they had paid the phone bill this month. Maybe an educated man like Charles could get them all organized. Heck, she didn't know. Was it wise to hire somebody just because he made you feel good all over? Staring at the two flower children throwbacks beside her, the question was just too obvious to ask!

Chapter Three

"You're back here again?"

"Yes, of course." Charles bristled as Hilton charged into his office later that afternoon shortly before four o'clock. He'd changed back into his dress suit and was in the process of packing up his briefcase.

"Why, Charles?"

"I work here, remember? Vice president of Fraser Advertising, forty-third floor of the Capshaw Building on West 40th?"

Charles knew he was going overboard, but he did indeed feel as if he were clinging to the side of a very rocky boat. After a lifetime of cool distance he and his father were finally managing to build a relationship of sorts. Sure, it was based mostly on their mutual interest in the family business, but Charles didn't mind all that much. They had common goals, they were a team. Finally, Dad had seemed proud and satisfied with his surviving son.

Until now, with another more attractive option on the horizon.

The fact that Hilton was capable of deeper feeling all along was something Charles had deliberately put out of his mind. That all the meatier emotion had been reserved for Dean alone was a closed issue best left behind. Charles had never experienced such depth with anyone and figured he was better off. Emotions led to insecurity, risk and heart-ache. A man was better off as a closed corporation.

But now Hilton was opening up his heart all over again. Their dignified arrangement would no longer satisfy. He was bound and determined to relive Dean's glory years by taking over little Lucas.

Hilton finally broke the silence by slamming the office door with a mighty thud. Charles continued to rifle through the papers on his desk, tossing some of them into his at-taché.

"So, how'd it go at the Weldons?"

Charles remained stoic. "I really can't say."

"Yet," Hilton was quick to clarify with some knowledge of his own. "Rose has taken the bait. She's calling the references on your résumé."

Charles took up a file folder and flipped through the contents. "She said she was going to."

"I had separate phone lines set up in my suite and I hired actors to play the roles of your previous employers."

Charles's cool mask slipped a bit. "Really, Dad! You didn't go that far!"

"I can't take any chances of you losing out. And look at it this way—I'm boosting the economy by employing people off the street," he cleverly rationalized. "The calls are being recorded and my personal secretary will type up the transcripts for you. Can't have any slipups in your story later on once you're in, either. I've made it as simple as possible, centering your experience around your bogus studies."

"It's not like you to trust outsiders on something so delicate."

"I had no choice. But rest assured I'm being very careful. Dorleen's been my gal Friday for thirty years and the actors have damn near signed over their heirs in a confidentiality agreement."

"Heirs must be looked after." Charles sighed deeply, staring into his briefcase. How tempted he was to blow the whistle on his own father. Sweet little Rosy seemed so helpless up against a dynamo like Hilton. He was reasonably sure she was a caring mother, a loving woman in general—if he was any judge, which he probably wasn't.

Auntie Daisy was a different story altogether. She was an odd blend of carefree bully, with the innate swagger of a champion boxer. Certainly tough enough to go head-to-head with Hilton. Hippie versus hardhead.

Oh, yes, he could express plenty of reservations about *her* influence. For starters she left him with the eerie feeling that she was picturing him buck naked. There was supportive evidence in the chubby form of one Mr. Pennyfoot, standing out in the open on the staircase, draped only in a sheet. What sort of man would allow himself to be posed and scrutinized that way under the dubious umbrella of art?

Then there was Aunt Violet, in delicate counterpoint to Daisy, though quite obviously heavily under her influence. In her own gentle way the younger, softer sister was even more dangerous to him than Daisy, bearing the insight to examine him beneath the skin, clear down to his naked soul!

He had to admire the aunts' protective instincts and their good intentions. Those qualities would mean nothing to the Hilton, though. He'd bottom-line it in his own characteristic way, and suspect nobody was minding the store. Which, come to think of it, was a fair observation, one deserving analysis.

But was Charles up to the job? Father figure to an innocent boy... The enormity of it all made him tremble in his shoes. Then again, it was supposed to be a job the average nineteen-year-old could do. Or a detective.

The option of a private eye lingered on. One could be easily coached on the finer points of the situation, given a glowing résumé too. An easy out for Charles. But he couldn't let a hired hand close in on Rose. For all his doubts, he simply couldn't. He was a Fraser with some bottom lines, too!

"So, how did you find the hen house?" Hilton asked abruptly. "Speak!"

"The dining room chandelier was dusty, the front door rickety, and the psychedelic swing set a little shaky at the joints," Charles reported smoothly. "That the kind of stuff you want?"

The dashing executive was visibly impressed. "Not a bad beginning. You'll make a decent spy, after all."

"A third-rate heel, you mean."

Hilton's tone sharpened. "So you liked Rose. With all you know…"

"I don't dislike her yet," Charles said easily.

Hilton stepped closer to the desk, gripping a paperweight in his hand. "How did she strike you? Give me your adman's encapsulated opinion."

Charles moved over to the window overlooking West 40th, and concentrated on raising the blinds to hide the flicker of basic male interest that had to be set in his eyes. "Young. She struck me as young."

"But she's your age."

"Give her a bra and a uniform and she could slip into any high school cheerleading squad across America." Charles shrugged his large shoulders in the wake of Hilton's bluster. "Sorry, that's how she struck me."

"Braless," Hilton growled, pulling a small gold notebook and pen set from the breast pocket of his black suit jacket and began to scribble. "I'd better keep track of all this." He leveled a terse look at his son. "You didn't mention the bra before. You better keep sharp. Overlook nothing."

Charles had in fact noticed everything about Rose, but knew it would be conceived as a weakness. That's what she was all right, a weakness to the Fraser boys. He could now understand Dean's initial interest. She was honey to the bee on a basic sexual level.

But he wouldn't be his father's son if he didn't swing back with some balance of logic. There was the possibility

Dean had come to regret making such a clean break, that he may have resented Rose to some degree over it all. Who knew how he'd see the present raising of his son, the need for a hired father figure.

"Let's see, what else did you say? Dusty light fixture, rickety front door, psycho swing set…" Hilton jotted it all down in tiny, stark print.

Charles turned to stare down at the library across the street, shaking with suppressed laughter. Fraser Advertising's high-powered clients, who depended upon them to concoct clever ads to sway millions of people into spending billions of dollars, would be flabbergasted to see the masterful Hilton collecting these petty tidbits like a frustrated schoolmarm.

"Is that everything so far, son?" he asked anxiously.

"Well, there is the matter of some arrests."

"Arrests!" Hilton paused, the lines around his mouth deepening. "Oh, there would be those, wouldn't there?"

Charles slowly turned round. "What do you know about it?"

"Those aunties rarely missed a protest rally. The whales, the minks, nuclear power, the Vietnam war." He waved a hand in dismissal. "Hardly a worthwhile avenue of pursuit, small potatoes in today's world."

"Your priorities confuse me. Arrests are superceded by loose screws?"

Hilton cast him a patronizing look. "Just dig and report everything. They'll be plenty more once you're on the inside."

Charles felt the tremble beginning in his shoes again. *On the inside.* He'd never been on the inside anyplace. Playing the worst-case-scenario exercise, he recalled the nude modeling tidbit. He decided to keep it to himself for now, fearful Hilton would storm the place with a SWAT team. "I hope you won't flip your lid if I don't make the cut," he mumbled.

"I have to believe you will. Getting close to that boy is

a must. It's killing me, not knowing all the little things about him. You should've tried to meet him——'' He broke off then. "No, it would've been too obvious."

"Oh, I did meet Lucas."

"What!" Hilton's voice was thunder, his fist pounding the desktop with a lumberjack's swing. "Why didn't you say so in the first place?"

Because of that resurrected glimmer of vulnerability in your eyes so long denied me.

Hilton's ruddy features began to soften with the possibilities. "So, c'mon, give. Does he favor me?"

"Not really, Dad. He resembles his parents. He's got Dean's bone structure and dimples, Rosy's round face and blue eyes."

"You're calling her Rosy?"

"That's what Dean called her. A slip of the tongue is all."

"Well, keep that tongue in neutral from here on in. A slip like that could sink the whole scheme."

Visions of slipping his tongue over Rosy's lips overwhelmed him suddenly, leaving him bumbling for a mere semblance of his suave self.

"How did he speak?" Hilton grilled with spell-breaking force. "Did he sound like a Fraser?"

"His voice was small and husky, like his mother's," he reported. "But he did have Dean's laugh."

Hilton released a shaky breath. "I think I love him already. Don't you love him already?"

Charles swallowed hard. Could he cross those kinds of emotional lines with anyone? A sense of obligation was more his style, what he felt for the Fraser cause. What Hilton felt for him.

A knock on the door interrupted them. Charles's secretary, Marcia Haines, entered with his new small red cell phone in hand. A long-term employee in her forties, she'd known Charles for years and had proven the ultimate helpmate. What he loved most about her was her unaffected attitude toward Hilton. Marcia could get any one of a dozen jobs around town and considered pandering to office hierarchy against her principles.

"Call for you, chief."

Charles's eyes widened. "How did you get ahold of that phone?"

"You left your suit jacket on a chair out front and it began to ring. I investigated and found this in the pocket."

Hilton met his son's eyes. "Is that what I think it is?"

"Yes, Dad. My connection."

Hilton glared at the secretary. "Did you have the audacity to really answer it, woman?"

She smiled sweetly. "Seemed the cordial thing to do."

"Fine time to start behaving cordially."

Marcia's temper was climbing hot and fast, so Charles intervened with even tones. "The party's on hold, isn't it?"

"Certainly, chief."

"What did you say, exactly?" Hilton barked.

"Uh, I believe I said hello." Marcia preened, smoothing her red curls.

"Did you or did you not, just say, hello?" Hilton mimicked the salutation in a high musical voice. "Nothing more?"

"Nothing," she assured flatly. "What's this all about, Charles?"

Hilton glowered at his son. "Charles has some girl trouble right now, which he prefers to keep private."

"Well, the caller did seem surprised by my answering. Now if I knew exactly what was going on, I could—"

"Get out!" Hilton thrust a finger at the door.

Marcia handed Charles the phone. "I have half a nerve to quit."

"You're no quitter," Charles scoffed with a wink.

"And you do nothing by half, Ms. Haines," Hilton raged. "A man would drop dead with your nerve in his tooth!"

Marcia paused blissfully, as though envisioning Hilton doing so, then whisked out the door.

"Dad, lighten up on Marcia. I couldn't bear to lose her."

"Ah, she quit on me dozens of times. I just kept giving her raises."

Charles rolled his eyes and depressed the phone's On button. "Hello... Yes, Rose... No, that was my pal's new bride," he quickly improvised. "Yes, they're back early... Oh, you do? Great... They'll be thrilled all right." He frowned at Hilton as his father began to mouth questions. "No, Sunday is better... Okay, see you then."

Hilton pounced as Charles signed off. "Who'll be thrilled?"

"I got the job," he announced smugly.

"That's obvious. Who's thrilled?"

"The fictitious roommates who supposedly want me out."

"If she'd take you tomorrow, why wait a day?"

"Because Saturdays are mine. Handball and lunch with the guys."

"But to waste time getting started—"

Charles raised a palm. "Leave this to me."

"I can't bear to keep my hands off."

"You know you need me as a go-between. These women are smart. If they get suspicious, they'll quickly make the connection. It's already risky. They know Dean had a brother named Charles. Actually, Dad, I'd like your promise that you will not try to come near Lucas at all until I'm through. No drive-bys, no phone calls—nothing!"

"That's unreasonable!"

"But necessary. Also, I want it clearly understood up front that I'll be keeping up on business matters here at the agency."

"But how—"

"I'll be expected to attend so-called classes at Columbia; I intend to pop in here instead."

"I hadn't considered your being back at all."

That wriggled under Charles's cool fast. "Thanks a lot! I'd like to think I'm indispensable."

Hilton reared in genuine bewilderment. "You are, of course. But this is the biggest deal you'll ever make in the Fraser name. And I've already doled out most of your accounts."

"You didn't!"

"It's temporary—"

"What about Jed Calhoon?"

Hilton studied his thunderous son. "We'll handle him together."

"You gave him to me!"

"I know. You've done well getting his two new spots into shape, outlining the concepts, executing the commercial shoots."

"When's he coming to see them, Dad?"

"I'm not sure. Soon."

Furious, Charles hammered out his position. "It's fine that you want this child in the fold, but my career is my life. I can't lose what I've built here. Especially over some simple little glorified baby-sitting job."

For the first time Hilton looked a little uneasy himself. "*Simple* is a word you should remove from your vocabulary right now. Nothing will go down easy with those women. Absolutely nothing."

ROSE FELT LIGHTER than air Saturday night as she tucked Lucas into bed.

"You sure he's gonna come, Mommy?"

Her soft heart-shaped face brightened. "Definitely, honey. Tomorrow morning."

"Real early or kinda early?"

"I don't know."

"How come you don't know?"

She tweaked his nose. "How come you keep asking me questions?"

"What if he changed his mind?"

Rose's pulse jumped over the unthinkable, but she kept her smile steady. "He won't."

"How do you know?"

She grew pensive in the glow of Dean's old cowboy lamp. "Can't explain why, exactly, but there's something very special about that man."

"What?"

"It's a *feeling*." A wonderfully warm feeling that left her safe and unsure all at once, the way Dean used to in his own strong and teasing way. Daisy was overzealous as usual in her afterglow observation, but Rose couldn't deny that her secret buttons, so long untouched, were immediately pushed by Charles, leaving her aroused, feeling desired.

She plonked down on the edge of his mattress. Boy, oh, boy, did she need a life! She sounded like a desperate spinster.

"Think he'll like me?" Lucas wondered.

"He already does."

"And Beastie Bichon?"

Rose stroked his forehead. "What's not to like about the Beast?"

His forehead furrowed beneath her touch. "What about Aunt Daisy?"

"Well..." she faltered. "Maybe you and Beast can protect Charles from Daisy."

Lucas beamed. "Yeah..."

"Yeah..." Rose bent over to give him a big lip smack. "The sooner you go to sleep, the sooner you can wake up."

"Maybe I should sleep out on the porch. So I don't miss him."

Rose made an exasperated sound. "Good night, Lucas."

Lucas giggled. "Good night."

Rose patted his cheek, clicked off his lamp, and headed for the door.

"I love you, Mommy."

She smiled broadly in the dark. Didn't he just?

Chapter Four

"Charlie! You came!"

Charles had taken a taxi from the suburban subway station the following morning to the Weldon's canary yellow two story. He was standing on the curb between his two duffel bags when he heard Lucas's whoop.

"Hey, man." Charles handed the driver his fare through the open passenger window and turned to watch the boy scampering down the front sun-dappled walk, a threadbare blanket in tow. The welcome wouldn't have troubled him at all if Lucas wasn't dressed only in short cotton pajamas.

He stopped at the boulevard, sleepy and shy. "I just woke up."

Charles stared up at the porch swing, spotting a pillow on the wooden bench. "Hey, you weren't sleeping out here, were you?"

"Not all the time. C'mon. Hurry!" He tried to give one of the canvas bags a tug, but found it was far too heavy for his spindly arms. With a chuckle Charles slung a bag strap on each shoulder, urging Lucas to lead the way.

"He came! He really came!" Lucas burst inside the house like a miniature tornado, his feet pattering on the old wooden flooring.

Charles eased off his bags, and sauntered round the foyer, inhaling the welcome smell of cooking food. He peeked into the dining room on the left of the staircase, then into the parlor on the right, conceding that the old place had a welcoming feel about it with its worn tapestry furniture, scattering of fringed rugs, and variety of oils and prints taking up most of the wall space.

He was admiring a rather strange wooden coatrack near the front door when he heard a feminine sound. He whirled around to find Rose standing on the last step, clearing her throat for a second time.

"Good morning."

Charles stared in wonder. She was the softest creature he'd ever laid eyes upon, bundled up in a pink chenille robe, her blond hair in fluffed disarray around her smooth white face. "Hello."

"You're...prompt."

"Always keep my word." He closed his eyes briefly, hoping lightning didn't strike him dead for all the lying words he'd be keeping.

She removed a hand from a pocket and stifled a yawn. "We don't get started around here very early on Sundays."

Bedroom eyes. That was the term for Rose's eyes, hidden as they were behind a fringe of pale lash. Certainly enough to get his motor running any dawn of any day. Charles closed his own eyes, quickly assailed with visions of lounging around in a very large bed with Rosy, stroking her petal soft skin, feeding her strawberries from the garden out back. Good grief, he'd be a sight here in a minute if he didn't take control.

"Did you know that Lucas was sleeping on the porch?" he asked gruffly.

"No way!" With an indignant flash of temper she alighted from the step in her small pink slippers and clattered across the foyer. She gave the front screen door a hard push and barreled outside. She was wide awake as she snatched up the pillow and spun back around. Anticipating her moves, Charles was holding the door open. Wide.

"Lucas!"

Lucas came trotting down the hallway from the rear of

the house, the Beast in his arms. The small white dog wiggled as he clutched it close to his small chest. "Hi, Mommy. He came, just like you said."

"I also said you shouldn't sleep out on the porch, Lucas."

His lower lip drooped. "I was out there six minutes, that's all."

"Oh." Charles faltered. "Sorry. It just seemed a dangerous situation, with the porch being wide-open to the street."

Put off by Charles's brusque entrance, Rose took some secret pleasure in knowing that Lucas was snookering him good. But in an objective sense she had to admit Charles's sense of reason was correct. Lucas could indeed use a firmer hand than hers. Adjusting might be tougher than she anticipated though.

Daisy appeared in the child's wake then, dressed in a red-and-gold caftan. "So you're here." Her eyes traveled Charles's length appreciatively.

Lucas tugged at the caftan's flowing satin folds. "Tell them I didn't sleep outside, Aunt Daisy."

"How preposterous!" Daisy exclaimed. "I'm all for faith in my fellow man, but you can't trust a boy to be safe outside all night. Hope those aren't the kind of silly notions you're going to have about child raising, Charles."

"I won't. I don't!" Charles raked a hand through his dark, neatly clipped hair, sadly missing the respect his employees gave him on the job.

"Let's eat," Rose suggested, flashing him a sympathetic smile. "The aunts made a special Sunday breakfast just for you."

Violet was already stationed at the stove in the kitchen, frying something in a pan. She absently greeted Charles with a flutter of her spatula.

"Something smells wonderful," he complimented, allowing Lucas to guide him to a seat at the large Formica table.

"Soy links," Daisy replied as she moved to fetch another place setting.

Charles chuckled. "You've got to be kidding."

"Certainly not. You didn't think it was some kind of *meat*, did you?"

He tugged at the collar of his blue knit shirt. "Well…"

Rose sat beside him, giving his hand a small pat. "We're vegetarians. Suppose I should've told you."

"Why?" Daisy balked, rounding the table with a pitcher of juice. "Small healthy adjustment at worst."

He gestured to his glass as she filled it. "And this adjustment is…?"

"Guava juice." The silvered blonde gave him a hearty slap on the shoulder. "Where you been living, a cave?"

"New York City," he couldn't resist retorting.

"Then you've lived with diversity," Daisy observed, her narrow face thoughtful. "And as a student, you'd have a wide-open mind, I imagine." The observations brought a light to her eye that unsettled him.

"Your point?"

"There are so many things we can teach you, of course!"

"Daisy," Rose said as sharply as Charles had ever heard her, "give him reasonable time to ease into our routine."

Daisy sat down with a plop. "Routine and reason are for suckers."

Charles scanned a coffeepot. "How do you feel about java?"

Violet shuddered. "Poison!"

"Coffee's all the rage these days, from East Side to West."

"Yuppies everyplace." Daisy bared her teeth. "Even Greenwich Village. Credit card pushers, plastic bohemians. Bah!"

"Don't even own a coffeepot," Rose translated.

Violet approached the table with her pan. "How many links, Charles?"

He gulped. "I think I'll pass. Do you have any bread I can toast?"

Violet's round face stayed merry. "Of course. The toaster's rather touchy, though, so I'll do the honors. What shall it be, berry walnut, or molasses chestnut?"

"Surprise me," he whispered.

Violet winked. "I'd love to."

"HOPE THIS WILL DO." Rose led him into a bright airy second-floor bedroom a short while later, moving to the two large windows to push back the neon striped curtains.

"It's...a room all right." He dropped his bags on a large white throw rug, blinking at the floor-to-ceiling murals of nature scenes covering every inch of wall space.

"It was a family project years back," Rose explained. "Violet and I did the backgrounds and Daisy did the detail work."

"Neat pink-and-orange dresser complement."

"The brightness shouldn't stop you from sleeping. I mean, your eyes will be closed."

"That's tough to argue." He ran a hand along the bed's ornate footboard, staring at the swirl pattern in the white chenille bedspread.

"This was my room while I was growing up," she told him half-apologetically. "It hasn't been done over since then."

His eyes crinkled teasingly, giving the soft mattress a push to find it had bounce. "I'm surprised you don't sleep in here yourself."

The personal question startled her, bringing back her vow not to allow him any closer, to keep their focus on Lucas alone. But it seemed an impossible policy to keep with his gorgeous face alive with genuine interest. "Dean—my late husband—and I used to stay in here together sometimes when we were in town for the holidays or something. We relocated to California for a few years. Until I returned for good after his death." She twisted her hands awkwardly.

"A tough spot to camp out in now?" he asked huskily.

"Yes!" She exhaled in relief. "That's it. Those old and newer memories mingled together are a bit too much to face with every new day."

He smiled tightly, thinking how it would rip Hilton's soul open to know that Dean had been so close to home for some of those last precious holidays gone by. They'd assumed Dean never returned under any circumstances. Naive in retrospect. But what would they have done even if they'd known?

Suddenly the soft mattress before him looked like a bed of quicksand. How quickly he'd sink away from any concise thinking if he let it all get to him! Hypnotized by her huge blue eyes, he suspected he wouldn't feel a thing. Until Hilton got his hands on him again!

He started, realizing she was searching his expression for insight. "If it's too wild to your tastes I'm sure we could rearrange things," she ventured, eager to please. "Daisy and Violet each have small rooms down the hall—"

"No need to trouble them, calling extra attention their way at all!"

She wrinkled her nose impishly. "They don't upset you, do they?"

He stared at the toes of his deck shoes. "*Upset* is a pretty strong word. But I sense they want to rattle my cage. Maybe force me to give up and go?"

She was genuinely surprised. "Not at all. They didn't think too highly of my placing the ad in the first place, but they've come to accept you as the one." As usual, she too was mystified by the unpredictable turn, but she'd learned to accept her aunts' behavior with patience and tolerance.

"Have you, Rose?"

"Have I what?"

"Accepted me." He knew he shouldn't be continually teasing her, but he found he liked to watch her fumble with their chemistry the way he was.

"I've just fed you and delivered you to my old bedroom!"

"You did try to shock me to my senses during the interview."

She squeezed her fists in exasperation. "That was then. That was *the test*. Had to know if you could take the heat around here. You're in now, Charles. All the way."

Her passionate play put the squeeze on him in return, just as he deserved. Another Fraser boy on the *inside* with Rosy, soon to be tucked into her old bed. He wondered if she knew how her lower lip puckered sensually whenever she was amused. He wondered if it ever puckered at other times....

Finding the air stifling between them, Rose strolled over to the neon dresser under the lemon-lime curtains. "These drawers are a little sticky, but they're lined with paper and fairly deep. If you need more space—" She paused when she felt his hand on her shoulder.

"The room is fine," he said gently. "I won't be spending a lot of time in here, anyway. I don't require much sleep in general, and there will be some nights I'll find a place to stay in the city, crashing with pals."

She whirled around, distressed by the message there. "Really? Why?"

"Ah, because of my studies," he lied. "If I have some work to do on campus, it'll be easier to stay over."

It sounded as if he were seeking an escape hatch already. Her body began to tremble.

He couldn't help but notice. "Naturally I intend to do my job with Lucas. I won't let you down."

"I hope not, Charles. He's depending upon you to be there for him!"

"Don't worry so, Rose."

She gave him a pitying look. "I have to worry big time. He's already attaching himself to you. You're his first close male role model."

"Certainly other men have—"

"Other men are none of your business," she said hotly. It took her a whole three seconds to launch into an explanation anyway. "What I've managed to do is keep dates away from the house, unless they made the cut."

"What cut?"

"The *cut*," she snapped. "Any man who shows real potential."

"And no one's made this cut?"

She folded her arms, burning over the trap he'd set for her. "Not yet. A few have reached the aunts, but not Lucas. I'm very careful about who and what I expose him to."

Too careful maybe? Her policy struck him as overboard. Again Charles felt trumped by his own tricks. A little pressure and she'd opened up in an emotional flood, encouraging him to form personal opinions he'd intended to avoid. He was supposed to be here as a mere observer.

"What's that frown supposed to mean?" she demanded warily.

"Nothing, really."

"If it's concerning me, I want to know."

"Well, you don't feel you might be a little too protective, do you?"

That stung. "I take it you had a father in your home," she challenged.

"Yes, but it was no picnic."

"Well, I'm sorry to hear it, but Lucas has missed the experience altogether. He was a newborn when his father died. Though he has no memories, he does feel a general sense of loss, especially when he sees other boys with dads. Surely you can understand how urgent your role is."

"You sound as though you expect the sun and the moon from me."

"As well as the stars."

And so she should, Charles conceded. He was suddenly ashamed of the escape hatches he'd been trying to set up in their arrangement, ashamed of their arrangement in general. He wanted to do them right during his short stay, but he did like his life as it was, and didn't want to jeopardize it by going overboard. Fraser Advertising was all he had. The sum total of his achievements centered around creating the clever campaigns he pitched to clients. He couldn't bear to let any of it slip through his fingers.

Rosy was the sort of woman men made crazy sacrifices for, though. And as it happened he knew just how he could win her over right then and there: a quick confession now about Hilton's plans. Sure, he'd be out of a job, a family, an inheritance. And she'd probably soon discover she couldn't stand the sight of him for his part, and subsequently boot him out. But at least for a short delicious moment, he'd be her hero.

Decisions, decisions. He could use a cup of strong coffee right now!

"I'm sorry," she said in the lapse. "Guess I'm the one having the most trouble adjusting to my own plan. I've just handled everything for such a long time. Leaning on someone new, it's going to take some time. I'll…leave you to unpack now," she said, turning in the direction of the door.

"And then?"

She paused with a lovely smile. "I thought you and Lucas could walk me to work."

"You're tied up today?" he asked bleakly.

"I work a lot of weekends at the gallery. But my hourly wage has gone up two dollars an hour since I started, so I really can't complain, can I?"

Lord, could she ever!

"It's probably for the best," she reasoned brightly. "Give you a chance to bond with Lucas."

Exactly what he hoped to avoid.

"LET'S RUN!"

Lucas, sandwiched between Charles and Rose on the residential sidewalk, was tiring of their leisurely pace. He was holding tight to their hands like a frisky monkey, urging them on with tugs and whines.

Charles was glad to let Rose rein him in with an excuse about her neat work clothes and impractical midheel pumps. Not only would he be too embarrassed to trot after a child on a public street, but he had a small worry of his own. They were a few blocks from the Weldon house and Charles suspected that the gallery in which Rose worked was located at the shopping center where he'd instructed his limo driver to park yesterday.

Some covert agent he'd make! People had stared at his car, at him. Hopefully no one would make the connection.

Sure enough the center was the same one, located in the heart of the community, serving a variety of needs with a grocery store, beauty salon, pharmacy, and a small pub-style eatery. Rogue's Gallery was on the corner beside the eatery, making use of its expansive window space with post art displays.

"Remember, Lucas, don't touch anything inside, okay?"

Lucas hung his head with a dramatic flop that sent his fine blond hair spilling across his forehead. Rose grasped him under the chin and combed back the strands with her fingers.

"And don't call Mr. Pearce Mr. Rogue, honey. He doesn't like it."

"But Mr. Beevee calls his drugstore Beevee's," Lucas noted. "Why does Mr. Rogue use two names?"

"It's a different situation."

"Why'd he do it, Mommy? He's got one name already."

"We've had this conversation before."

Lucas wiggled as his mother tucked his red T-shirt into his white shorts. "Charlie wants to know, I bet."

Charles had been examining a print of the Hawaiian Islands, and turned their way at the sound of his name. He failed to completely swallow back the chuckle bubbling up his throat.

"Don't look so smart, mister," she chided. "This is the kind of stuff I hired you to take over."

He laughed loud and hard then. "Hey, I'm stumped myself. Why this place isn't the Pearce Gallery is a mystery."

"Boys!" With a huff and fluff of her ruffled hem, Rose whirled inside.

A discreet bell tingled upon their entrance. A well-dressed gentleman with a goatee emerged from a room in the back. "Ah, Rose." With the grace of a dancer he wended his way up front through the shop. Charles noted that the place was Manhattan chic, with tempered lighting, textured walls and professional displays.

"Charles, this is Mr. Rogue—I mean Pearce." Rose reddened profusely in the wake of her son's giggles. "I am so sorry, sir, Lucas has me in a spin as usual. Osgood *Pearce,* this is Charles Johnson, the man I told you about."

"Pleased to meet you." Charles made the first move, shaking Pearce's hand, returning his subtle inspection. It was difficult to stay cool under the older man's jaundiced eye. The picture Charles was portraying—the carefree student, with wind-tousled hair, dressed for a sport in navy shorts and white polo shirt— wasn't going to garner the instant respect he was so accustomed to. His eyes were as keen as ever though, as was his firm and smooth handshake. Pearce was mildly puzzled, but kept a polite businesslike smile.

"So you're the father figure."

Charles kept his features pleasant. "That's right."

"I do suppose a child should be exposed to more of the rough-and-tumble at some point in time," Pearce said with mild distaste. "If only to wean it out of the system."

"Many elements make up the sum total of a male," Charles bantered easily. Suddenly an image of Pearce's goatee dripping egg yolk appeared in his mind. That would certainly take some of the starch out of his pomposity!

Distress marred Pearce's high smooth forehead. "Certainly a thinking man's theory. But in this case, I imagined someone younger putting the boy through his paces. That's what Rose led me to believe."

He had it bad for Rose. The force of that less than subtle reality slammed hard against Charles's chest, nearly knocking the wind out of him. Pearce was pursuing her in his own pretentious way, drawing out her confidences, keeping tabs on her moves, all the while paying her cents above the minimum wage. Charles's smile dissolved to a slit as he took a closer, harder look at the shop owner. Fortyish, peevish, thinning blond hair, most of his strength in his yapping jaw. How Charles wanted to take him to his 34th Street gym and use the simpering fop as a punching bag!

He was overreacting of course. The city was full of guys like Pearce. The advertising agency catered to a steady stream of them. Just because this one happened to like Rose... And what a sneak, easing in between the cracks of her date-filtering system under false colors. It was clear he'd used his position as her employer to get close to the family.

Never mind that Charles was doing much the same thing, under the guise of an employee. This was different. Pearce had only his own lecherous interests at stake. Charles was trying to do a little good for Lucas.

"When shall we come back for you?" Charles asked lightly as he turned toward Rose, standing nearby beside a pedestal holding a Chinese vase.

She managed a lopsided grin as his eyes singed her with a territorial heat. "I'll make my way home. You boys go knock around on your own."

For a brief, tense moment Charles couldn't take his eyes off her, so delicate was she in her blue-and-white floral sundress, her bouncy hair spun golden on her shoulders. The pricy vase at her elbow looked dense, heavy, and dime-store cheap in comparison. He didn't want to leave her here.

He was behaving irrationally, he realized. This was her life, her routine, her meal ticket. He had no right to barge in and trash her arrangement, jeopardize the only income that rambling house of fools had.

One thing he could do was make Pearce come out of the shadows and state his intentions as his brother Dean had, be man enough to go through her filtering system as her other dates had. That would give Charles the chance to tromp him fair and square.

Rose wondered why he lingered. "So, Charles, do you think you need some ideas for the afternoon?"

Pride lifted his strong chin. "No, I think we can manage, can't we, Lucas?" He gave the boy's head an awkward pat.

Lucas smiled beatifically. "Sure, Charlie. I gots some ideas."

Ideas… Charles skimmed the present company—Rose's hopefulness, Pearce's coolness, the boy's dimpled cheeks. Seemed everybody had ideas.

All in all, he had never felt more cornered in his life!

Chapter Five

"You still looking at that stuff, Charlie?" Lucas came screeching to a halt in the center of the hardware section of the Beevee's Drugstore, one worn tennis shoe clamping down on Charles's brown deck shoe, the other butting up against his shopping basket full of a variety of screws and household tools. "Mr. Beevee's got all kinds of better stuff."

Charles was in a crouched position at a shelf full of door locks, making it convenient to confront Lucas on his level. "You shouldn't be wandering around this place without me." He removed the boy's shoe from his, then slowly rose to his full height.

Lucas rolled his eyes. "It's okay. I know all the people in here and Mr. Beevee's been helping me shop."

"Shop for what?" The question had an absentminded quality as Charles studied the dead bolt in his hands, reading the installation directions on the package.

"Good day to you!" a male voice boomed. "Mr. Beevee at your service. You must be the father figure from the ad."

"Yes." Charles stared at the rotund man towering over him. Charles was six foot three, so he figured Beevee had to be a good six-six, weighing in at 250 pounds beneath his khaki clothes.

"This is my good friend, Charlie," Lucas said cheerily,

aiming a thumb at the owner. "Mr. Beevee, like it says on the sign. *His* name is on his store, like it's s'posed to be."

"Been down at Pearce's again, haven't you?" Beevee chuckled, gently cuffing the boy's chin.

"Mommy hasta work there." Lucas curled his lip in disapproval.

"Mr. Beevee," Charles interjected, holding up the dead bolt. "I'm looking for the best kind of lock for the Weldons' entry doors, front and back."

The clerk's balding, egg-shaped head bobbed. "Excellent idea. I've asked the flower sisters many a time if they needed reinforcements." He edged in between man and boy, his bulk sending Lucas into an exaggerated stumble. "That one you're holding is okay. It's the most expensive—"

"I don't care about the cost."

Beevee's smile widened. "I'll show you the best, of course. But it's this one." He held up a box. "It's easy to install and works as well as that more expensive type. Doesn't come with as many keys, but I can make copies right here cheaply."

Lucas patted Mr. Beevee's beefy arm. "You're a good guy."

Beevee was openly pleased. "I try."

"You're a good guy, too, Charlie, don't ya worry."

Mr. Beevee tapped his chin with a heavy finger. "You know, Charlie, you're familiar to me somehow. Spent any time in these parts?"

"No, never. I'm taking graduate courses at Columbia, and am strictly a city dweller—until now," he added.

"Oh." Beevee lifted his huge shoulders. "I rarely go there."

Charles gritted his teeth behind a smile, reasonably sure that Beevee had seen him at his limo yesterday. Hopefully, he wouldn't be busted on such a small technicality.

"Charlie's a real good guy," Lucas announced. "He's finding all the loose screws in the house."

Humor skittered through Beevee's dark marble-size eyes. "Give them both my best, Charlie. Now you guys come up to the register, I found those other items you were looking for."

As the clerk lumbered away, Charlie caught Lucas by the shoulder. "What were we looking for?"

"What we *need!*" Lucas said in exasperation, dashing ahead.

"A baseball and mitt?" Charlie set his basket on the old wooden checkout counter moments later, staring down at the additional purchases.

"Sure," Lucas called out, skipping back toward the sporting goods section. "Wait here."

Charles balked. "Hey, man!"

"Be back in six minutes!"

Charles rubbed his lips together, suddenly realizing that Lucas dropped that six-minute time frame on adults whenever it suited him. He wondered how long the boy had really been keeping watch out on the porch that morning.

"He'll be fine," Beevee assured. He pointed to a mirror clamped above Charles's head. "I've got a clear view of him up there."

Charles smiled ruefully. "He's tough to keep up with."

"I understand why you're surprised about the child-size glove," Mr. Beevee said, leaning over the counter in a conspiratorial way. "The county is nearly picked clean of them at this time of year, with all the junior leagues starting up. I found this one in back." He paused wistfully. "Well, maybe I was hanging on to it for the kid, hoping upon hope that things would change in the Garden of Eden."

Garden? What had he called Daisy and Violet? The flower sisters? He tried to piece things together. "Are you trying to tell me the flower sisters don't want him playing ball?"

"I reckon I am." Beevee's large features clouded. "That won't stop you, will it?"

Charles rubbed his chin. "I don't know. What's Rose's opinion?"

"Don't know. She's always trying to please those ladies."

"Can't see how a ball and glove could do any harm," Charles mused, amazed at the number of judgment calls forced upon him.

"And you are the male mentor, right?" Beevee challenged man-to-man. "I mean, if Rose wanted her son planting posies and posing for paintings all day, she wouldn't have hired you, right?"

"Makes sense," Charles said hesitantly.

The clerk seemed puzzled by his reluctance. "You did come in here for this stuff, didn't you? The way Lucas sounded—"

"Sure," he abruptly lied. "It's my job to make the boy happy."

"That's the spirit, Charlie."

Lucas appeared on the front aisle again, another glove in his hands. "Found it, Mr. Beevee!"

"This one's way too big for you," Charles protested as Lucas plunked it on the counter. "The other—"

"It's for you, Charlie."

"Huh?"

"Why sure, I can't play catch with just me. I need you." Lucas clamped his hands around Charles's midsection and hugged him fiercely.

Charles could feel his heart squeezing painfully as memories rushed to the forefront of his mind. Dean trying to teach him how to swing a bat in Little League. Charles whacking out Dean's front tooth. Hilton had been livid, beside himself with fury. Dean was more merciful, having had taken the blame for standing behind him.

Big brother had ended up with the finest false tooth available to mankind, but Hilton didn't let it go for long. Somehow he'd convinced Charles he was an inept athlete, dangerous in all fields of play. To this day, Charles stuck to handball, never picking up a club of any kind.

"Aren't there any little boys around here you can play with?" he asked lamely.

"I happen to sponsor and coach a T-ball team, Charlie," Mr. Beevee ventured. "I'd hoped to get Lucas involved in that time."

It was clear the pair had set him up big time, but Charles clung to the latest turn like a life raft. "There you are, Lucas. Kids your age, knocking 'em around."

"I need to practice," the boy protested, his arms falling free of Charles.

"He really should," Beevee agreed solemnly. "Most of the others have had a year with me already."

"But T-ball is fairly simple."

Lucas tugged on his belt loop, his face both sly and earnest all at once. "You want Mommy to keep you?"

Charles was instantly stricken. "Of course I do."

"Then you better make it two gloves, Mr. Beevee," Lucas piped in with authority. "And put it on Aunt Daisy's charge account."

Mr. Beevee laughed in an air-sucking bellow as he began to ring up their purchases. "I'd be half tempted to if she'd paid me anything since 1989."

"We'll pay cash," Charles said dourly, reaching into his back pocket for his wallet.

"How 'bout a bat too?"

"No, Lucas!" Charles cleared his throat, managing a small grin as he handed Beevee a large bill. "Let's leave the hitting for the field."

"Practice is at the playground over on Grange Avenue," Beevee said, handing Charles change and a receipt. "I'll let you know when."

"Guess we'll see you there."

Lucas trailed after his brand-new temporary father with a puzzled wail. "Why can't we have a bat?"

Charles pushed the glass door open with his hip. "Let me think about it for six minutes."

Lucas marched outside with hands on hips. "Hey, that's what I say!"

Charles pulled his sunglasses out of his shirt pocket with a smirk. "Guess a fella's never too old to learn a new trick! C'mon, man, let's go find me a decent cup of coffee."

Lucas's eyes danced with intent. "I know just the place. They have coffee *and* the best hamburgers in town."

ROSE RETURNED HOME that evening around seven to find the front door fastened—with a whole new lock. She rang the doorbell, tapping on the bright yellow porch planks with an impatient shoe. Lights were on inside; she could hear the faint murmur of the television. She paced fretfully, gulping humid air. A curly gray head suddenly looming in the parlor screen startled her. "Aunt Violet! I can't work the lock on my side. Let me in!"

"I would love to, m'dear, but I can't seem to unlatch it, either. Go around back."

"Where did the lock come from in the first place?"

"Charles."

"Charles! Why would he fiddle with our locks?"

"Because they were too easy to crack, so he said."

"What good is a lock that *we* can't crack?"

"I'll teach you the basics," came a male voice with a velvet promise. Rose whirled around to find Charles standing beside the porch in graying light. He looked fit and sexy in ragged jeans and a tight white T-shirt, a little defiant with a cocky tilt to his stubbled chin.

Rose descended the wooden staircase with hard-heeled clops, until she reached the bottom step, which put her at eye level with him. How she hoped she'd overestimated his affect on her. The only way to be sure was to put herself to the test, steel herself against his charms.

Some woman of steel. The same old tingle swiftly chased up her spine, sizzling against the beads of perspiration rolling down her back. He sensed her condition like a panther, pressing just a little closer.... She leaned back into the rail. "What are you up to, playing handyman?"

"The boy's education is in my hands, isn't it?" He wiggled his fingers in her face. "Can't go wrong learning how to put in a new dead bolt."

Rose took short, puffy breaths, inhaling his manly scent of aftershave and sweat, vowing she would do this over and over again until he no longer affected her. No matter how many long summer days and nights it took, she was going to get some level of control....

"Charles, this isn't what I had in mind for you." At his look, she stammered, "F-for Lucas, I mean."

Charles's features narrowed but he didn't press her. "None of you were safe with those toy doorknobs dating back to the Truman administration."

"I suppose you do have a point—about security. And Daisy must've—"

"She was busy in her studio," he admitted.

"Oops."

"You just wait, Rosy, wait until I get ahold of your...garage." He smiled as she gasped during his deliberate lapse, only to realize that he'd called her Rosy and shouldn't have. Such a slip might be too much, he could very well have Dean's inflection in his voice. Stupid and risky.

She wrinkled her nose as a faint internal bell rang in her head. "I hope you're not disappointing Lucas with this turn to chores."

"He's learning you work before you play."

"When does the play begin?"

"Oh, we've been whooping it up around here, too. Come and see—"

"Hey, Charlie, come back." Lucas came charging around the house, his glove hanging limply on his hand. "Oh, hi, Mommy."

"Hi, yourself. What are you guys up to?"

"Baseball."

"Baseball!"

Charles steeled himself for a tirade like the one he'd gotten from the aunts, but amazingly, she was gasping with joy.

"Finally, Lucas, somebody who knows the rules of the game!"

"Beevee signed him up for his team. Hope that's okay."

"Yes, I guess. I should've done it myself, but the time never seemed right. The aunts... My Dean..." She gave him a helpless look.

"Let's show her how we catch," Charles suggested, shooing Lucas on. "Go round back and get ready."

Lucas zipped off and Charles slipped his arm into hers, slowly guiding her across the grass, around trees and bushes. "I'm glad you approve."

"Very much so. My late husband and I had season tickets to the Yankees. Dean liked to play some, too." She started with recollection. "That reminds me of a crazy incident. Dean's clumsy little brother bashed his tooth in with a bat! I've never mentioned it to Daisy and Violet, though. They already think all organized sports are akin to war games."

Charles sobered. Was that one tooth incident all Rose knew of Dean's little brother? Curiosity overwhelmed him, as did a feeling of being treated unjustly. "I imagine your husband would've wanted Lucas to give this a chance, though, don't you think? I mean, he and his brother must've made up."

"Oh, yes. Dean was extremely fond of—" She paused. "You know, his brother's name was Charles, too. Didn't like to be called Charlie though, like you do. Unfortunately, Dean lost touch with Charles. There were several years between them in age, and there was a falling out in the family. Poor Dean simply didn't know what to do but cut all contact with them."

"This other Charles must have been fairly young. Maybe he needed a big brother."

"Yes, but his father is such a tyrant! Dean just figured it could get messy for Charles if he tried to have a relationship with him. You see, Hilton Fraser has a great deal of money, a thriving business. Dean didn't want Charles to find himself disinherited on account of him."

"I see."

"Life is full of tough decisions, isn't it?"

"Oh, yes." Charles stared up at the darkening sky, the awakening stars. Dean thought about him, wanted the best for him. Even missed him. It did so much to validate the times they'd shared as good, memorable, meaningful.

He rubbed a hand over his shaky lips. If he weren't careful, he'd find himself breaking down in a most embarrassing and revealing way. What would a stranger ask her at this point, he asked himself. Surely there was something to bridge this awkward gap. "So, ah, is this Hilton still around, doing his thing?"

"He's too mean to die," Rose said vehemently.

Charles silently conceded the point. Hilton could be damn mean. But his rights as a grandparent were another issue entirely. There was a dynasty at stake, the Fraser family name. He couldn't help but wonder how set against Hilton she was.

"This father have any contact with you and Lucas?"

Rose paused midway along the side of the house beside a maple tree, her mouth dropping open in horror. "Certainly not! A man that controlling, that selfish would only hurt Lucas—as he hurt me!" She took a deep breath, forcing a smile. "I'm sorry. I didn't mean to sound off that way. We mustn't let thoughts of Hilton Fraser spoil our evening—or our summer for that matter."

Charles was stupefied. The soft woman he'd come to know had turned into a tigress before his eyes. But that was what a good mother did, or so it seemed from his observations. It was just as he'd suspected in theory. She'd been devastated by Hilton's actions and wanted to shield Lucas from the pain.

They moved on, making their way to the well-lighted, fenced-in backyard. Rose opened the creaky gate, clearly on the rebound as she merrily thanked Charles for not bolting that, too. She was trying to rebuild the cordial shield between them, set him back a step where he belonged. He understood. It was the end of a tiring day, and they barely knew each other. The logic didn't buffer his disappointment, however. He found himself drawn to her with increasing strength. The more he discovered, the more he wanted to know. The closer he inched, the more urgent his need.

By all appearances, Lucas had all but forgotten them, running circles around a frisky, yipping Beast.

"They have an incredibly short attention span at this age," Rose remarked, noting his surprise. She cupped her hands to her mouth in an effort to add volume to her naturally soft voice. "Toss a few balls, then it's bath time and to bed. You've got school tomorrow."

Lucas brightened at the sight of them, picking up a glove from the grass. "Watch, me, Mommy. I'm good already."

Charles retrieved his glove and the ball from the picnic table and played a game of catch with the excited child. Lucas caught three and missed two, seesawing between jubilation and frustration.

Rose waited until Lucas threw a ball way out of Charles's range, then approached her son, taking custody of his glove, steering him and Beast toward Violet who waited at the back screen door. Lucas obeyed, waving good-night to Charles.

Charles prowled across the grass with a playful frown. "Hey, who am I supposed to play with now?"

Rose clutched the glove to her middle. "A sensitive jock? What's the sports world coming to?"

"Put that thing on," he dared, gesturing to the mitt.

"It's too small!"

"Naw, bet it isn't."

"Whadaya bet?"

He wiggled his dark brows wolfishly. "Whadaya got?"

Rose pressed her thighs together shyly as the breeze lifted the full hem of her dress. His lopsided grin was devastating. How did he manage it? Playing with Lucas one moment, flirting with her the next? Then it struck her that husbands and fathers did just that every day of the week. "It just so happens, mister," she claimed saucily, easing off her pumps, "that I got a lot!"

"Put some spit in that leather and let's go!" Charles was concerned that he was letting loose too soon, pressing their friendship. But he couldn't seem to help himself. It all seemed so right. She happily fit the glove like a lacy fashion, then stood poised, as though hailing a cab. "You look like a girl out there!" he lamented.

She stared down at the glove and punched it. "Don't think I can spit."

"Just squat a little and catch with both hands." When he finally did release the ball it floated up with all the force of a slow-moving cloud.

"You threw harder to Lucas!" she complained, leaning forward to catch it before it fell to the grass.

"Well, I didn't want to make the boss look bad on my first day."

They played catch for quite a while under the yard lights, tossing and lunging and laughing. Charles tried to pry information out of her about her day, expanding on her job, her ambitions. She admitted to wanting a gallery of her own someday, right there in White Plains. He imagined himself gallantly presenting her one.

They finally called it a night when the mosquitoes overtook the field. It seemed natural to Charles to wind his arm around her shoulders as they sauntered toward the back door, he with the equipment, she with her shoes.

"That was great fun," she said, leaning against the stoop

rail, cradling her pumps. "I could kiss you for hooking Lucas into it so fast."

"Maybe it's Mr. Beevee who deserves that kiss."

Rose gasped, overcome with gulps of laughter. "As if! He's more like *my* father figure."

Charles sighed in resignation. "Okay, I'll play proxy for the swell old guy." Cupping his hand under her delicate chin, her raised her mouth and bore down on it with his own.

A taste of honey. That was what Charles's kiss was like. Rose hadn't been kissed so deliciously, so thoroughly since her marriage. Her heart fluttered wildly as he held her just close enough to touch, then skimmed her mouth with gentle, unhurried passion. She probably shouldn't have given in, but the spontaneity of the gesture made it seem like so much good clean fun. It felt so good to feel so wanted.

He finally released her with a peck on the forehead. "Suppose it's time to call it a night. Lucas isn't the only one who's beat."

"Parenting is a big job." She laughed softly, giving the knob a twist. "This doesn't want to turn."

"It's locked, Rose. That's the way the dead bolt works."

Rose rapped on the door. "Hey! Anybody there?"

Violet appeared in the glass, pushing aside the curtain. "Can't open back or front now," she mouthed in distress.

Rose's face crumpled. "Is this right? We're trapped? They're trapped?" She seized Charles by the shirt in a fiery panic. "Do you have any idea what you're doing around here?"

"Of course I know what I'm doing!" It was the biggest lie he'd told yet. He was swimming in confusion over Rose's subtle sensuality, her hunger for his advances.

She sensed his predicament. "I'm talking about the locks here."

"Locks I know." He turned back to the pane. "I told you, Violet," Charles stressed on his last thread of patience. "A key is necessary on both sides."

"How preposterous!" the older woman grumbled.

"Oh, for Pete's sake!" Charles shoved the gear under his arm and dug into his shorts pocket for his keys. With deft movements he slipped the proper one into both locks, top and bottom, and the door swung open.

Daisy was just entering the kitchen as they barreled inside. "Lucas is all tucked in and drifting off."

Violet was ecstatic to see her big sister. Pressing a hand to her ample chest, she said, "Oh, my, this door is impossible, just like you said!"

Daisy pushed some faded strands of hair from her vision, centering upon the flushed couple. It was likely that she was gauging the advancement in their relationship but chose to let it lay. "Violet and I discussed this boobytrap, Charles. You really should've asked before you went to such extremes."

Charles knew they'd been fuming over his handiwork, and it seemed they were waiting for Rose to return before letting him have it. Unable to completely keep up his facade after his long day, he stared Daisy down with sternness. Here was a fine example of what Hilton feared, that the aunts weren't near up to guiding Lucas, with all their restricted diet and unrestricted views, their heads in the clouds on important matters like this. He was compelled to speak plainly.

"I think you may need a lock on the inside first and foremost. The idea that Lucas was camped out on the porch this morning for mere minutes is a joke. I've come to realize that his six-minute line is obviously a routine excuse for everything. Something you already knew," he accused.

"He may be daring," Rose argued, "but I'm sure he doesn't sneak out a lot."

"How do you know?"

"I keep track."

"You have to sleep sometime, Rose," Charles reasoned.

"We are capable of looking after one small boy!" Daisy snapped.

"But you do have a problem here that's already in full bloom. Lucas knows he can sneak out and he has the guts to do it. It's necessary to accept that, to work on correcting the problem. In this case, the inconvenience is minor at most."

"He's got a point," Rose interjected as Daisy arched her hands like claws. "Lucas is too young to understand all the dangers involved. At his age, it seems wise to simply put up the necessary barriers."

"Lucas is brilliant, capable of understanding anything. You know how strongly I believe in reasoning with the child rather than stifling him. Don't we, Violet? Reason is the way."

"Oh, my, most certainly," Violet gushed worriedly. "It's the way we raised you, Rosy."

"I wasn't as adventurous or obstinate, though," Rose admitted, torn between fronts. "Lucas is a wanderer, a handful—all boy!"

"All the more reason to listen to a man like me!"

Daisy's lip pruned, her eyes aglitter. "It does trouble me some, Charles, that you're more interested in fixing up the doors and the swing set than in nurturing the child."

"That's not so!" He was only more comfortable with it. "There's something to be said for blending work with play."

"It's also troubling that the *play* portion of your day centered around scarfing down hamburgers and tossing around a baseball."

"Is it so wrong to give him treats that kids all over the country are enjoying?"

"What I think is that you're Lucas's biggest chump yet!" Daisy hooted. "He's led you around by the nose all day, indulged in the things he believes are missing from his life, and you, wanting to play big shot, gave in at every turn!"

The women watched him, the aunts triumphant, Rose distressed. "I guess you've seen right through me,"

Charles said stiffly. "When I wasn't hiding behind nuts and bolts, I was out to win over Lucas in my own clumsy way. On that insightful note, I think I'll say goodnight, ladies." With a stiff nod, Charles strode through the kitchen and into the hallway. The ball bounced to the floor, but he didn't pick it up.

Daisy's narrow face pinched in anger as she reached for the ball. She gave it a near seam-busting squeeze before setting it on the counter between the napkin holder and the toaster. "This man goes so against our grain. It makes me wonder if he's an awful mistake."

Rose sank into a chair at the table. "We may have been too impetuous. Though I am delighted about the baseball—and even I feed Lucas burgers."

"He's taken so much upon himself in a very short time," Violet said.

"One day here and he's trying to change everything," Daisy exploded in exaggeration. "Hardly what you were after, dear. You wanted a complement, not a makeover."

Here it comes, Rose thought, passing a hand over her face. The rigorous lecture on who ruled the canary-colored roost. Daisy was angered by anybody who didn't automatically fall under her tutelage, and Charles's outburst tonight was the crowning jewel on a day of mutiny. Rose found herself torn between Charles and the aunts and didn't like it.

Violet set three juice glasses on the table and filled them with homemade grape wine, as well as an eye dropper of impatiens-clematis extract so conducive to curing bouts of anxiety. Rose took a healthy sip of hers.

"Men are generally dolts who can be fashioned to fit a woman's design," Daisy stated, clinking her glass against Rose's before taking a swig. "Nature's grand plan in my opinion."

"Perhaps we should've advertised for a dolt." Violet giggled.

Rose thought again that the hired hand probably

should've been a nice pliable teenager. Charles was so forceful when roused, so dynamic all the darn time, way beyond the untried student type. If she didn't know better, she'd have sworn he was the executive type, comfortable with clipping out orders and making things happen.

Ironically, Daisy was something of the same steely sort beneath her liberal views and hippie garb. It was no wonder they'd clashed so quickly. Dean had given neither of the aunts a millisecond of trouble, fitting so snugly into their open-minded ways and free-love philosophy.

But Charles was bound to make all kinds of trouble if he stayed on. Delicious trouble for her personally, judging by his playful mood tonight. Lucas wasn't the only one he was trying to impress.

Was it so wrong to enjoy his company? Not if her feelings clouded her common sense. Was he the best man for Lucas? The hand holding the glass shook a little. He came on so self-assured, the handsome Prince Charming. But there was an urgency swimming just beneath the surface. It was plain that he was looking for gratification of his own. But why here? In the end, it all came down to trust and intuition.

"Please don't be offended," she finally said. "But I would like to make the final decision about Charles. Just leave it to me."

CHARLES MADE A QUICK trip to the bathroom, dressed only in his jeans. As he stared into the mirror, brushing his teeth, he decided he'd blown the whole deal. Would they even let him stay the night, he wondered.

Simmering down, it occurred to him that he was mostly to blame. He should've played it more lightly. But this boy was a Fraser! His own nephew. As awkward a mentor as he was, he had rights and obligations.

Then it occurred to him that a man had to stake a claim before he began to demand rights. In short, he'd first have to reveal his true identity. Until then, it seemed he was at their mercy.

Admittedly, they had made some valid points. It was mighty humbling to accept that a pint-sized kid had manipulated him all day long. Like the ladies, he found it tough to resist that cherub-faced operator. Stuffing his toiletries back into his leather case, he marched down the hallway to his room, hoping to dive into bed, unchallenged, until morning.

"Psst! Hey, man!"

He drew to a stop at a darkened door that had to be Lucas's. "Hey, man," he said with forced cheer. "You're supposed to be asleep."

"Can't sleep without my mitt, Charlie. You got my mitt?"

"It's in my room. Hang on."

Charles padded back and forth, dumping his case, retrieving the glove. Surely he couldn't get into much trouble serving this one last need of the night. It wasn't as if he were installing another lock or force-feeding the boy meat. Though a cold cut submarine sandwich would go great right now.... Back at the Fifth Avenue apartment, he had all the necessary ingredients. By the looks of things, he'd be banished to the city by this time tomorrow.

As he crossed the threshold of the boy's room, Dean's lamp with the cowpoke base clicked on, bathing the small plain room in light. There wasn't much on the shelves over his dresser, just a few model cars, a few books and some board games. Beast had a small bed of his own near the maple rocking chair, lined with a handstitched quilt that matched the one on the boy's bed. Odds were the aunts made those, too.

Lucas stared groggily into space, reaching his arms out. "Gimme."

Charles sat on the edge of the mattress, dropping the glove in the boy's lap. "Catch."

Lucas smiled dreamily. "Yeah..."

Charles pressed him back gently to his pillow, tucking him in snugly.

"Know a good story, Charlie?"

"Ah, not really."

His small hand popped back out of the sheet and patted a book on the nightstand. "There's some in here."

"Okay. A short one."

Charles twisted around, scooped up the book, and made the short transfer to the nearby rocking chair positioned in the glow of the old familiar lamp. He sat back and flipped through the pages. "Let's see…" He inadvertently looked up at that point, nearly toppling out of the chair as his eyes lit on the wall opposite the headboard.

The wall held a huge dramatic mural of Dean!

He couldn't stop staring. A youthful, happy Dean, a glitter in his eyes, his dark blond hair parted a little off center. Daisy's work for sure. And she'd done a marvelous job, capturing his late brother's strength and humor. Charles couldn't stop staring, admiring. *Feeling.*

Rose's confidences came back to him in a rush. Dean had cared about his younger brother, so much that he'd left him to Hilton and the family fortune. Dean had been happy though, the portrait confirmed it. The smile was real, just right.

There was a creak of the bed springs and a rock of the chair as Lucas climbed into Charles's lap with his mitt and blanket. "That's my daddy's picture," the boy whispered. He touched Charles's cheek. "You cryin'?"

Charles blinked. "No, no, just got something in my eye."

"That mean you can't read to me?"

"I can do it." Charles blinked hard and dove into a story of the boy's choosing, about a clown with a hamburger stand.

Lucas rested his head on Charles's chest and listened…until they both drifted off.

"YOU'RE GETTING IT. Slide it in, then out again. See how easy it fits?"

Charles's silky murmurs floated up the staircase the following morning, capturing Rose's avid interest as she made her descent. What was he doing downstairs? A smile of relief brightened her face at the sight of him showing Daisy and Violet the finer points of dead bolt operation. They were behaving like a couple of giggly girls, hunched over his sturdy shoulders.

So what had changed since they retired for bed last night?

"Slide it in and turn," He guided Violet's plump hand holding the key.

Rose took a steadying breath, as erotic fantasies spun recklessly in her mind.

"I did it!" Violet whirled around to find Rose crossing the foyer. "I mastered both keyholes."

"Remember, ladies," Charles said, rising from his haunches to push back the inside door. "If you want fresh air during the day, just put a stopper behind here and hook your storm door like always."

Violet quickly removed a gold chain from her neck, unfastened it and slipped the key on it. "I shall wear this around my neck so I'm never at a loss."

Charles stepped up from behind to assist Violet with her fastener. "Would you like your lesson now?" he asked Rose with a wink.

"No, I can't take any excitement this early." Scanning his tan slacks and green knit shirt, she realized that like herself, he was dressed to go out. "Classes today?"

"Uh, yes. I intend to go into the city quite a lot during the week, especially when Lucas is in school."

"I did hire you for evenings and weekends," she said understandingly.

"So, I'm still hired?"

Rose looked around the foyer to find that the aunts had

disappeared. "Yes, of course. Daisy and Violet seem to have no objection, either."

"Can't explain it," he confessed. "They were giddy when I came down this morning. To tell you the truth, I was all packed, fully expecting the grand heave-ho."

Rose bit her lip, finding no argument to his logic.

"But they were absolutely charming, anxious for a dead-bolt lesson."

"Their way of making amends for last night's row," she surmised.

"But why, Rose?"

"I don't know. But I did tell them I'm in charge of you and—"

"You really said that?" He savored the idea with twinkling eyes.

"Oh, knock it off." Rose fidgeted under his teasing look, tugging at her form-fitting yellow shift. "You know what I mean, the agreement's between the two of us."

He nodded solemnly. "Yes, of course."

"Say, you didn't make any rash promises, did you? About visiting Daisy's studio in the attic?"

He watched her innocently. "No, I didn't say or do a thing. Just appeared my usual, wonderful self."

Lucas came charging up the hallway in blue shorts and an orange T-shirt, his hair styled with some fragrant mousse. "Time to go to school, Charlie. Violet's driving us."

"I was planning to take a taxi to the station."

"Those daily fares would break you," Rose protested.

They heard the rumble of a choked up motor out in the driveway. Charles peered out to find a vintage Volkswagen van, replete with flower power and peace signs!

Lucas called for Beast, gave him a quick cuddle and slipped his small hand in Charles's. "Time to go, man."

Rose tucked her fair hair behind her ears, leaning over to give Lucas a peck on the cheek. "Be good."

"Have no fun with Mr. Rogue." With a cute smile, he

tugged Charles through the screen door. Charles followed him across the porch and along the walk to where the family vehicle was idling. "You gonna be here when I get back, Charlie?"

"Afraid not."

"How about dinner?"

"I'll try."

"But what if I need to talk to you real bad?"

Charles stopped Lucas, pretending to straighten the boy's shirt. "That reminds me," he whispered, "I left my little red cell phone under your pillow. You can call me if something important comes up. My number is taped to it. Got all that?"

"Course I do. I know lots of numbers. Want me to count real high?"

The van's horn tooted and the passenger door swung open.

"No time for counting now." With an easy swing Charles hoisted the boy onto the bench seat and climbed in after him.

Rose stood in the door, wondering what man and boy had been discussing. Whatever it was made Lucas very happy. How she hated missing any secrets involving Charles. Well, there was one secret she could crack without delay. She marched into the kitchen for a showdown with Daisy.

Daisy was at the sink, taking a variety of vitamins. "Oh, it's you. How about some oatmeal?"

"What happened here this morning?" she asked shrilly. "Eight hours ago you were ready to dump Charles in the nearest recycling bin, then I find you playing with his keyholes."

Daisy regarded her calmly. "I know. But, well, things can change."

Rose crossed her arms and lifted a brow. "Like what!"

"You wouldn't have seen anything last night, with your bedroom at the top of the staircase, but Violet and I stumbled upon the most moving scene, Charles and Lucas in that old rocker I got at a flea market last summer.'' She glowed in remembrance. ''You just had to be there to get the impact. After what we put that man through, all but firing him on the spot, he carried on, cuddling Lucas in his arms like a prized possession. Lucas was glued to him with such dreamy contentment. Charles possesses such sensitivity, looks so vulnerable in slumber. I must say, it's almost as revealing as a nude session. By the way, did you ever say whether I could ask Charles to pose?'' she asked innocently.

''I said no. You know I said no.''

''Maybe he'll want to volunteer.''

Rose squinted at her. ''Daisy, find your own little friend.''

''But I'm warming to yours, dear.''

''You haven't even had the courtesy to ask if I intend to keep him on.''

Daisy smirked. ''You do. That slide of key left you panting.''

''Arrrr.'' She clenched her fists and spun around. ''I have to go to work.''

''Can we expect Mr. Pearce for Monday night dinner as usual?''

She paused at the counter where she'd left her small leather purse. ''I suppose so. Guess I forgot about him in all the excitement.''

''Mustn't ever forget Osgood. Any week now he's going to agree to my one-woman show in his gallery.'' Her graying brows furrowed. ''Now you wouldn't want to stand between an artist and her big break, would you?''

''No, the show must go on.''

Daisy gestured to the wall clock. ''Better hurry, dear, or you'll be late.''

''So you'll be here to handle Lucas this afternoon, then?''

"Thought we'd practice calling Osgood Pearce by his correct name."

"Practice all you want. Lucas already knows the difference."

"Think Charles will be back by then?" Daisy asked nonchalantly.

"I don't know. Probably not if he finds out about Osgood. Somehow, I got the vague feeling that they didn't care much for each other." She shook her head in bewilderment. "Perhaps it's because they have nothing in common."

Daisy shook her head, murmuring softly at Rose's retreating back. "You're such a dunce about men, dear. What they have in common is you."

Chapter Six

"Good *afternoon,* Mr. Fraser."

Charles breezed into his offices later that morning with a doleful eye on his secretary, Marcia Haines. "It's still morning by a long shot," he said with good humor.

She glanced up from her typing to the pendulum clock hanging on the mauve wall. "Technically speaking, I suppose so. Though you must admit that ten's normally considered the shank of the day to workaholics like us."

"I was forced to drop by my apartment for a suit," he explained, moving through the connecting door to his own quarters.

"Drop by from where?" she anxiously called after him.

Charles turned back, nearly bumping into her as she came up quickly carrying a brass watering can. He inhaled as though to make a full confession. "From where I was, of course."

She leaned over his desk as he sat down. "You've got a new girlfriend, haven't you?"

"Marcia, don't you have some work to do?"

"I'm watering the plants." She raced over to his sill to douse a sad-looking begonia, plucking off some of its dried pink petals.

"Seen my father this morning?"

She cast him a sympathetic look. "He's been pacing the floor over you."

"Oh. Well, the Calhoon Soup account is heavy on his mind."

"Or so I thought, until he said, quote, 'blast that Calhoon!'"

Charles thumbed through his phone messages, trying to conceal his surprise. Another emotional outburst from the man of steel. All because of Lucas, of course. And Hilton hadn't even as much as laid eyes on the boy yet. "So," he said with forced vigor. "Did *you* hear from that blasted Calhoon?"

"Not a word." She straightened, smoothing her black Chanel suit, about to bust. "What's happening with you Fraser men? Have you finally found the daughter-in-law of your father's dreams?"

Charles broke into rare genuine laughter. "Definitely not!"

"Then what gives? You're out of touch all Sunday, after leaving me the message that you're to be temporarily incommunicado during the off hours."

"That's the way it has to be for now, me checking in on occasion."

"But that's totally out of character. Don't you know how I depend on your constant communications, tossing around your brainstorms, chasing down your tips on potential clients?"

"I only started this blackout yesterday—"

"When I needed your beep the most! I was at my parents' for dinner, hoping, praying you'd have the decency to interrupt!"

His eyes twinkled in empathy. "I am truly sorry. Are they on the march again about your terminally single condition?"

"Naturally! You wouldn't believe what a grand exit I could've made out of one tiny beep. I could've pretended this place was on the verge of ruin!" she said with a flap of her arms.

"Easily solved. Give me notice next time and I'll ask

Dad to beep you.'' He made a notation in his appointment book, ignoring her gasp of indignation. "I think I have time for some correspondence. Would it be easier if I use the recorder?''

"No, I'll get my steno pad. Who knows, you might slip and give something away.''

They'd gotten through five letters when Hilton showed up.

"Charles! You're holed up in here!''

"Yes, Dad,'' he greeted wryly. "Hiding out in my own office.''

Charles tipped back in his comfortable leather chair and directed Marcia to carry on. Hilton followed her to the connecting door, making sure it was firmly closed in her wake. He returned, rubbing his large hands.

"So, how goes the snooping?''

"Fine. Lucas is a wonderful little guy.''

"How did you spend your time?''

Charles gave a rundown of their day, hitting on the vegetarian fare, the baseball hookup through Beevee despite the aunts' objections, and Rose's respectable job at Rogue's Gallery. He tried to keep his inflection even throughout. He did omit the touchy points of the nocturnal argument nearly leading to his dismissal, the mural of Dean and the way the cooing aunts took Lucas from his lap, then guided Charles down to his own room, tucking him in like another groggy boy. Even in his sleepy state he'd sensed their reservations giving way. And why not? He was proving as susceptible to Lucas's charm as they were.

"Imagine, forcing the boy to abstain from meat!'' Hilton raged, no doubt set to tear into every fact Charles unearthed.

"It's not as bad as it sounds. He's pretty crafty and well acquainted with the restaurant menus in the area. Rose treats him to his favorites.''

"But is it often enough? The very idea of denying him protein,'' Hilton pressed. "Starvation tactics!''

"Oh, c'mon! The boy's healthy."

"Still, it could cast reasonable doubt in court."

"Unless you land a vegetarian judge."

Hilton was nonplussed. "Hadn't considered that."

Charles rubbed his neck, looking away. "Well, you should."

"About this baseball stuff…"

Charles stiffened in his chair, squaring himself for the blow.

"You haven't forgotten how inept you are with bats, have you?"

"No, father," he said on a sigh, "you've never let me forget my ineptitude. But if Lucas wants to play, it seems only fair he be allowed."

"Of course, I'm all for it. Dean loved the game despite his injury and would've wanted the same for Lucas." He shook a finger. "Just as long as you're careful. When's practice start?"

"I don't know yet. Beevee from the drugstore is going to call."

Hilton's heavy brows gathered as he hunched over his son's desk. "Think he's satisfactory coach material?"

Charles laid a hand on his crisp white shirt near his heart. "You're trusting bungler me on that?"

"You're capable of making an observation from the bleachers."

"Dad, this is T-ball. It's my guess that patience is the most important factor in a coach at this level."

Hilton tramped around like a penned-in bull. "Probably so. Naturally I'll take note that the aunts were against it."

Naturally.

"Your description of Rose's job seems to jibe with my preliminary check."

"Yes, I suppose so. She's in sales, framing. An all-around assistant to the owner, one Osgood Pearce." Charles failed to keep a snarl out of his voice as the name roiled up his throat.

Hilton mistook his tone for pay dirt to his own cause. "They horsing around? Passing illegal goods through that place? What—what?"

"Pearce is the most painful sort of snob," Charles reported. "He may very well be interested in Rose—" he held up a hand to fend off his father's glee "—but believe me, it won't do you any good. Just the opposite. He'd be a most credible witness for the defense. I can see him now, going on about Rose's attributes in grand, convincing soliloquy." *All the while thinking of how he was going to trap her like a helpless kitten for his trouble.*

Hilton took the blow grumpily. "Seems he is better off dismissed."

Charles melded his fingers into a knot on the desktop. "Definitely."

"Must admit, you've made progress fast," Hilton said on the upswing.

"You'd need more than a few firecrackers to prove your point," Charles felt the need to caution. "You'd need TNT."

"Just keep at it," Hilton said with rare and open confidence.

Charles appreciated his father's faith in his ability, even in these odd circumstances. After all these years, he did on occasion still ache for an overall stamp of approval. It would probably never come, he knew. Though getting the TNT this time would go far to put him in favor.

On the other hand, the fact that getting these explosives was his ultimate mission at the Weldons was something that pricked him like a tailor's pin stuck in the seat of his pants. He shifted around, rolling his chair back and forth, finding no comfort.

"I've already been to the lawyers about some of the other flaws you've found," Hilton thought to confide. "The bad locks for instance—"

"Oh, I fixed those."

"Fixed them? How could you!"

Charles balked at him. "Dad, you can't stand there and tell me you wouldn't want that child kept safe?"

"But it was evidence. How about the swing set?"

"Fixed that, too," he admitted with an eye roll.

"Oh, son." Hilton rubbed his forehead with a mournful sound. "You're putting me in moral dilemmas I never knew existed."

"Yeah, well, misery loves company."

A silence pervaded the dignified office. Hilton picked up Charles's engraved letter opener, running his finger along the silver blade. He finally spoke with effort. "Look, don't feel bad about the handiwork you did."

"Gee, I'll try not to."

Hilton seemed to miss his son's sarcasm. "Whether you fixed that stuff or not isn't the issue. It needed fixing when you got there, and you can testify to that much."

"Testify!" Charles jumped halfway out of his chair, raw panic in his face. "Me? Personally?"

"Naturally," Hilton barked, clenching the opener. "What did you expect?"

"Not to testify personally."

"What did you plan to do, whisper it in my ear and have me whisper it to the judge?"

"I don't know! I thought you'd handle it all, as is your habit."

"A smart businessman knows the value of a personal pitch, son."

"I'm not sure I'd be very convincing in this particular case."

Hilton drilled him sternly. "You're not going soft, are you?"

Soft? Charles knew he could no longer clearly define himself as the razor-sharp executive with the ready answers. He knew the Weldons mopped the floor with him. He did sound a mushy version of his old self at that.

"Charles? Answer me!"

He stared up at his father, tense with fury. "Huh?"

"Are you going soft?"

Charles grew hearty. "A Fraser? C'mon!"

Hilton glowed with parental pride. "So, do you have plans for lunch?"

"Eating in. I have to work."

"Oh." Hilton slowly ambled to the door, giving him time to reconsider.

Charles busied himself at the computer, resenting Hilton's ploy. For the price of a sandwich the old man wanted to further pick his brain about their precious new heir. "I'll take a rain check," he called out in farewell.

"See you at the Calhoon meeting then," Hilton finally relented. "Two o'clock. Bring the storyboards."

Charles's hand fell still. "*You* spoke to him today?"

"Of course. He's settled in at the Marriott and looks forward to seeing our ad campaign."

Charles bared his teeth as the door thumped shut. Jed Calhoon was supposed to go through him personally. Couldn't his father keep his nose out of anything? Charles stopped typing jibberish and leaned back in his chair, his mind drifting to Lucas. Was he wrong to help Hilton get a stake in the child's life, take it over as he was trying to do his?

The pros and cons played in his head. The riches at stake were enormous by anyone's standards. There was the money, of course, but also the Hilton wealth of knowledge and experience, his power in social and political circles, his capacity for gruff love. The kid was bound to find the old man a pain in the behind quite frequently, but any achievement was worth a little discomfort. There were so many doors an acknowledged Fraser could have opened to him.

Didn't Lucas deserve the opportunity to give his birthright a once-over, decide what might be useful to him? He was incredibly young now, of course, but in no time, he'd be grown and wise to the world.

Charles hated being the sneak, the man in the middle. But it was too late to stop this tilt-a-wheel in motion. He was in the nest, and Rose had made it clear she had no interest in giving Hilton a break. He was getting that quick-sand feeling all over again.

JED CALHOON HAD the body of a whipcord, slim, spare. A born and bred Texan, he could easily be mistaken for a genuine ranch hand in his western wear. But he was crafty, wily and every bit as successful as the Frasers. He always said he knew his soups and the Frasers knew just how to push 'em.

Charles was extremely grateful when his father had given him the reins of the prized account last year. If only Hilton would dismount completely. Whenever Jed galloped into the Big Apple, Hilton's breath was right there on his son's neck.

If only the soup empire didn't need so much at this juncture. Charles was in the process of shooting two very important commercials for Calhoon's newest soups. It was a lot to think about, on top of his newfound extended family.

But business was business, and this was a workday. He skipped lunch altogether to go over his presentation and made it a point to be in the boardroom early, pressing Marcia back from a short lunch to help him set up the storyboards.

Naturally, Calhoon arrived in Hilton's care, arguing about the performance of a German-made sports car. Charles hid a smirk as Hilton gave in to the Texan after a modest fuss. That kind of surrender was pure thespian skill on the adman's part, bull reserved exclusively for clients.

"Nice to see you again, Charles." Jed Calhoon's voice was modulated with a hint of a twang.

Charles shook his hand, matching his grip. "Good to see you, especially at such an exciting time for Calhoon Soup."

"Yep, we're proud as can be of our new line."

"More stew than soup." Charles bounced off the approved slogan he'd come up with for the company's heartier blends.

Jed Calhoon beamed. "Like it better every time I hear it."

Several other executives joined them at the long walnut table, and one of Hilton's male interns served coffee from a small stainless steel refreshment station in the corner. Once everyone was settled, Charles went through the concept of the first commercial.

"We're doing something completely new with this one, Jed. A grandmother type is stirring a big gleaming kettle on the stove full of Calhoon's Beef Burgundy. She doesn't want her family to know it isn't homemade, so every time a family member comes into the kitchen to check up on her, she pretends she's planning to add something else, like an onion from the fridge, some seasonings from her spice rack. Each relative in turn stirs the kettle and says, 'Don't tamper with perfection, Ma.' Then the voice-over says, 'Don't you tamper with perfection, either. Calhoon Soup, etcetera, etcetera.'"

Jed ran a hand through his thinning black hair. "You're a marvel, Charles."

Charles's chest puffed a little under his suit jacket. "The second is a carryover from our other campaign. The fictional Harris family in despair over a quick, hearty meal after a game of touch football. Everyone groans over the idea of soup, until Mrs. Harris brings out the new, heartier line of Calhoon's. The two kids start tossing around bread sticks and crackers, setting the table, all while Mrs. Harris is grinding open those cans with wide eyes and contemplative nods of approval. The husband asks about dessert and Mrs. Harris suggests he wait and see if he has room for it."

"Again," Calhoon said, "I'm mighty impressed."

"We don't have the daughter back. She's done some sitcom work and is impossible, throwing fits on the set and demanding too much money."

Jed's bony shoulders lifted beneath his chambray shirt. "I leave those details to you folks."

Charles tried to conceal his relief, as that was the only hang-up he knew of. "Excellent, Jed. Give me a minute here and I can tell you exactly how long it will be before both commercials will be completed." With Marcia's help Charles thumbed through the papers stacked on the table.

Suddenly a muffled ring filled the silence. There were many surprised expressions around the table. Hilton didn't allow cell phones into these meetings. Charles approved and gladly complied to show a good example.

Before Lucas, anyway. Ah, uncomplicated life before Lucas. Just last week, if memory served him right.

Charles reached into his jacket for the little red instrument nestled in the lining pocket. This was his own fault, really. He'd given the boy the phone and being a curious youngster, he'd decided to use it. Surely it was something important, though. He'd told Lucas to think important. On second thought, maybe he should've said emergency.

"Yes, hello," he greeted with enough briskness to avert suspicion.

"Hi, Charlie," the small chirpy voice greeted.

Charles wore an even smile as he met curious eyes up and down the table. "What's up?"

"Not much."

"You sound...different."

"That's cause I got peanut butter stuck to my tongue."

"Peanut butter?"

"Yeah, you like it?"

"Sure, I like it."

"Do you click it up and down in your mouth?"

"Not lately."

Lucas made a gulping sound, his voice clearing. "You ever get peanut butter stuck anyplace?"

"I don't think so."

"I'll save you some."

"That would be fine." The cords in Charles's neck tightened just above his crisp white collar, aware that people were listening intently. The seconds were passing like hours.

"I'm home from school."

"Yeah, I figured that out. Look, I'm rather busy right now."

"Don't you wanna talk to me?" Lucas whined in disappointment.

"Of course I do," Charles said thinly, rising from his chair with an apologetic expression. He moved away from the table, thinking that the room had never seemed so small before. Was there really only one door? "What's going on this afternoon?" he asked softly.

"I wanna play catch. Can you come home?"

"I can't right now. I'm doing some work."

"You got a really mean teacher?"

Charles gazed over at his father, looking especially masterful in a charcoal suit and a bloodred tie, a death ray gleam in his eye. "I sure do."

"So when are you coming home, man?"

"Late, I think."

"Dinnertime?"

Charles paused at the coffee station for a refill. "Probably not."

"Mr. Rogue's coming to dinner."

"What!" His exclamation ricochetted off the papered walls and the packet of sugar he'd been peeling open plunked right into his full, steamy cup.

"He comes every Monday. Didn't they tell you?"

Using his body as a block, Charles edged the cup with the floating packet behind one of the large silver urns. "How long's that been going on?" he asked in an urgent whisper.

"Six minutes."

"Very funny."

"Ha-ha, Charlie. Bye-bye."

"Hang on!"

"What?"

"I'll be there," Charles promised rashly under his breath. "For dinner."

"Hot dog! And boy, would I like a hot dog, Charlie. Let's buy some."

"It's a deal." Charles disconnected then, slipping the phone back in his pocket. The room was quiet with a hollow, expectant tension. Charles returned to the table. "Sorry, another negotiation in the works."

The sea of faces went blank with acceptance, save for Hilton, who knew damn well who was on the line, and Marcia, who desperately wanted to know.

The meeting went on for another hour without a hitch. Charles was grateful for once to leave Calhoon in Hilton's hands as he made his escape. Marcia, however was impossible to shake, as they shared the same suite.

"You've got yourself a girlfriend after all!" She snapped her fingers, trailing after Charles as he strode back into his inner office.

He sank into his chair. "I told you before, no."

"You said no to the daughter-in-law of your father's dreams. That's different from finding a girl of your own. A lot different, I imagine."

"Different how?"

"Yummy peanut butter..." She smacked her lips. "Can't picture your daddy indulging in a hot time like that. Can't imagine why he didn't protest that call, either."

Normally Hilton would have raised hell over such a strange interruption. Marcia was right and knew way too much for the Frasers' good. Viewing her as an annoying big sister, however, did give him the right to speak plainly about family affairs. "You're doing to me what your parents are doing to you."

Marcia gasped. "What a terrible thing to say."

"But true," he insisted, aiming a pen at her with slitted eyes. "You are prying into my romantic life uninvited. I want you to cut it out."

"May as well. Judging by that call, I'd say this fling won't last anyway."

His brows jumped. "I was nice! Real nice."

"Tense. Real tense." She took on an airy resolve. "Never mind. Go on with your tense conversations, keeping your late office hours—"

"That reminds me, I'm leaving the office at four today."

She nodded approvingly. "Good. Spread it real thick—both the peanut butter and the sweet talk."

"It's not what you think!" he raged.

With an unconvinced look, she waltzed away.

He rested his chin in his hand, feeling a dimple similar to Lucas's forming on his cheek. Dimple sightings were rare at his age. It took something especially crazy to make it happen.

He massaged the spot thoughtfully. Now if Rose ever managed to bring the dimple out in him, that would really be something. Forgetting himself in her... That would really be something.

Chapter Seven

"Daisy, are you sure this new casserole recipe is a tasty one?"

Daisy stopped Rose as she was about to open the oven door for the third time that hour. "It's delicious. You know I treat Osgood Pearce to the best we can afford. This week's creation is a cheddar rice bake, full of fresh broccoli crowns, tender green onions, plump firm mushrooms." She closed her eyes, obviously in the throes of creative visualization.

Rose couldn't help but think how pretty Daisy looked then, much younger than the sixty years, with her complexion pink and soft, her silver-blond hair swept back loosely with a barrette, a purple crepe pantsuit more tailored than most of her billowy garb. She'd pulled out all stops to impress Osgood Pearce, one of the area's few bona fide art dealers with enough vision to understand a bohemian talent like hers.

Daisy was looking over Rose's appearance, too. "I'd say you've gone all out. New outfit, your hair in a *très chic* knot." Daisy pinched her chin. "On behalf of my cause, I thank you for the extra effort."

Rose smoothed the new pale green dress over her hips, giving the skirt a little swirl. In truth, her efforts were for Charles. He was coming home for his first official family dinner. She'd fretted through the morning, wondering if he'd bail out someplace in the city.

Then the personal phone call came through to the gallery. Her son's string of babble held the all-important message. "Guess where I'm calling from? A secret place. Charlie's coming home for supper. Can we have hot dogs? Does Mr. Rogue gotta come?"

The world was a wonderful magical place again for Rose. After all this time, she found herself infatuated with a man. A man with little more than a sterling résumé, simmering brown eyes, and a sensual hunger that matched her own. She discovered Lucas wasn't the only one with yearnings and unfulfilled places in the heart.

But a serious romance between her and Charles would complicate matters greatly, give them all a lot of crazy ideas. And if it didn't work out? Nothing was sealed in stone. At any given time, Charles could go out for a hot dog and never come back. So much for her date-filter system.

Her more impetuous side scolded her reluctance. Had she learned nothing in Dean's passing? Warnings of extreme caution were best suited for road signs. Life was full of rough surprises, but good ones, too. If fate had delivered Charles to her, why not relax and enjoy him?

She jumped a little as a male hand weighed on her shoulder, spinning her around. A gasp caught in her throat as she found Osgood Pearce standing before her.

"Violet let me in," he said, pleasure lighting his features. "Don't you look lovely, Rose."

"You just left me an hour ago at the gallery, Osgood," she protested with forced gaiety. "I can't have changed much."

"But you have." He inspected her thoroughly, as though discovering a real gem set among rhinestones. "You're quite different. Truly."

And it truly pleased him to no end, Rose realized, trying not to flinch. Osgood was the controlled type at the gallery and it suited their limited, working relationship just fine. Restraint suited him in general, really, from his orderly clipped goatee to his manicured nails.

Could it be that he'd always viewed these innocuous weekly dinners as some kind of a slow courtship? The idea seemed preposterous. Osgood was much older than she, showing only a vague interest in Lucas—in the mere concept of children, for that matter.

She'd long suspected he greatly enjoyed playing her Henry Higgins, introducing her to art, fine wines, and important people from the city. But Daisy was the one who'd instigated these dinners, all in the hope of landing a showing at his shop. The surface amenities had seemed enough for Osgood, until now.

Admittedly, two things had upset the status quo they'd enjoyed last Monday night: Charles Johnson and her quick interest in him. Obviously Osgood had seen the fire in her eyes in this unguarded moment when she thought the new man of the house had come home. He was taking full advantage of her weakness, ravishing her with a look reserved for his favorite Van Goghs.

Common sense cautioned her that she'd have to be very careful in handling Osgood. Rebuffing him flat out would do nothing for Daisy's chances of an art exhibition—not to mention putting her own job in jeopardy.

Darned if he wasn't going to kiss her! Rose braced herself woodenly, keeping her lips tight. Much to her relief his pucker landed on the downy spot between her brows. She giggled in spite of herself.

"I think I love that giddy sound." He cocked his head as though listening to the wind. "Yes, I think I do."

She pressed her forefinger to her temple, half smothering a full laugh. "Your goatee tickled my nose."

He grasped her shoulders. "You are so wonderful!"

"Osgood," she said with sweet firmness, "slow down, to the comfortable speed we're used to."

"Oh, that's been fine and well for the gallery—for far

too long. Your cool, brisk ways in the store are perfect, of course," he was quick to add. "But here and now, you're like the most glorious bud, all soft, fragrant and—"

"Rosy?" Charles ambled in through the back screen door. "Isn't that what you were about to say, Pearce?"

Osgood stiffened, lines marring his high forehead. "Why, yes, I suppose I was about to impose on my close nexus with the lady, by making such an observation."

Rose sized up Charles with undying gratitude, absently noting that his clothes were as fresh and unwrinkled as when he'd left that morning. Odd, she didn't recall him wearing black oxfords this morning though.

Charles followed her gaze down his body to his feet. His shoes! How stupid could he be? He was so intent on beating Pearce back here that he hadn't taken care while he changed. A quick check confirmed that everything else was okay though. Thankfully his gold tie clip wasn't dangling from his belt buckle or anything.

Even in his rush, he hadn't managed to discourage this pass by Pearce. The pompous art dealer was just the kind to play it safe until he was given a nudge from some serious competition. And Charles was the type to instinctively nudge hard. Ironic, as setting fire to Pearce's bony backside was the last thing he'd wanted to do. Charles only wished to unsettle Rose's life-style if he could better it.

Fine attitude for a turncoat spy!

"Back from school then?" Osgood queried with schoolmaster superiority.

"Yes," Charles replied pleasantly. "Home sweet home."

The gibe hit home just as Charles hoped, causing Pearce's eyelids to twitch. "Don't let us keep you from your homework," he drawled.

"But we're about to eat," Rose interjected graciously, stepping in between the men for a comical body block.

Charles smirked, thinking how she looked as refreshing as a pastel mint candy in that dress, how easily he could hoist her over his shoulder and saunter off into the sunset. "Something smells great," he said casually.

"You shouldn't be standing that close to her," Osgood snapped.

Rose blushed. "He means the casserole, Osgood."

"Oh." Pearce sagged a little.

"I wonder where Lucas has gotten to." With hands on hips, Rose looked around the kitchen for any signs of her son or his dog.

Osgood joined in with forced interest. "Yes, where is my favorite lad?"

Charles suspected that Pearce wouldn't trade even a lesser Bordeaux for the answer, and judged by the surprise on Rose's face, she was having similar thoughts. He hoped she was, anyhow. Surely she couldn't take this jerk seriously.

Suddenly he felt her gentle hand on his bare arm. "Charles, your briefcase is ringing."

It was his turn to be usurped. Striding for the table, he opened up the case and reached for his new red phone. It had to be a wrong number. "Hello," he said silkily.

"Hi, Charlie."

"It is you! Why call me here and now?"

Daisy appeared just then to check on her oven. She did so quickly, then joined the circle forming around Charles.

"If it's important, we can leave you alone," Rose whispered.

"He can leave us," Osgood objected.

Charles raised a hand to fend them off. "Exactly where are you?"

"I'm chasing Beast around the house. It's a race."

"Didn't I tell you these are special phones for special times?"

"This is special, man," the small voice huffed. "You came home to play, didn't ya?"

"Sure. But as for the phone, I think you should be keeping it someplace safe, like under your pillow—" Charles broke off, aware that Rose was frowning curiously. Like his secretary, Marcia, Rose automatically assumed he was talking to a woman. But in all fairness, he was the type of man to give a fire-engine red phone to a woman for some games. "Just simmer down now," he commanded, causing Rose's thin brows to jump even higher. "We'll have a long talk later. Just come in to eat."

"What—" Rose paused. "Is that Lucas?"

"Yeah," Charles admitted, disconnecting the call.

She charged up to his open briefcase. "You gave him a telephone?"

"I loaned him one." He quickly closed the case, realizing there were some telltale Fraser Advertising folders inside.

"But the expense—"

"It's part of my humanities study, funded by the university," he said, hastily preparing an explanation.

Just then Lucas charged through the back screen door, his red cell phone in his hand, the fluffy white Beast trotting at his heels.

Rose quickly took the phone from the boy. "This is a very expensive instrument."

"It's my instrument!" Lucas squealed with the stomp of his tennis shoe. "Charlie gave it to me 'cause we're pals. He's the man. He said—"

"That's enough," Charles directed, ruffling his hair. "Big guys don't scream at their moms."

"Indeed not," Pearce chimed in loftily. "Especially not a nice mother like yours."

Lucas glared up at Osgood Pearce, his small face screwed up, his eyes snapping blue fire. "Only Charlie can yell at me, 'cause Mommy pays him to."

Though Charles wasn't receiving any money, the general idea was correct, and hit home with Pearce. He nervously stroked his goatee. Charles could tell his rival was weighing his options, deciding how much abuse at the hands of this youngster was worth his while.

When Pearce spoke it was with intelligence and control. "There, now, Lucas. We're friends from way back. It's my pleasure to employ your mother so she can in turn provide you with...*him*." He was triumphant as he mapped out the pecking order, placing Charles at the bottom.

Charles grimaced. This chump was in for one rude awakening about whom he was dealing with. Taking back the reins, he collected the extra phone, the briefcase and the boy. "Let's go wash up, Lucas." With a polite nod, he steered the boy through the doorway.

Dinner was delicious, the hot, bubbly cheese casserole, the steamy crusty bread. The conversation centered around Lucas's adventures and Violet's run-in with a runaway shopping cart at the grocery store. Charles chewed and listened and laughed, more as an observer than a participant. A pattern quickly formed, he noted, to his own relief and amusement. Whenever one of the Weldons would try to query him about anything, Osgood would turn the discussion another way, more often than not to himself. The maneuver suited Charles just fine; he learned to time his swallows, so that Pearce had enough room to beat him to the punch.

As dessert closed in, however, Pearce found himself in a trap of his own making. Not for the first time Daisy was trying to wangle a precise week out of him for an exclusive showing of her paintings.

Pearce sipped his herbal tea slowly, picking at his cheesecake with a fork. "Must we talk shop at a gala meal like this one?"

"Shop is all you talk about!" Everyone gasped when Daisy leapt up in a flash of purple. "I insist we take this conversation up to the studio at once!"

Pearce dabbed the corners of his mouth with his napkin. "I know exactly what you have, Daisy. And I've told you that when the time is right—"

"But I've set things up to create an atmosphere," she protested.

Pearce looked around the table for an ally. Rose and her aunts were pinning him with defensive, daring stares, insinuating that their hospitality should have some rewards. Charles took a gulp of water, relishing watching Pearce squirm.

"Oh, c'mon on!" With her bell sleeves and pant legs billowing, Daisy led the parade on its way. With the timing of ballroom dancers she and Violet swept Osgood Pearce up and along.

Lucas sidled up beside the lingering Charles. "You coming?"

Charles gulped. "Up there?" The last thing he wanted to do was tramp up to the attic for a look at a portrait of Mr. Pennyfoot—and presumably others like him—posed in the buff.

"Why, sure."

If Hilton got wind of any of this *art*... Charles shuddered in dread. It would help if Lucas was at least banned from the studio. "Maybe you have homework to finish down here," he suggested.

Lucas tipped his round face up to him, beaming like sunshine. "Not in kindergarten, Charlie. Don't you remember how kindergarten was?"

"Uh, not really."

Charles found that Rose had lingered in the doorway and was studying him strangely. What would she make of his behavior? She moved in close, setting her hand on his solid biceps. "It's all right," she whispered.

Charles wanted to think so. Her warm breath on the sensitive curve of his ear caused him to shudder again, this time in exquisite pleasure. That, along with the smell of her skin, sent a burning ripple through his blood. It was as if a torch had been set to his infatuation, turning up the heat that he knew he should be keeping on a low flame.

This was the last woman on earth he should be playing with.

And it made the attraction all the more exciting.

As if burned, she pulled back her hand and stepped away. "What I mean is I've noticed that Daisy's bluntness, her earthiness, unsettles you a bit. But Lucas is well acquainted with her artistic flare-ups and finds it all rather commonplace. He may as well come along if he likes."

Charles drew in one last fortifying breath of her intoxicating scent. "Lead on."

The attic was amazingly airy, bright and spacious, a long rectangular room of varnished pine, with ornamental windows which opened at front and back, and newer skylights set in the slanted roof. Charles took in the picture, thinking that much of what Daisy made on her art sales had to be reinvested right here. Frames, canvases, and colorful paint littered the area in no particular rhyme or reason.

There was some sense of order in the center of the room, however. Daisy had put together a crowded display of her work on easels. Much to Charles's relief and amazement, it was not some kind of lusty display, but a wide variety of subjects—nature and Parisian scenes, human figures—all of which were in some state of dress. It didn't alter the fact that Daisy did do nudes, though, and that she did on occasion regard Charles himself with an X-ray vision that burned through his B.V.D.s.

Charles felt torn about keeping Daisy's shenanigans from Hilton. But so far he'd reasoned that he wouldn't be expected to report such fishy goings-on to Hilton if he didn't see it firsthand, or wasn't asked to participate. Until now, all he'd seen was a hulking man standing on the staircase in a sheet, all he'd heard was Daisy's lament for some flesh-colored paint. That was hardly enough to throw the book at anybody in a court of law.

Osgood Pearce, meanwhile, was pacing around the small display, nervously rubbing his slender ivory hands together. "I see you've been working very hard."

Rose watched her aunt's anticipation and moved in beside her, hugging Daisy.

It was so unlike Osgood to even agree to this viewing.

But Rose suspected it had something to do with his coming on to her earlier this evening, and his agitation over seeing Charles. Osgood perceived himself as the king of the jungle around the Fraser-Weldon household. But would that be enough to force an act of generosity out of him?

"Daisy," Pearce said as he paced some more, "I would like to comply but—"

Rose noticed beads of sweat glistening on his domed forehead. She was actually enjoying watching him squirm.

"—but my most recent exhibitions have focused on the abstract...and on a single theme."

"Yeah, like the one with all the feet, or the eyeballs," Lucas piped up. "I thought that was cool, all those eyes staring." He struck a bug-eyed pose that sent Charles into chuckles.

"See," Osgood said with an edge of desperation, "even this child, this unmolded flesh—"

"Hey," Lucas shouted, "don't call me names."

Pearce gave the boy's head an awkward pat. "Whatever." He dismissed Lucas with a wave of his hand. "Suffice to say I'm looking for the unconventional, Daisy. Something you aren't anymore."

That did it. Daisy's nostrils flared as she gulped in air. She wrenched free of Rose and stormed over to a three-paneled screen set off in a corner. "I'll show you theme. I'll show you unconventional. I'll show you all the body parts on one glorious canvas!" With a flourish she whisked out a large frame, and made to tear off the sheet covering, no doubt, the naked likeness of one Mr. Pennyfoot. Before he could even draw breath, Charles dove at Lucas and clamped a hand over his eyes.

Chapter Eight

"Doesn't this family ever sleep the conventional way, in their own beds?"

"Oh, Charles. It's you."

Rose, seated on the porch swing some hours later, was startled to find him easing out the front door in some low-hung pajama bottoms. Even in the dim light of the yellow porch bulb, it was evident by the lay of the wrinkled cotton that they were straight out of the package. It made her wonder if he was in the habit of wearing pajamas at all, and if not, what he usually wore to bed.

Hoping to conceal the glint bound to be dancing in her eyes, she busily tucked her peach nightshirt around her thighs and moved to one side of the bench.

He pointed upward as he sat beside her. "I heard a creak through my window and thought I'd better investigate."

She caught her breath as his solid, bare biceps brushed against her upper arm, causing a delicious friction on her dewy skin. "I suppose you thought I might be Lucas on the prowl again?"

He shook his dark tousled head with a chuckle. "The idea crossed my mind, but I couldn't believe he'd really cracked our new security system." He turned slightly, angling an arm over her shoulders as though seeking a more comfortable position for his large frame. "Then when I found the inner door propped open by a heavy bust of some dead president, I figured Lucas was cleared."

Rose's pulse jumped as his fingers touched her collarbone. "The bust is of a man named Jerome Kenmore, one of Daisy's old flames, done during her clay period back in the seventies. She's always immortalized her lovers in one form or another."

"Wouldn't that make for a unique theme at the gallery?"

Rose chuckled. "It would be an interesting collection of artwork, I'm sure."

"So what brings you out here so late? Insomnia?"

"Could be I'm restless 'cause I think you're gonna make a break." She smiled as his brows rose. "Seems we torture you at every opportunity."

"Maybe you'll end up sweeping me off the property," he half joked.

She sat forward, causing the swing to rock. "Why would we ever?"

Let me count the ways. For starters, there was his duplicity. How he hated being torn between her and Hilton, trying to decide what was best for Lucas. She'd no doubt throw him out when—if—she discovered that. Not that he wished it was anytime soon. "For complaining about policies, of course," he improvised. "For starters, you had to notice I was unhappy that Lucas was exposed to that ruckus with Daisy. Wouldn't it have been simpler to leave him downstairs?"

Rose brushed a stray bug away. "He's up there constantly."

"But Daisy seems so centered on provocative expression—"

"She's harmless, really." Rose was all at once touched and offended by his concerns and it put a huff in her tone.

"But to whisk out that painting in front of the boy—"

"There was nothing risqué about it, Charles. Admit it, Mr. Pennyfoot was posed from a side view, and any strategic areas were covered by his extended Viking shield."

He summoned the preposterous vision to mind. "Well, yes—"

"He was never nude through the whole sitting."

"But the whole idea—"

"Is a blend of Daisy's tall tales and your overactive imagination."

Charles found it hard to not to let his imagination run wild right now, what with her hand posed on his knee.

"Didn't you happen to see Mr. Pennyfoot on the day of your interview, standing on the staircase, wrapped in a sheet?" she speculated.

"Yes, I did," he reluctantly confessed.

"And overheard some of our conversation?"

"Yes, yes. But I have to tell you," he said soberly, "what gets to me most is the unshakable feeling that Daisy's been viewing me as…as a potential figure for her painting!"

"She does do that," Rose admitted, setting the swing off again as she pushed off with her feet.

"A *nude* figure," he clarified.

"Uh-huh."

He tapped his chest with a finger, his voice dropping to a hoarse level. "I am the *father* figure. Completely dressed as a rule." He fumbled under her amused survey of his low-slung pants and bare chest. "This isn't funny, Rose!"

She didn't stop laughing. "I'm teasing you in only the most affectionate way, Charles. You've been wonderful about everything. And you wear plenty of neat clothes at all the right times. You don't know much about accessorizing your shoes, but you can learn."

The sexy little tease. It seemed insane to kiss her now. But she was asking for it, with those luminous blue eyes, moist parted mouth, soft flyaway hair. He desperately wanted to consume her, to bond with her, to feel, for even a brief spell, that he had control of her—all of her thoughts, all of her reactions. He wanted to know that when she laughed again, it was because he was deliberately witty.

Damn plenty to expect from a single kiss. He'd have to make it good.

He stroked her delicate cheekbones with his fingertips, then capturing her chin in his hand, he drew her mouth to his for a deep lazy kiss.

Rose caught her breath, held it tight in her throat as Charles kissed her deliberately, thoroughly. His hands skimmed the flimsy fabric of her nightie, as if committing to memory her every curve. She held his shoulders, delighting in the feel of his solid muscles. This was the way it was supposed to be between a man and a woman. Frantic, hungry, impulsive.

When they finally broke apart, they were both breathless.

As much as Lucas needed Charles, Rose was growing certain that she needed him more. Their instant attraction had struck like lightning, with a rush of elation and seduction, and the promise of fulfillment. The chemistry was pure magic.

A rueful smile twitched her mouth. No wonder Osgood had jumped out of the dugout into the batter's box. One look at Charles, and the play-it-safe Pearce was swinging a hot bat in the hopes of guarding the little stake he'd half-heartedly made.

Thank goodness Osgood had been too conservative to make a bid before now. If he'd been more forceful during her leaner times, she might have given in—for financial and security reasons only.

Even if Charles wasn't the man for her, he was proving fast and furiously that life with Osgood, or any of the other men she'd dated of late, was *not* a step up from being alone.

"I suppose it's time to call it a night." Charles spoke tentatively, hoping Rose would climb into his lap for another taste, or the very least invite him to stay and enjoy the starry night. But she'd already taken some mental distance from him, breaking the spell of his kiss. He rose shakily and leaned against the porch railing to gather his wits.

She watched him in appreciation as he flexed his body against the length of the wood and folded his arms across his chest. Sure he was still brooding over her aunt's antics, she tried again to comfort him. "Please don't worry so much about Daisy's influence on Lucas. She was someone to reckon with thirty years ago, peddling her art in a Greenwich Village shop full of carefree hippies, but she's more talk than action now, believe me."

"But your boss has lit that old fire in her again, hasn't he?" He hated to bring up Pearce, but he needed answers. Daisy's huge ego made her a weak link in the Weldon crew, the one that Hilton could most easily break in his attack. If she got involved in some provocative project, it could mean big trouble.

"Osgood's no saint," Rose said slowly. "But he probably would sponsor Daisy if she came up with the goods."

He pulled a tight wary smile in the shadows. "You like to dig for the best in everyone, don't you?"

The question rang like an accusation, taking her off guard. "I was raised to do that, unless I'm proven otherwise. Weren't you?"

"Not exactly." Fearful that she might pursue the issue, he kept on course. "If only we could steer Daisy on to other, better-dressed games...."

Rose studied him coyly. "Say, I wonder if she'd get this whole nude concept out of her system if she had one virile volunteer to call her bluff."

"Whoa..." Charles put his hands out and slowly inched toward the door.

"Oh, c'mon, what's a little bluff in the buff between friends?" With a bewitching look, she rose in pursuit, backing him through the screen door and over the threshold.

"Not me! No way!"

"Even if it would put a stop to all of this? Even if you'd be the hero?"

He came to a halt in the dim foyer and gave a grunt of satisfaction when she plowed right into him. Before she could think, he snaked a hand underneath her tide of hair, and held her firmly by the neck for one last kiss. He released her, then, his voice husky, his eyes teasing, said, "I'm just not the kind of guy to reveal that much of himself. And I'm certainly no hero."

Charles's last words lingered in Rose's mind as she crawled back into her bed for another attempt at sleep. He was revealing more about himself than he knew. He perceived himself as one hotshot bachelor. Outside of his duties with Lucas, of course. Though he was making an obvious attempt to temper his ego, it was still there, putting a strut in his step and a gleam in his eye.

Buried deeper was a fierce sense of caring that revealed itself at stressful times, such as the confrontation with the aunts over the locks, and coming upon Osgood making a pass at her. He'd made a better recovery over the latter, sizing up and striking in a near flawless stroke that left Osgood reeling. Charles had been so sexy and masterful as he burst through the kitchen door like a contented daddy bear who owned the place and everyone in it. She suspected Osgood wanted to die right then and there—and that Charles would've obliged him with his bare hands.

Like it or not, Charles was sizing up as just her kind of hero.

She pulled her covers up to her chin and snuggled into her pillow. She closed her eyes to dream, cross the lines into a flawless world where Charles was her man, a permanent father figure to Lucas. It took little effort to embellish on his kisses, to envision them as passionate caresses.

Maybe some dreams could come true. Given time...

"THE UKRAINIAN BRONZE sculptures, Rose! They've arrived at last!"

Rose entered the Rogue's Gallery delivery entrance Friday morning to find Osgood in a spectacular mood as he unpacked a wooden crate of long-expected art objects.

Some of them looked rather heavy, but he refused her offer of help with a jaunty macho grunt. The image hardly worked, she thought with a jab of sympathy. He'd taken off his gray cashmere jacket and rolled up his shirtsleeves as a laborer might do, but his small chest and weak shoulders marred the desired effect.

Osgood had been strangely jovial since Monday night's dinner, as though determined to prove that he, too, could be the reckless sort of guy who now seemed to appeal to both her and Lucas. Though they hadn't talked of the night, it was growing clearer with each passing day that Osgood saw Charles as a direct threat.

Rose could barely believe it. He was a stodgy precise, reserved man.... She might have been amused by Osgood's turnaround if he were anyone but her boss. But she needed this job! Why did he have to suddenly make romantic overtures toward her in particular when there were so many single, childless women flitting in and out of the gallery each week?

She watched in concern as he hoisted a large bronze elephant from the crate. The grin pasted to his mouth all week was in place even now, as sweat pooled on his upper lip. She couldn't resist dashing up to help him lower the piece to the floor.

"That's the last of it," he said reedily, dusting some packing material from his pleated trousers.

"Shall I call your list of bronze-happy patrons?" she asked teasingly.

"Yes, eventually." He busily unrolled his sleeves. "When Fred gets back from his deliveries, you can tell him to clean up this mess, too."

"Certainly, sir."

He regarded her warily on the unusual formality, then moved to a freestanding mirror to adjust his tie. "You had a visitor a little while ago."

"Oh, who?"

"Beevee." Pearce sneered, glowering at his own reflection. "Dressed in that tattered uniform shirt of his."

Rose stepped up behind him, her surprised expression joining his disgruntled one in the mirror. "What did he want?"

"Didn't say—wouldn't say," Pearce clarified with strong displeasure. He turned to her then, brushing some strands of hair up on his high forehead.

Rose wavered under his probing look. "Maybe I should run down to the drugstore."

"He said he'd return. And I need you here, to make those calls. In the meantime," he confided with mounting excitement, "I plan to display our treasures."

Rose was seated at the teakwood desk organizing orders for frames about an hour later when Mr. Beevee merrily lumbered into the posh gallery, a pharmacy sack under his arm. "Morning, Rose."

Rose stood, rounding the desk in cheery welcome. "Hello."

He'd paused to study the cluster of bronze figures set out on plaster pedestals. "What's something like this go for?"

Osgood Pearce, standing at the wall adjusting an abstract print, spun round with a condescending look. "Interested in Ukrainian talent, Beevee?"

Beevee barked out a laugh in good humor. "The local talent keeps me busy, Osgood. All the kids are interested in playing ball." When Pearce turned away, Beevee leaned closer to Rose. "Not that I couldn't afford one of these crummy hunks of metal."

"I'm sure you could," she murmured sincerely. She gestured to his sack. "So, did Violet call in another order for some organic shampoo? One of her homoeopathic remedies?"

"Neither." He dipped a hand into the bag and produced a kelly green jersey and a matching cap. "This is Lucas's team uniform. They don't get much at the T-ball stage. But

I thought I'd drop it off here and double-check on your approval.''

She held up the small shirt, studying its white lettering, Beevee's on the front, and the number ten on the back. All the while she was aware that Pearce was edging closer to eavesdrop, straightening pieces as his cover. "I approve," she assured magnanimously. "I should've encouraged this myself, but I've been busy, and…well, I didn't know much about baseball.''

"Well, that's what your father figure's for, right?" His large features beamed. "That Charlie seems nice. And Lucas is quite taken with him.''

She folded the shirt in half and draped it over her arm, then took the cap from Beevee. "It's been a week since I hired Charlie, and I have to say I'm pleased so far." He and Lucas had shared a splendid week, renting movies, popping corn, playing catch. And as for herself…. Well, Charles had proven a master thief at stealing kisses when least expected. About the only line he'd drawn was with Daisy and her constant pestering for a modeling session. Rose was quite certain her aunt would faint dead away at the sight of Charles in his nude glory. She, on the other hand, was sure she'd remain conscious.

"Know if he's played any ball?''

Beevee's anxious question startled her. "The subject never came up. But he can catch. We've been playing a lot of that.''

"I'm looking for an assistant coach, you see. Matt Levitt moved to Jersey last month, so he won't be around to help out.''

"I don't know for sure, but the odds seem good.''

"Charles gets along so well with Lucas, I thought maybe he'd enjoy it. Important that the coach like the job.''

Suddenly Osgood Pearce was nearly on top of them, his frame dwarfed beside the bulk of Mr. Beevee. "I just may be interested in that position myself," he said with a defiant tilt of his pointy chin.

Beevee barked with laughter again. "May you really?"

Pearce fingered the knot of his silver tie. "I don't appreciate your attitude. I'd think you'd respect a serious offer."

Beevee worked to control his amusement. "Sorry. Can't blame me for being stunned out of my senses."

Pearce reared back. "Why, I never!"

"That's just it," Beevee said firmly. "You never did before. But I'll keep you in mind." As if dismissing him, Beevee turned to Rose. "Practice is tomorrow at ten at the rec center."

"Okay!" She gave his hand a squeeze. "And thanks."

Beevee departed, whisking his bulk gracefully out the door.

Rose folded her arms over the bodice of her blue shirtwaist dress, waiting for her boss's rebuttal. It was a matter of seconds as his chin set to quivering beneath his goatee.

"Beevee has a nerve," Pearce huffed, "insinuating that I'm not equipped to assist him."

"You must admit, it does seem out of character for you, Osgood, dashing around after baseballs."

"I thought it common knowledge that I'm always willing and able to help you in family matters."

They'd skirted the romantic turn of Monday night all week long, just as they had the blowup in the studio, but Rose knew something would eventually trigger it. But how to discourage him without wounding his pride...or losing her job? "Osgood, I would feel awful if you didn't know up front that I'm not sure we could...uh...you know, ever get together in a serious way."

He regarded her as one might a child insistent upon avoiding her cough syrup. "I've given the matter intense thought, and believe I am the one who's made the mistake of not speaking up sooner. Things have been so comfortable between us, I simply took things for granted, made assumptions."

"Things have been very pleasant," she assured.

"I should've taken the reins of Lucas long ago!" he spouted, causing Rose to flinch. "Then that—that student wouldn't be tromping all over the place."

"Charles is doing a fine enough job."

"And teaching Lucas what? To slap a hand in a high five instead of shaking it. To call adults 'man.' Hardly refined behavior."

All things Dean would've done had he lived for the chance. "I appreciate your interest—"

"That's a beginning, then," he gushed. "Allow me to be of service—that's all I ask."

A wily twinkle brightened her eyes. "Helping Daisy would be the best beginning." With that, she moved back to her desk.

To her surprise, Pearce kept his bearings and trailed along. "I already made my position clear on that front. All Daisy has to do is express herself in an inventive way and I'll gladly back her up."

Rose sank down in the deep leather chair and went about depositing the hat and jersey in the bottom drawer of the desk. Not to be brushed off, Pearce hovered close. An annoying truth bubbled up through her thin reserve as he leaned over the desk into her air space. "I really feel that you went too far in pushing the nudes. It's made for an awkward challenge to Daisy. She really doesn't do them anymore—"

"I don't ever *push* anything. I guide, I advise."

"Still…"

"It's the best of what she's done," he argued, tipping his head cockily. "If she can come up with something as inspired, more power to her."

It seemed a rather slippery exit for a man who'd lit Daisy's erotic fuse, but Rose saw no value in putting up an argument. "I'll relay that message."

"As you wish. Now, as for the baseball—"

"Mr. Beevee asked for Charles," she said, taking pleasuring in cutting him off for a change.

He kept a jaunty demeanor. "For the sake of argument, let's say that Charles can't or won't be able to show."

"He'll show. Thrilled and ready to go. Guaranteed."

Rose went home at the noon hour to give Lucas the news about the practice. She swept through the back screen door to find him still dressed in his school clothes, seated at the kitchen set, munching on a peanut butter sandwich. Beast was poised at his chair on his hind legs like a circus dog.

It took Lucas a full two seconds to acknowledge the jersey and hat she was carrying. "That's mine? For real?" He scrambled off his chair to charge her with gooey fingers.

Rose held the shirt out of his reach. "You need to finish eating first. And wash those hands!"

His milk-rimmed mouth formed a protest.

"Go on, finish," she chided gently.

The child obeyed, returning to eat the last quarter of his sandwich. "When is practice?"

"Tomorrow at ten, at the playground."

"I can't wait to tell Charlie."

Nor could she. It was all happening so smoothly, but in reality it was such a tremendous milestone in their lives. Lucas was finally one of the guys.

She'd finally managed to reach out beyond the feminine parameters of her strong-minded aunts. They'd raised Rose herself fine, no doubt, but a boy had different needs. Until now she hadn't been strong enough to push Lucas out into the masculine world. It was a world she knew nothing about, a world she had depended upon Dean to introduce their son to. But Dean never got the chance. And her son had had to spend these years without a male figure to indulge him in the rough-and-tumble activities that boys loved.

There was nothing that could hold back the man in Charles Johnson. He made a fine example for Lucas to follow, a role model to respect. Truth be told, she'd done her own share of admiring as well.

In a very short time Charlie had managed to leave his

imprint on the household, cutting a wide swathe with shaving cream in the sink, giant shoes on the doorstep, cuff links on the windowsill, and tools on the counter. He'd made their space his. Made himself at home.

She sauntered around the room with an air of anticipation, discovering one of his watches on the refrigerator. She turned the large silver face around in her hands, slipped the wide loose band on her slender wrist, relishing its size, its weight. Everything about him was so strong, so large, so sturdy.

"Watcha doin', Mommy?" Lucas was watching her intently, his plate and glass empty.

Dreaming big dreams again, a cottage built for three. "Thought maybe Charlie might show up early," she said pensively, returning the watch to the place she found it. "With the weekend coming and all."

"No Charlie yet." Lucas slipped off his chair and washed his hands at the sink. He turned back, a wily smile curving his mouth. "Hey, maybe somebody better call him up."

Still distracted, Rose handed her son a small checkered towel. "You mean disturb him at school?"

"Yeah, everybody likes to get out of school to play."

"Adults sometimes would rather stay and learn." She tried not to laugh as his eyes and mouth grew round in disbelief. "Still, I suppose he would like some advance notice about the practice."

"I'll call him on our special red phones!"

"Okay, let's do it."

Lucas led the way to his bedroom, pushing aside some books on his shelf to produce the compact instrument. He climbed up on his bed and patted the mattress in invitation to his mom. He carefully opened the phone, stared at the number taped to the inside flap, and began to punch it in on the keypad.

"I could do that," Rose offered.

"I done it before," he retorted, wiggling to shake her off as he dialed.

"Quick," she urged, "see if it's ringing."

"I will!" Lucas pressed the phone to his ear and his cherub face lit up. "It's ringing, Mommy."

Chapter Nine

Charles was seated at his desk, about to dig into the deli
sandwich before him when the familiar bleep of his new
cell phone filled his office. Glancing up to make certain his
office door was closed, he reached into the briefcase at his
side and scooped up the red instrument. "Hello, Lucas."

"Hey, Charlie."

The boy's soft voice piped up clear and sweet, tugging
at Charles's heart. He was surprised at how glad he was to
hear from him. "How's it goin', man?"

"Good. You done studying yet?"

Charles looked over at the cluttered desk. "Nope, still
working."

"I've got a surprise," he said in a singsong voice.

Charles chuckled. "Lay it on me."

"Guess."

"Aw, c'mon, Lucas."

"Got my shirt and hat for T-ball!"

"Hey, that's great!"

"Guess what color it is."

"Pink."

Uncontrollable giggles filled the wire. "Green."

"Sounds perfect."

"So we gotta practice."

"You sure do."

"*We* do, Charlie."

Charles took a sip from his soda can. "Oh, yeah, right. When?"

"Tomorrow."

"Saturday!" Charles didn't mean to boom, but, *Saturday?* His day of rest. His day of play. His very own day.

"You mad, Charlie? Don't you like Saturdays?"

"I love Saturdays," Charles quickly assured, dabbing at some cola he'd sloshed on his gray trousers. "It's just…a lot of things. It's—"

"Charles?"

He stiffened at the sound of Rose's voice. Miles away and he could gauge the inflection with no trouble. She'd been standing by Lucas, listening, judging, wondering. "Hello, Rose."

"Sorry if we disturbed you."

"Not at all. Lucas has permission to call me anytime."

Rose leaned back on the maple headboard, frowning at the disparity of his tone. He sounded unusually hurried, distant. She instinctively patted Lucas's knee as he edged closer, nuzzling Beast for support.

"So Lucas is set to play ball, is he?"

"Yes," Rose said carefully, pleasantly. "Mr. Beevee brought his uniform into the gallery and I dashed home with it on my lunch hour."

"That's great. Lucas will do great."

There it was again. The remoteness, a sense of haste. "Lucas was so excited," she said gamely. "He just wanted you to know."

"Rightly so."

"Is something the matter, Charles? Can't you make it to tomorrow's practice?"

"Actually, I was going to call you later—about my plans. About my staying overnight in the city."

"Tonight!" When was he planning to report in, she wondered angrily.

"Hope you're not inconvenienced. I did tell you this would happen on occasion." In truth, he intended to do it every Friday night to pave the way for his standing Saturday morning handball date, and had in theory figured it wouldn't make much difference. His stay with the Frasers was so temporary that he couldn't see sacrificing his court time and jeopardizing his arrangement with his stockbroker partner over it.

Just his luck that this T-ball deal would conflict. Unfortunately, Charles had never had to compromise his playtime for anyone before and he was having a hard time with it.

"It seems we'll just have to rethink things on this end." She kept her tone even, devoid of emotion.

"I could be back by two o'clock," he offered.

"That would be too late," she said briskly. "Practice is at ten."

"I am so sorry."

"If it can't be helped…" She trailed off, hoping he'd reconsider.

His sigh of relief was audible. "It can't be. A standing date, really."

What date could be more important than the responsibilities he'd taken on here, she longed to ask. But did she really want to know? Could she handle the truth? Charles had to be popular with the women. A jolt of pride gave her new resolve. "I suppose we'll manage."

"Yeah, you're a great mother." The old comfortable warmth was back in his voice now that he'd won, making her all the angrier. "I'll be back by two tomorrow," Charles promised jovially.

Too little, too late. Rose bit her lip, suddenly tempted to tell him that Osgood was raring to step in and prove himself, then ultimately decided against it. She didn't want to make a contest out of this, didn't want him racing back just to keep his new nemesis at bay. She wanted Charles to volunteer gladly, to find her and Lucas irresistible.

If only Charles could see that this particular event meant so much to Lucas, that finally having a male alongside him was so very important. Not to mention the fact that she'd half volunteered him to Beevee as an assistant coach! How naively enthusiastic she'd been. Too enthusiastic all around, it seemed. She'd be wise to put on the brakes a little, proceed with caution.

"Look, this call is getting expensive," she said.

"Tell Lucas—"

"Goodbye? Of course." She signed off abruptly then. It was out of character, but she was the one left holding the discontented boy, presently crawling into her lap along with his powder puff dog.

Her poor little Lucas. He'd once again be showing up at the playground without a male at his side. It was bad enough at the informal parties marking the holidays, or the occasional picnics held by the chamber of commerce. But this was different. Lucas never would've agreed to play ball if he didn't have Charles. And now, with everything set, Charles bailed.

She only hoped he had a reasonable excuse. Funny, he didn't sound like a man just run over by a truck.

"So, Mommy, is he coming? Did you make him?"

"No, honey."

He pounded the mattress, making Beast yip. "You should've! You make me do lots of stuff!"

"I know, but I'm responsible for you, Lucas. Charles is a grown man who can do whatever he pleases."

They sat in silence for a while, Rose stroking Lucas's golden hair, Lucas stroking Beast's belly.

"Don't be sad, Mommy."

"I'm fine," she said, kissing his forehead. "How about you?"

"I'm fine, too." His velvet brows crunched over his vivid blue eyes. "But the Beast is very disappointed in Charlie. Very, very disappointed."

Rose's mouth thinned ruefully. Lucas often assigned his true feelings to the dog. "You can still go to the practice, of course."

"With *you?*" he squealed in affront.

Rose tried not to take offense. "Well, sure."

"Maybe Charlie will be just a little bit late," Lucas hastily decided. "Six minutes late."

"I don't think so, champ. Say, I could offer to help coach."

Lucas buried his face in his hands. "No way! No girls allowed."

"Girls play ball."

"Not with boys."

"I'm pretty good. If the boys see that—"

"I'm not going anymore!"

She clasped her hands together in prayer. "Oh, Lucas, please. You felt so left out last year."

"I don't care. I need a guy to take me."

"Hey, I know what," she said excitedly. "Let's ask Osgood Pearce."

His glare would've dropped a soldier at twenty paces. "Mr. Rogue? Yuck!"

She rocked his trembling body against her. "He tries with you, honey."

"He likes you, Mommy. That's all."

Out of the mouths of babes. Rose clenched her teeth as a swell of sadness overwhelmed her. "Maybe Osgood just needs more practice with children," she ventured hopefully. "Everybody needs practice at things."

"He can practice on some other boy!" Wriggling out of Rose's embrace, he tumbled off the bed.

She sat there bleakly, holding the soulful-eyed pooch. "Lucas, please try to understand."

"That's all you ever say!" He stomped his feet in disgust, his eyes teary. "You shoulda fixed this."

"I tried—" The claim died on her lips as he charged out the door.

Had she tried hard enough? Had she tried hard enough to find the proper mentor in the first place? Charles had a nerve conning her into hiring him when he wasn't prepared to follow through.

Again she wondered if she wanted him more for herself than for her son. With his disarming smile and subtle strength he'd done everything but scoop her aboard his handsome white charger. In one fell swoop he'd put her in touch with her loneliness and given her the remedy in himself.

Maybe he was the wrong man for the job. If so, it would be best to dismiss him while Lucas was still good and mad.

CHARLES RETURNED to his Fifth Avenue apartment building that evening, pausing on the sidewalk to exchange pleasantries with Duane, the night doorman. Charles was weary after a long and full day, but managed to put up a decent front anyway. The tall, regal man in the snappy burgundy uniform had been on night duty at the Blecker Towers for years, and deserved his respect.

Charles first met Duane as a boy while visiting his father's city digs, and they had struck a fast friendship. When the time came for Charles to rent, Hilton had pulled some strings to get him the apartment adjoining his, insisting it was near impossible to get one at all. Duane had discreetly put him on to an available one almost a dozen floors away. Charles had never forgotten the favor, and had bestowed upon him a generous Christmas bonus ever since.

Duane knew the people he served, knew the human condition in general. Charles had always aspired to such wisdom, and thought himself one smart operator—until the Weldon mission that is. With each passing hour, he felt he was losing ground. He tried to move with his usual confidence under their domain, but more often than not, he felt bamboozled by their family politics.

"Haven't seen much of you this week," Duane observed.

Charles shifted from one foot to another, smoothing his wind-tossed hair with a free hand. "Life's been busy."

Duane adjusted his hat. "Figured you'd be along tonight, though."

"Why?"

"Your father's gathering, of course. When he herds in the cashmere suit crowd, I know Fraser Advertising's up to something big."

"Sure, naturally," Charles faltered.

Duane gestured to the house phone just inside the double glass doors. "Shall I ring him and announce you?"

"That won't be necessary." He stared up at the dark sky, the slice of moon, wondering what his father was up to. "Did there happen to be a cowpoke in that herd of suits?" he asked.

"Yup, pardner."

Hilton had been crowding Calhoon all week long, showing the Texan a rip-roarin' time around town while the staff toiled on the soup campaign. Charles should've been the one running the schmooze, but Hilton was having such a tough time handing over his old and cherished client.

Taking a bolstering breath, Charles patted Duane's shoulder, gesturing to a Lincoln full of matrons easing up to the curb. "I'll leave you to your own rodeo. 'Night now."

With his shoulders squared, Charles strode through the plush lobby to an open elevator. He stood alone inside the car, staring at the glowing numbered buttons. Hilton roomed on thirty-two, he on twenty-one. Where to go? He hadn't expected this kind of quandary tonight. Playtime, then bedtime. Fridays were like that.

It had taken an almighty effort to put both his jobs on hold while he followed his treasured Friday routine, meeting some of his bachelor pals for dinner at Elaine's on Second Avenue, followed by some club hopping. Pushing aside the firm's accounts was usually fairly simple, except for the bigger ones like Calhoon Soup. Calhoon's wizened face—topped off with an oversize Stetson—flitted by his mind's eye a few times. Rose's lovely intelligent face had been a tougher one to forget, floating on the surface of his martinis, metamorphosing into Lucas's round dimpled mug.

Were they angry with him over the ball practice deal? Rose had sounded rather cool over his rejection. But it was one small date he couldn't make, for pity's sake.

The four matrons from the Lincoln crowded into the elevator, pushing a button in the high thirties. Perfumed, oiled, and draped in Anne Taylor, they ogled him without shame. Forced to choose a floor, he jabbed thirty-two. Instinct warned him he wouldn't get a wink of sleep without checking up on Hilton. The timing seemed right for a showdown about Calhoon, too. He'd catch them partying and stay on to officially get back the reins of the account.

Suddenly his thoughts drifted to Dean. As a young executive, trapped between Hilton and Rose, his brother had to feel as suffocated as Charles did right now. With each passing day, he grew to more clearly understand Dean's viewpoint, how he had to sever all strings or have Hilton forever trying to pull them his way. How tough it must have been for Dean to choose, when Hilton loved him so and wanted only the best for him.

Charles was trying his best these days to imagine Hilton giving Rose a chance, soothing her hurt and anger over his past deeds with a fresh beginning. Such an altruistic goal gave his presence in the Weldon house substance beyond Lucas's well being.

Charles the peacemaker, the fixer. Everybody's hero.

Would it be enough for Hilton, though, to accept that Rose was doing a fine job raising the boy and that he might be grandfathered in, so to speak, without too many conditions, or questions, or accusations. How badly Charles wanted to keep this out of the courts, away from the glare of public scrutiny.

When had life gotten so blasted complex?

The car landed on Hilton's floor with a discreet ping. The steel doors glided open. Charles nodded at the ladies, who were giddily discussing some investments they'd made. They silenced, all aglow.

Did every woman over fifty mentally strip a man naked

these days, he wondered, pausing to check his reflection in a brass-framed mirror on the floor's small lobby. He adjusted his tie, combed his hair, and decided Daisy's X-ray vision was making him way too crazy.

Hilton's apartment was at the end of the corridor facing Central Park. Soft jazz could be heard as Charles approached the door. He rapped just firmly enough to be heard. Hilton's houseman, shipped in from the Connecticut abode, eventually answered, giving him entrée.

Charles moved through the foyer to the living room, his eyes trained on the dignified Oriental rug in an attempt to hide the surprise that would be obvious in his eyes. It was evident that no more guests were expected, least of all him.

The palatial space was decorated opulently. The furniture was gilded eighteenth century French, the paintings Miró and Picasso, and the golden candlesticks adorning the marble fireplace bullion-bar pure. It seemed the perfect setting for the tinge of fragrant cigar smoke and the mingle of rumbling voices and music coming from the dining room.

In a bygone era their game might have been whist. Today it was poker. Seated at the round oak table going clockwise was Hilton, Fraser executives Templer and Kapon, and the soup king himself, Jed Calhoon. The admen were peeled down to their shirtsleeves, with ties loosened and collars unbuttoned. Jed was duded up for the occasion in an Aztec-pattern yoked shirt of black and red, and stiff blue jeans. There was a concho button bolo with horsehair tassels at his collar and a huge silver buckle at his waist.

No wonder Duane had remembered him well.

Five card stud was on with a vengeance. Or so it appeared. Charles smiled winsomely, noting that, lo and behold, Calhoon had a ransom in poker chips, while the others were simply surviving with a pittance. Funny how Hilton could be a good loser when it suited him.

"This is a surprise, son." Hilton clamped a fresh cigar between his teeth, struck a match to it, and puffed like a mighty engine.

"I was in the neighborhood and—"

"Really, Charles?" he barked incredulously. "In the neighborhood?"

"I do have an apartment here, remember?"

Quiet prevailed. The creases in Hilton's ruddy face deepened, smoke curled round his head. "Thought you'd be staying on in the suburbs."

"It is Friday, Dad."

Hilton was unimpressed as he flicked ashes into the small crystal bowl at his elbow. "Comes once a week so I'm told."

"I always meet up with my friends on Friday nights," Charles said stubbornly. "Then stay over to play handball."

"Leaving the henhouse untended?" Hilton asked in an annoyed slur.

Charles couldn't believe how his father was venting his feelings in public, until he realized that they were all sloshed. Each heavy-lidded man had a two-piece crystal place setting of sorts, ashtrays full of ash, matching stout glasses puddled with whiskey. Bottles of Jack Daniel's and soda lined the wet bar, a Chinese cloisonné humidor brimming with Cuban cigars lay open. Given the cards, it was an adult sandbox scene, for the express entertainment of the soup king. A glance to his watch told Charles it was nearly two o'clock. They'd probably been at this a long while. Too long.

"Dad, if I could have a brief word—"

"Not now!"

"But, Dad—"

A bark from Hilton brought the houseman in from the kitchen. Without a word, he dutifully freshened drinks, fishing a lighter out of his white uniform jacket to light the stogies.

"Pull up a chair, Charles," Jed Calhoon invited. "Feel we've barely had a chance to talk this week."

Charles grimaced. Wasn't that the truth, with Hilton spiriting the mogul away each day with a list of tourist distractions.

Still determined to force Hilton to either fish or cut bait with Calhoon, Charles wedged a chair in between Kapon and Templer. Pausing at the bar to fix himself a very mild drink, he sat down to watch them play out their hand.

Calhoon studied his cards, then focused on Charles with bleary eyes. "Your father says the commercials are set for an audience preview."

Your father says. "Really," Charles murmured, clenching his glass, raising it to his mouth for a long, slow sip. "I was around this afternoon, I'm surprised Marcia didn't relay the message."

Hilton waved a large, gold-ringed hand. "Jed and I were touring the departments and Sally from Public Relations took me aside and told me personally. No big deal."

Charles could feel Kapon and Templer quaking at his sides. Both were good men who tried to play Hilton's game without betraying the son and heir. It was a precarious tightrope to walk, Charles knew. He wasn't surprised when the pair decided to bet the last of their chips on this—what they hoped to be—their final hand.

The young executives vacated the premises within minutes, making a smooth exit, Charles thought, relinquishing their chips to the boss with just enough regret, followed by hasty farewells.

Charles was glad to see them go, but it unfortunately brought him no closer to a confrontation with Hilton. Jed remained planted in his chair with a fresh drink and smokes, ogling Hilton's chips. Charles was forced to join the game then, cursing his own nosiness and stupidity. He should've guessed a binge like this was going on. That Hilton would be in no mood to talk rationally and Calhoon would be in no hurry to leave. Now he'd be trapped here forever and left dirt tired for his handball game.

"I unnerstand you've been very busy this week, Charles." Jed's words sounded a bit slurred.

Charles shuffled the cards with a neat and clean snap. "Always have time for you, Jed. Given the chance..."

"Known your daddy here for a bushel of years," Jed droned, winking at Hilton. "Guess we know how to play well together...while you're too busy."

How could he hope to ease into Hilton's shoes someday if he was kept a full pace behind? Charles silently fumed. "You'll like those commercials, Jed," he said pleasantly, dealing out cards with a sober, experienced snap of the wrist. He noted that Jed had some difficulty holding onto his cards. How much had he drunk? No matter. However much he had, Charles realized the time for talking any kind of business was long gone, something Templer and Kapon no doubt already knew as they exited with their helpless looks.

If only he'd pushed the button to his own floor when he had the chance.

"So, you left *them* to their own devices, eh, Charles?"

Charles frowned at Hilton as he took a swig of whiskey. Hilton could get mighty petulant in his condition, and by the looks of his glassy eyes and droopy mouth, Charles had the feeling he was in for it.

"Dad, I wonder if this is the time or place to discuss that matter."

"Jed's a parent, Jed knows all the ins and outs."

But was Jed trying to wage a custody battle with the most beautiful woman in the world? Charles sat back in his chair and sipped whiskey along with his elders, studying the battle and the fact that he'd automatically dubbed Rose the world's best mother. Again he wondered if she was angry with him.

The game seemed secondary now, the shank of the evening long gone. Jed set his cards flat on the table and ambled down the hall toward the bathroom.

Hilton awkwardly rolled his sleeves a little higher on his muscular arms, and leaned forward. "Level with me, son," he said brusquely. "What the hell are you doing in the city with that hangdog look?"

"Hangdog? You've been spending way too much time with old Jed. And speaking of that, he's why I'm here. I want to hand you back the account. I'm through playing second fiddle."

"This is no time to discuss that, not when you've abandoned your post."

Charles felt himself going on the defensive and even though he didn't like it, felt propelled along as usual. "Dad, there is no reason why I shouldn't keep up my own relationships. Everything at the Weldons is under control."

"What happens next? Anything? Well—well?"

Charles sought to give the old man a bone before he blew his stack. "Lucas's first T-ball practice is tomorrow—"

"What time?"

"Uh, ten. Ten o'clock."

"You'll have to fly to get there."

"I'm not going—"

"What!" Hilton's thunder nearly brought the ceiling down.

"They'll manage without me this once."

"We know you can't be trusted with a bat, but to miss it…" Hilton's chest expanded with rage. "What if that nutty Daisy tries to take him! He'll be the laughing stock of the town!"

"I told you the aunts are against all organized sports."

"Did you? I don't recall." Hilton swayed in his chair, dazedly looking around. "I should write that down for my list."

Charles glanced down the hallway as he heard the bathroom door open. "Don't worry about it now, Dad, please."

Jed returned then, looking a little startled. "Everything okay?"

"Certainly," Charles said pleasantly.

Hilton's grimace didn't waver. "We gotta set this kid

straight, Jed, tell 'em. Tell 'em how a boy needs his father
at baseball practice.''

"Well, sure," Jed agreed in mild confusion. "But you
aren't married, Charles, are you?"

"This is a hypothetical case," Hilton hastily inserted.
"Now wouldn't you say that if a boy was counting on a
mentor to be there, he damn well should be?"

"Naturally," Jed concurred. "I'm leadin' my own two
young grandsons around, teaching 'em the ropes."

The proud grandpappy took over, elaborating on the
blessings of grandsons. Charles figured it was good for Hilton's blood pressure to fall back in his chair and listen for
a change.

Unfortunately, the subject didn't calm Charles any.
Damned if Hilton didn't find a way to chew Charles out in
front of Jed without giving Lucas's existence away. Hypothetical was the term all right. Not in Lucas's case, but
in direct reference to Charles himself! To Hilton, the boy
was already larger than life, someone to nurture, indulge.
Charles was and always would be a distant consolation
prize. A son couldn't get much closer to being a simple
hypothesis than he!

Charles broodingly listened to the fatherly babble, a dull
ache pounding his temples. Hilton had been so busy with
business, he'd never once appeared at any of his sporting
activities. But that didn't stop him from shading the past
now to suit his image. "All's fair with a client," would be
Hilton's excuse, if confronted.

Suddenly, the center core of the Weldons' situation hit
him squarely. Sitting here, in the role of the son, feeling
every bit a small, neglected child, Charles unwittingly
found himself in Lucas's place.

The resulting jolt of pain catapulted him to his feet. He
was doing the same thing to Lucas as Hilton had done to
Charles as a child. He was missing the boy's T-ball game.
The kid had to be devastated by his father figure's rejection.
That was the only word that fit really, there was no way to

squirm out of it. And Rose, in turn, had been feeling her son's loss. Naturally, she would blame Charles for reneging, being that he'd initially shown some interest in the ball team.

Even though he had every right to some space, per their arrangement, it was the wrong thing to do. The selfish thing to do.

Wouldn't Hilton be thrilled to know that he was helping out by acting as a bad example? Charles couldn't begin to imagine what a judge in a custody hearing would think of that! Damned if he couldn't stop wondering which of the older set was the worse for Lucas, the hippie aunts or the iron-willed gramps.

Hilton stared up at him, his fists clenched on the table. "What the blazes are you doing, Charles, standing there like a lightning rod?"

Charles regarded his woozy father with sad impatience. "Deciding where best to take my next dose of lightning, I guess." Oblivious to his father's responding bluster, he bid them both a good-night.

Chapter Ten

Rose got a lot more than she bargained for when she went out to the porch for her Saturday newspaper.

"Charlie!"

Charles, drowsing on the slatted porch swing, quickly came to life. She'd never called him Charlie before. No woman had ever used that tone on him before either, a sleepy blend of desperation and exasperation. He raised himself up on his forearms to thoroughly enjoy it. "Don't you know any better than to parade around in your nightie?" he asked gruffly.

"What!" She placed a hand between her small breasts, provocatively outlining them against the sheer knit of her top. "I—I only meant to step out a few inches. Then—then you—" She clamped her mouth shut and rushed the swing. "You're the one who should be talking hard and fast here, mister, popping in now—this way!"

Sitting up, he snaked an arm around her waist to tug her down.

Rose breathlessly toppled against him, pale hair flying, bare legs akimbo. She was swiftly aware of his beating heart, the bristle on his whiskered chin, the hardness of his denim covered thighs, the softness of his simple white T-shirt. She squirmed in his lap like the family's frisky bichon frise, wondering what had brought the flicker of bedevilment to his eyes. "What's that look all about?"

"Who, me?" he taunted.

"You're living dangerously, Charles."

So it was back to Charles again, was it? Cupping her chin, he pulled her close for a long, luxuriant kiss. They were both on even breathless ground once he released her. "Now that, sweet Rosy, is living dangerously."

"Do you think that's going to get me off track?"

"It's the best diversion I've got," he whispered hoarsely. Feeling her soften against him, he kissed her again, urgently, raking a hand through her hair, holding her head firmly while he explored the recesses of her mouth and savored her essence.

Rose's heart fluttered wildly like a butterfly testing its wings. Hearing her nickname on his lips was as seductive as their steady pressure. She allowed herself to slip into a warm, blissful state of arousal over the burn of his whiskers, the tickle of his tongue. She barely recognized the sex kitten who was kissing him back, hooking her arms around his neck, tasting him, and moaning in contentment and hunger.

Not since Dean had a man called her Rosy. Amazingly, Charles's tone was a near mimic of her husband's. Or did she simply want to believe so?

"See, you are glad to see me," he crooned in the curve of her ear.

His confidence jarred hers with a nagging fear that Charles enjoyed making love to women and had most likely had his fair share. She struggled to keep a sensible perspective. Though he was indeed playing the gallant rescuer, he shouldn't have hesitated in the first place. It seemed smart to remember that he'd proven unpredictable, fallible.

It took incredible willpower, but she managed to break free of his spell and slide onto the bench beside him. She shook her head in exasperation as he regarded her in wounded shock. "I have to know, Charles. Exactly what brought you back here today?"

He tweaked her cheek playfully. "The subway?"

"You know what I mean."

He did. And it made him squirm like his naughty little charge when he was caught dozing on this very swing. He tried to counteract his discomfort with a wolfish gleam. "Your charms had something to do with it."

"This is about Lucas!" she huffed in frustration. "What made you change your mind? Honestly!"

He brushed some tendrils off her brow, grazing her forehead as though checking for a raging, disorienting fever. "Your timing is awful."

"So is yours sometimes, like yesterday." She tipped her chin defiantly as he reached for her again.

His jaw slacked helplessly. "I can think better when we're snuggling."

"Liar!" With a rueful look she caught his anxious fingers in midair.

"Hey, you guys!" Lucas came barreling out the screen door in his shorty pajamas.

"Hey, man!" Charles opened his arms as the boy charged the swing. The chains creaked and the planked box swung as he bounced into the tiny space between the adults. He looked up to his mentor with shiny blue eyes.

"You sleepin' out here, Charlie?"

"Just waiting for someone to wake up," Charles hedged. "Didn't want to ring the doorbell too early."

Lucas twisted on the seat to face his leery mother. "Don't be mad at him, Mommy. I bet he was here for only six minutes."

Rose smiled thinly. "I'm sure."

Lucas squeezed her knee in a panic. "You didn't fire him yet, did ya?"

"No—no," she stammered, blushing.

Charles felt an inexplicable ripple of betrayal and disappointment. Despite the fact that he was flying under false colors, he couldn't believe she'd been doing some undercover planning of her own. So she'd been contemplating sacking him. Sat right here and kissed the daylights out of him, holding a pink slip over his head. How could he have missed the energies fueling her? He swallowed hard, staring her down in bewilderment.

"Are you thinking of firing me, Rose?"

"I was...but, well, I've reconsidered," she replied in a hurried fluster. "It was a rash decision I made last night as we argued over my taking Lucas to the playground. He flatly refused to accompany me—" She inhaled, trying to catch up with her skittering nerves while she avoided his dark, hooded gaze. "Darned if he didn't try to take your side against me when *you* were the one who was hurting him!"

Charles fell into a penitent silence. That did have to sting—loyal parent versus hired mentor. "Your mom was right to be angry with me, man," he admitted quietly. "She was right to assume I wasn't coming."

Lucas's small face screwed up in discontent as he leaned closer for a confidence. "Gotta tell ya, Charlie, I tried to make you look good 'cause we're pals. But I didn't think you were comin', either."

Charles hung his head in misery. How this pair touched him! And how eager he was to please. He rubbed his hands together between his knees, struggling for words. "Guess I sometimes get too wrapped up in my work—er, studies— and I make mistakes. I did get smart though and rearranged my schedule for you, man."

Lucas squinted in deliberation. "Okay, Charlie," he finally said. "But you should feel bad. Mommy took the day off from work and was going to drag me there. I didn't want to go with a girl, but she was going to *make* me."

"I am sorry!"

With a huge sigh, Lucas scooted off the swing. "Guess I'm hungry now," he said simply.

"I'll be along soon," Rose promised as he bounced through the door.

Charles stared mutely. "That's it? He's suddenly hungry?"

"Little boys are satisfied with the simple truth and open remorse."

"Oh." Pleased, Charles shifted on the seat to keep Rose pinned in place. "What about big girls?"

"They take more convincing." *Once they clear their heads,* she thought with some embarrassment. What must he think? Her giving in to his advances, when she'd tossed and turned all night, contemplating his heave-ho. She guessed they both had some reason to feel awkward around the other.

"Can't we declare a truce for now?" he asked softly. "And get you inside and dressed?"

Rose had to concede she'd outstayed her welcome as the street was coming alive with morning activity, the mailman loping from house to house with his heavy leather sack, dog walkers along the sidewalk, vehicles rolling along the street. "Guess you're off the hook for now."

Charles exhaled wearily, feeling as though he were ending the day rather than beginning it.

"HELP, help, Charlie!"

Charles strolled into the kitchen at twenty minutes of ten to find the aunts hovering over Lucas like a couple of plucky hens, tugging at his green baseball jersey, massaging his small limbs, urging a cup of tea to his lips. Careful to hide his annoyance, Charles asked the women what they were doing.

Daisy glanced up at Charles as though he were a pesky fly. "Trying to prepare him for the battle, of course!"

"Battle? What battle?"

"That is how we view rough-and-tumble sports of all kinds." Setting the teacup on the table beside a clutter of remedies, Daisy tipped some liquid from a brown bottle and dabbed it on Lucas's wrists. "This is a special mint essence from the Far East, meant to calm the system."

Charles smirked as he spotted a familiar price tag on the cylinder. "Mint miracle via Beevee's apothecary."

Violet's soft round face clouded. "He is such a puzzle that Beevee. We expect ignorance on the issue of sport from a young strapper like you, naturally; but for our own medically enlightened druggist to involve himself in such violence is appalling. To show such sensitivity in homeopathic matters, then to devote his free time to rouse young innocents into ruthless competition!" She sank into a chair with an anguished cry.

"I can see how you might not care for the roughness of football—" Charles paused in the wake of their gasps of horror. "But," he continued firmly, "baseball, especially T-ball, is absolutely safe. The batter even wears a helmet."

"And one of those masks?" Daisy inquired hopefully, fretfully, massaging Lucas's small neck. "I've seen those. They seem to cover a lot."

"Only the catcher wears a mask."

"But couldn't some exception be made in Lucas's case?"

"No way!" Lucas squealed in mortification, trying to wiggle free of Daisy.

"It would be against the rules," Charles patiently explained. "And Lucas wouldn't be any safer, because his range of vision would be so small."

The aunts absorbed the facts, curious, wary and blessedly quiet. It gave Charles confidence to go on. "It's not like the professional games on TV. These kids are slow; they're just learning. Why, when I played as a boy—" He stopped as the picture of him smacking his brother with the bat took shape in his mind, but he quickly refocused on better times. "Just trust me when I say there's no huge risk. If things are properly supervised, if the kids are well coached, nothing goes wrong, honestly!"

The aunts smiled at each other. Daisy released her grip on a much relieved Lucas and regarded Charles with fondness. "We do have faith in you."

"You do?" Charles gulped, wary of their mood swing.

But he supposed their artistic temperaments had to be constantly taken into account.

Daisy winked slyly. "You've managed to put things in a practical light, with a lot of class—like the dead bolts and the rickety swing set. And your rapport with Lucas is evolving at a very pleasing clip. Even when you do stumble, even when we disagree, you keep coming back with an admirable spirit. That's the family way."

"A lot of people are put off by us because we're flamboyant," Violet confided, plowing her fleshy arm across the tabletop to collect their remedies.

"Really?" Charles gently mocked them to cover the tide of guilt swelling through his belly. Hilton was certainly one of their biggest critics. But Charles couldn't help noting with passing time that he and Hilton lived a similiar version of the "family way"—locking horns, backing off, then eventually drifting back to center ground. And people were put off by Hilton as well, as he, too, wore the same sort of gutsy independence on his sleeve.

Fraser conservatism versus Weldon liberalism. Were they separated by a gully or an abyss?

With her hands full of vials and bottles and boxes, Violet transferred the lot to a cupboard beside the sink. "What we're trying to say is that, though we have many reservations, we are willing to concede that if anyone can see to Lucas's best interests out on that field, it's you."

Charles tensed, sensing trouble. "In what way?"

"In the biggest way." Daisy's gaze keened shrewdly. "It's our understanding that you'll be at his side every minute, guiding, protecting."

"That takes the fatherly role a little far."

"Not if you're part of the team," Daisy murmured.

"What are you ladies talking about?" Charles demanded.

"I was going to tell you."

Charles spun round on his athletic shoes to find Rose standing in the doorway, a large shirt identical to Lucas's draped over her arm. "Mr. Beevee dropped this off for you at the gallery yesterday afternoon."

"For me? But I'm a spectator!"

"He would rather you help coach. Seemed reasonable—"

"So you took him up on it, without asking me first?"

"Well, sort of…" Rose sank her teeth into her luscious lower lip.

Fury mounted inside him until Charles was nearly smoking out of his ears. "You actually took that shirt when you were contemplating firing me?"

"You were what?" The aunts chorused in alarm.

"In the morning I said you might do it," Rose sought to explain. "Then he came back later with the jersey after you and I had talked. I was at a loss to shut him down then and there. You know you really should be flattered, Charles," she coaxed.

"About which part?" he croaked.

"About everything," she returned brightly. "About Mr. Beevee's interest in you as a coach. About my faith that you'd return to do the job."

Charles folded his arms across his wide chest with a dubious look. "I bet I was chosen through process of elimination, when none of the dads wanted to do it."

"Mr. Rogue wants to do it," Lucas grumbled. "That would be awful, Charlie, the guys would hate me for bringin' him."

"You're right about that, man." Charles barely recognized himself as he snatched the shirt from Rose like a roused bear. That pompous art dealer pushed buttons in Charles that he never before knew existed.

Rose watched him sheepishly as he tugged the jersey over his white T-shirt. "Hope you don't feel trapped."

His head popped through the neckhole. "Oh, no," he raved.

She sought eye contact. "I wasn't even going to mention

Osgood Pearce. And I really did try to dissuade him from participating, even when I was furious with you.''

"Sure, sure." He gave Lucas a gentle push. "Go get our gloves and your cap.''

"Yeah, man!" With a whoop of joy, Lucas raced off. It was clear that he didn't care how the deal was struck, just that it had fallen in his favor.

Was Charles ever given the chance to view things so simply, so innocently? Not that he recalled. Certain he might explode on the spot, he began to pace to work off his temper.

Rose wasn't feeling quite as impish over her victory as he moved in like a thunderhead, taking up an impressive amount of kitchen space.

The aunts made their exit in skittering haste, hands on their bosoms as though finding it hard to catch their breath in the impending storm. They relayed a swift silent message to their niece: This is your problem, your man for hire. Deal with it.

"The last thing I want is for you to have any competition, Charles," Rose ventured in a trembly voice.

"Really?" He stared her down, his eyes as dark as coffee on the bitter boil. "Hiring me to jump-start Pearce would've been a foolish game to play—on Lucas!" he added pointedly.

Charles looked away again, grinding his fist into his palm. He was determined to view everything around here through Lucas's point of view first from now on, and in this case it gave him the bonus, a shield behind which to hide his risky romantic stake. Was it possible that Osgood Pearce's attention was what Rose was after all along? Was part of the reason she'd ultimately decided to hire Charles, the older-than-average student, to get Pearce on his toes not only as a potential father, but as husband material?

Rose forced herself to watch the rage play out on his handsome face. He was struggling with his feelings for her, deciding how much to reveal without risking his dignity. Couldn't he tell that she was worthy of his trust by now?

She so badly wanted to pound his chest, force him to spill his guts and declare his intentions. But it was obvious he wasn't as ready as she for such a meltdown. Suddenly she remembered that Dean too had been the guarded type, more obliging during carefree moments. The Weldons were an impetuous people in all moods. When they saw something they fancied, they reached for it. She willed herself to take things slow, to lead with calm reason.

"Believe me," she ventured, sidling closer with a sway of her hips. "No one is more surprised than I that Osgood has become so...interested!"

"I think he's always been interested," Charles said tightly.

"Still, after all this time...I'm flabbergasted by it." She tugged at the front of his new jersey. "I had to literally rip this shirt out of his hands. It was like a cartoon tug-of-war!"

He curled his tight fingers around her slender arms with a sardonic smile. "Wow, I hope you didn't hurt him."

She closed her eyes, summoning control. She wouldn't let his touch affect her again, not when he was so determined to hold back himself. But the roughened touch of his fingers, pressing into her tender inner arm, was a subtle, but powerful temptation. "It was never my intention to pit you against Osgood, Charles," she quietly assured. "If I wanted to encourage that sort of triangle, I would've told you on the telephone yesterday that he wanted to coach, right?"

"Yeah. I suppose." He simmered down a bit, releasing her.

Rose stared down the open doorway into the hallway to make certain it was empty, then spoke in an urgent whisper. "Lucas should be the third point of our triangle, Charlie. Not Osgood."

Charles grasped her chin in his hand, relieved and

pleased. "A perfect geometric equation, honey." He was about to kiss her when he realized they had company again.

Lucas studied them innocently, a cap perched atop his head, his arms laden with the mitts. "There's guys goin' by already, so we gotta hurry."

With a resigned sigh, Charles released Rose and tugged the bill of Lucas's cap. "Guess we got no time to lose, not when we've got a ball team to whip into shape."

Rose calmed herself, moving to the counter for her purse. "Just give me a minute to fix my lipstick."

"Lipstick!" Lucas wrinkled his nose. "Are you coming?"

She turned to grace them with a savvy smile. "I am. I took the day off to see what all this was about and I'm going to follow through."

He sagged like a limp dishcloth. "Oh, Mommy."

"Pretend you don't know me if you like," she suggested merrily.

Smitten, Charles silently vowed that was one lesson the boy would learn at his knee. Never, ever deny Rose as a relative. Probably the last lesson any Fraser had a right to teach, but still, one that should be set straight.

They set out on foot down the old cracked sidewalk fronting the century old homes, aware of all the green-jersey-clad boys rolling by on their small two wheelers, accompanied by older boys and parents.

The threesome stopped at the first intersection for the red light. Charles pushed his reflective sunglasses farther up his nose, studying the mobile crew that had made it across on the green. "We should've taken your bike," he remarked offhandedly.

Lucas small face drooped. "Don't got one."

Rose caught Charles's eye as the Walk sign lit up. "The aunts…"

"Oh," Charles said flatly, needing no further explanation.

"I never had one, either," she added, scooting Lucas up the curb. "I grew up just fine."

Charles recalled the freedom his bicycle had given him. Though the Frasers were wealthy, it didn't mean that he had special transportation back then. Without bikes, he and Dean would've been stranded a great deal of the time. "Are you dead set against them?"

"Well, no, I suppose not."

"Then let's talk it over later. Definitely talk it over."

"Way to go, Charlie." Lucas gave him a pat on the waist. "You can get me a bike for sure."

"Slow down, fellas," Rose cautioned. "This matter will take some investigating."

"We could investigate by renting first," Charles suggested.

Rose stopped dead in her tracks, aghast. "*We?* As in me, too?"

"Certainly. It's perfectly safe."

"The aunts will boil you in polyunsaturated oil for this."

"They'll bend." Charles urged her along again, gesturing to the pack still wheeling up in the distance. "Look, most of those kids are wearing helmets. That precaution wasn't popular when your aunts denied you a bike. Maybe now they'll see things differently."

"Guess if anyone can convince them, it's you," she mused. "I'm forever amazed at how they've taken to you in such a short time."

Her tone insinuated that she appreciated it and shared the sentiment. How angry they'd all be when they discovered his identity. He couldn't bear the idea, what with their growing mutual attraction.

Charles followed mother and son through their suburban turf, falling into his own thoughtful haze. A wise man would put a hose to the fire growing between he and Rose. The hotter their fuse, the bigger the blast was bound to be.... The tougher the break would be.

But did it have to be that way? Wouldn't he end up a

hero if he could smooth out the ill feelings between their families? Somehow bring about a solution that would make peace? If only he could shape his image as the concerned snoop, rather than the traitorous spy. It was his stock-in-trade as an adman, after all, to slant public opinion, make the hard sell look effortless.

Tempering his hard sell to Rose was growing increasingly difficult. How badly he wanted her! Sampling her honeyed kisses, stroking her soft curves, basking in her longing was burning his insides raw. Charles wasn't accustomed to showing patience with women—never had to before! They'd always seemed to fall easy to his charm.

Here he was, after all these years, pitted against a man fifteen years his senior, with a highbrow air that kept him from seeing any humor in the human condition. In Pearce's favor though, he had that gallery to interest all the Weldons, and no deep dark secret threatening his courtship technique.

It would be easier if Charles wanted Rose simply because she was so unassuming and unique. But Charles already knew that he wanted Rose *just because.* He'd heard tell of *just because,* but he'd never experienced it before and doubted it truly existed.

Why did it seem for every lesson he taught Lucas he learned one of his own?

Chapter Eleven

The playground proved to be impressive in size, with four ball fields, a play area, batting cages, and a recreational center. Clutching his small glove to his chest, Lucas shot ahead to the field brimming with small green-jersey-clad players.

"He seems comfortable over here," Charles remarked as he and Rose took the gentle sloping grass at a slower pace. "Familiar."

"We do come here for things," she said defensively, gesturing to a cluster of swings and monkey bars. "He likes the playground and the craft projects in the center all year round. The aunts love to bring him for them. In fact, Daisy has even taught watercolor!"

"I didn't mean—" He broke off under her dubious survey. "Okay, so maybe I did mean it that way. But he doesn't even have a bike!"

She rested her hand on his solid arm, her fingers grazing through his growth of springy black hair above his watchband. "That's why I hired you, for the male point of view. Don't ever be afraid to express yourself. It's all part of the fun."

Fun? The skim of her filed nails on his skin was an act of wicked black magic, made all the more provocative by her gentle modesty. If he dared to imagine those fingers on the prowl to more intimate territory, he'd surely pass out.

The spell was broken as Lucas galloped back in their direction, his little bare legs pumping like mad. Charles fleetingly wondered how people managed to have more than one child when that child crashed into every black magic moment.

"Man. Oh, man." Lucas halted, arms flailing arms, chest huffing.

Charles squeezed his shoulder. "What's the matter?"

"He's here. Mr. Rogue. He's here."

The same fingers that had been tempting Charles moments ago stole to Rose's mouth. "I don't believe it."

"He's got a jersey and a hat." Lucas shook his head, breathing hard. "I told Mr. Beevee that's Charlie's hat!"

"Don't worry about it," Charles said more grimly than he meant to.

"We can go home if you want," Lucas said halfheartedly, staring back at the field.

"No way, man! A Fraser—a Lucas Fraser doesn't back off that easy." Charles glanced at Rose to see if she caught his slip, the inference that they were one under the Fraser umbrella. Shielding her eyes against the sunshine for a closer look at the field, she appeared oblivious.

Lucas tagged along at Charles's side for the trip to the infield. They approached the bench where the kids were clustering around Mr. Beevee. The druggist was holding a clipboard, taking roll call. He announced Lucas's name, beaming in surprise at the sight of Charles.

"I'm with him," Lucas said spunkily, easing up to his mentor's side.

Once the kids were sent to their assigned positions, the adults began to wander off or take seats in the bleachers. Only Rose, Charles and Osgood Pearce lingered near Beevee. Mr. Beevee promptly dug into his sack for another coach's cap and it handed over to Charles. "Always keep a spare."

"Looks like you've got a spare assistant as well," Charles remarked evenly, nodding at the art dealer, who was readjusting his cap on his high forehead. The manicured nails, the precisely clipped goatee, struck Charles as rather a strange complement to a sport where one had to do a share of sliding in the dirt.

"I thought I was needed," Pearce declared rather defensively, frowning at Rose. "Thought…" Resisting the urge to unload his anger, he compressed his lips to a tight line.

Rose was extremely uncomfortable, circling her fingers around the chain-links of the backstop. She knew she should say something clever to smooth the way for everyone, but she wasn't feeling the least bit witty. "So who's minding the gallery?" Rose finally asked.

Pearce tipped his head jauntily. "Denise kindly stepped in to help."

Rose gasped in amazement. "Your sister came in from the city?"

"Well, yes," Pearce admitted. "She enjoys framing prints, visiting with the customers. And she likes you, Rose," he added tightly.

Obviously she liked her enough to extend what she thought was a favor. Rose blushed self-consciously. "I'm sorry you were so inconvenienced. I never thought…"

"What was I to think?" Pearce whispered. "You went home at noon ecstatic, sure your 'father' here was a go. Then you returned crestfallen, refusing to speak of the team. The equation seemed simple enough."

Charles stared up at the sunny blue sky, thinking how everything was suddenly tinged a foggy gray around this pompus twit he wanted to hate. Rather begrudgingly he felt forced to extend Pearce some credit. This whole deal had to be tough on him, too. Charles saw how surprised Pearce was to see him, how Pearce winced as Lucas promptly claimed his man. Charles sincerely believed Pearce thought the path was clear.

Apparently the poor bumbler dove in to play the unlikely hero. Charles felt responsible for the mixup. He should've agreed to come in the first place.

"You don't have to stay if you don't want to, Osgood," Rose said politely.

"I'm here. I may as well."

Charles thought Pearce might head for the bench, but he didn't. Rather, he took the canvas-covered bases from Beevee's long equipment sack and brought them to the infield. The tee came in two pieces, a flat rubber base and a long hollow tube. Charles offered to assemble that.

Beevee tossed some baseballs to the boys, encouraging them to play catch. He hid a smirk as Osgood Pearce, who'd been lining up the distance between the bases like a surveyor on a construction site, suddenly switched to the hastier eyeball method of measure, darting back to home plate within seconds.

Cupping his huge hands to his mouth, Beevee called all the balls in, and explained to the boys that a coach would hit balls to them, and they in turn, would get it to first base as swiftly as possible.

To Charles's amazement, Pearce strode right up to the array of bats, checking them for weight. Choosing one, he told Beevee he'd gladly start them off.

And start them off he did. Tossing them into the air like a seasoned juggler, Pearce hit them with precision, calling out in a sure voice exactly which player should respond.

The kids went wild, including Lucas. This Pearce guy was dynamite with a bat. Who'd have thought it?

And then there was Charles. He looked the part, young, muscular, athletic—but so traumatized over hitting his brother, he hadn't touched a bat in years. As if Pearce were going to give him the chance anyway, hogging the limelight for himself. He even told an impressed Beevee where to position the kids.

Standing by with nothing to do, Charles felt his original resentment for his opponent resurface. Osgood Pearce was no befuddled overseer strictly concerned with Rose's well being. He was indeed on a campaign to outdo Charles, edge him out of the competition for the whole Weldon package.

Pearce's present maneuver to completely take over the assistant coach's slot couldn't be missed by any reasonable person, could it? Certainly not by Rose, who was at that moment trying to somehow evaporate by strolling over to the players' bench for a seat. It was so obvious now that Pearce was trying to prove Charles's father figure job obsolete, delivering his jabs slowly, like a conservative boxer dancing round and round the ring, patiently waiting for the best openings. Tough luck that Pearce had inadvertently managed to strike at one of Charles's weak spots.

A seasoned ad executive like Charles should've been prepared for this kind of sucker punch, of course. He should've gone with his original instinct that Monday night's dinner was a real and accurate glimpse into Pearce's cunning nature. This was the man who refused to step forward with a plan until Charles rocked the boat, who was stringing Daisy along about her art, just to keep those Monday night dates coming.

Why, a month ago, if somebody would've told Charles he'd be singed to the socks at a kid's playground, he'd have laughed himself sick. Now he was just feeling a little sick as the kids' squeaky cheers for ''Ossie'' rang on the warm spring breeze. Why did Pearce have to show up a batter of all things, when Charles could tromp him on a handball court or outrun him on any track in the land!

Suddenly he had to know what Rose thought. As he stood near the third baseline with arms folded, his sidelong gaze traveled the space between them. She was turned away, a shapely knee pressed against the sagging bench, pretending to dig through her purse. He shuffled his feet and cleared his throat. She stiffened with awareness, but did not turn around, probably hoping he'd give up.

He finally spoke to her shapely backside, with the steely force that the subject of Osgood Pearce deserved. ''He knows how to play well.''

''Yes,'' she called over her shoulder with a distracted air.

"Wonder why he didn't offer to help these little guys a bit sooner?"

She closed her purse with a distinctive click and stared off at something on the street. "I suspect it's because he's incapable of caring much for them." She turned around slowly then, revealing the distress she'd been hoping to cover up.

He turned back to the infield, rocking on his heels, hands clasped behind his back, a triumphant grin twitching at his mouth. It would take a tornado of a turnaround to make Rose view Osgood Pearce as a partner, not when he hadn't cared passionately for Lucas all along. It had taken competition to force him to put the boy first.

Rose Weldon Fraser would expect a lot of the man of her choosing. With fierce longing Charles decided he would prove himself that man, swiftly, forcefully, before there was a permanent wedge between them.

"First no man—now two!" Daisy's admonishment to her niece that afternoon was buffered by a dash of humor.

Rose, who was in the process of changing the sheets on Charles's bed, tucked in a corner and straightened to glare at her aunts. "I never should've said anything!"

Violet clucked, shifting her ample frame farther into Rose's colorful girlhood room. "Of course you should, Rosy. Talk of sex around here these days is sadly just talk. We're thrilled and jealous that you may be on the verge of something physical!"

"We'll see," Rose said briskly in closure. She couldn't help but be on edge about their location for this conversation. Smart women didn't linger in a man's lair to discuss men.

"Just don't let both of them get away while you're measuring pros and weighing cons," Daisy advised with a sage squint of her eye. "Each male has quality. Charles is mighty handy. Osgood has his gallery."

Rose shrugged, rather surprised by her aunt's choice of

utilitarian attributes. But she knew full well that both ladies valued security more than they let on, that having her and Lucas in the house made for added responsibility, even though Rose's salary helped enormously.

Bottom line, if they could see her settled, they would want her to be in a secure position that would free them up from excessive worry.

"I appreciate your concern," she murmured, absently flicking a summerweight blanket over the sheets. "But I would never choose a mate on the basis of those practical pros and cons alone."

"A balance of a hefty bank account and mattress prowess is ideal," Daisy gushed in agreement.

Violet made a cooing sound, swooning for effect. "I, for one wouldn't mind measuring Charles' prow—"

"Sh!" Rose squealed thinly, with darting eyes. "He'll hear you!"

Daisy's silver-blond ponytail shook with her denial. "He won't. He's showering."

"Well, he shouldn't come tramping in here to find a bunch of women hovered over his bed."

"He's hardly the monk type," Daisy drolled, winking at Violet.

Violet's round face softened dreamily. "Wonder if he'll be wrapped in a towel when he discovers us. One of the threadbare yellow-striped ones."

Rose surveyed the amorous pair knowingly. "I deliberately left several new oversize ones on the top shelf of his closet."

Voilet groaned. "Spoilsport."

Daisy worked her orange-painted lips into a smug purse. "It's all right, Vi, dear. I deliberately switched him back to the stripes!"

Rose looked to the closet with a gasp of indignation. "That was very, *very* naughty."

"Naughty can be fun," Daisy reasoned. "We have a

man under your roof who's emitting more heat than our ancient furnace. Why not enjoy it?"

"But to manipulate his towel supply for a little selfish pleasure? Next thing I know you'll have me keeping the keys to his room, encouraging him to parade around just for me." With a giggle, Rose paused to live the fantasy. The aunts were such a corruptive influence at times.

Violet cast a longing gaze to the casual clothing hanging in the open closet, then picked up a bottle of aftershave. "Must say, I'll miss Charles if he leaves us."

Rose gasped. "Why would he?"

"If you do pick Osgood, he must."

"I've never thought of Osgood in romantic terms, you know that."

Daisy shrugged. "Now you're forced to view him in a new and different light, though, aren't you?"

"I think he'd like to force the issue, but I refuse to encourage it."

"Won't hurt to play coy." With a smirk Daisy held up two fingers an inch apart. "Just a little bit."

Rose tossed her head, causing her blond mane to ripple down her back. "You want that exhibition pretty darn bad, don't you?"

"Not at any cost to you, Rose. Truly."

"I should hope not." Rose went about tucking blanket corners.

"Can't blame you for being more intrigued by Charles," Daisy conceded. "He is the ultimate male. And Lucas likes him much better."

"If you had the chance to unwrap one of them at Christmas..." Violet's voice trailed off.

"It would be Charles," Rose gleefully proclaimed. "And I don't mean it just sexually. That's part of it, of course. Of course! But I see so much restrained beneath—"

"Those tight jeans?"

"No! Well, yes," she retracted with pleasure. "I mean, I find him an utterly fascinating personality, too. I'm so anxious to discover all there is to know about him, decide if I am falling in love for a second time. Not that he needs to know this yet. There's something to be said for playing a little hard to get—'' Rose stopped short as Lucas appeared in the doorway, still wearing his jersey, his mitt tucked under an arm, a glass of lemonade clenched in a hand.

''No boys allowed?'' he asked tentatively.

''Sure, boys are allowed.'' Rose beckoned to him. ''Help with the bedspread.''

Lucas turned and stared down the hall. ''It's okay, Charlie. Boys allowed.''

He had to be kidding! With a wild cry Rose tore for the door. There, leaning against the adjoining doorjamb, stood a shivering, bare-chested Charlie. He struck her as resplendent, all sinewy six feet of him, glistening from his combed-back hair to his damp feet, a worn striped towel cinched at his lean hips.

For a fleeting moment she wondered if he might not have been eavesdropping all the while; but even with chattering teeth, he managed to bare a deliciously wolflike smile that steamed her legs to macaroni.

''I KEEP TELLING YOU, ROSE. You have nothing to feel funny about.''

Rose couldn't bear to look at him as she unclipped clothing from the backyard clothesline. Only twenty minutes had passed since their collision upstairs and her cheeks were still singed with embarrassment. She'd fled out here to some space only to have him follow in hot pursuit—after throwing on some clothes.

''It's no big deal. Honestly.''

She stared straight ahead, over the chain-link fence into the adjoining yard full of maple trees. ''No big deal? I don't know if I should be relieved or insulted by that.''

Determined to keep his sense of humor, he pressed his

hands together in an enterprising rub. "Why don't we go out to dinner by ourselves. I'll help you decide."

She continued along the clothesline, unclipping a row of her son's small colorful shirts, nudging the pink laundry basket through the grass with her foot. "Oh, sure, try to whisk me away to some secluded romantic setting after all the private intimate thoughts I shared! Get the girl while she's vulnerable."

He laid a hand on her shoulder then, speaking in a soft, desperate squawk. "Look, don't you think I suffered too, stuck in that drafty hall, then ushered in to the fray? There was Daisy, circling me like a hawk in my own private space—with my precious pants just out of reach—all in the name of art!" His brows drove together in consternation. "Those skimpy towels should be burned. Today. This instant!"

Rose had reached the end of the line as she dropped a pair of her shorts into the basket. Caught between his body and the steel end pole, she attempted a saucy pose. "You should be glad Daisy admires your form. Her opinion comes from vast experience."

"I get the feeling she'd like to gobble me up. Does that strike you as natural?"

"For her, yes. She studies people very thoroughly, imprints them in her photographic memory for future art projects."

He lifted a stern brow. "And never just for kicks?"

"Well, I'm not a mind reader," she teased. "But when she does date, it's the Mr. Pennyfoot type."

"I just wish she'd stop her games. It doesn't look good—"

"Look good to who?"

To anybody intent on suing. "I don't know..." He trailed off awkwardly, staring back at the pines where Lucas was romping with Beast.

"Daisy is accustomed to running the show. Never having married, she's always been the head of the house, always looked after her family. Considering the circumstances, you've worked miracles on her, winning her interest and respect.''

''She's constantly arguing with my ideas.''

''Ah, but even when you challenge her ways, you land on your feet. That impresses her. Take today, the way you brought Lucas back from baseball in one piece.''

''Still, she stares at me too much. And that towel trick was—was diabolical.'' His tone took a wistful turn then, as he brushed some tendrils from her forehead. ''It wouldn't have been so bad had you pulled it, though....''

Traces of merriment danced in her eyes. ''I apologize for not thinking of it first. It was the most tantalizing sight that's hit my old digs in ages. Still...'' She sobered as she tossed the clothespin bag into the basket.

''Still what?''

''Oh, I only wish you hadn't heard *everything* we said.''

He shrugged boyishly. ''Maybe I didn't.''

She inspected his face. ''You did,'' she declared flatly. ''Darn you!''

''I couldn't turn away on a conversation like that. For one thing, I had no place to go!''

She stomped her sandal in the grass. ''But you didn't have the right to know those things until I decided the time was right.''

Charles hovered over her anxiously, thinking how small and delicate she seemed, wanting to reassure her. ''From a need-to-know, basis, I have to tell you, honey, fate stepped in to pull me out of a very sorry state. Discovering how much you care, in such a fresh and delightful way, did my heart a world of good.''

With a tripping pulse, she placed a hand on his chest. He'd never stopped to dry himself properly and the white T-shirt molded to his skin in a very erotic way. Her fingers trembled a little as they grazed his nipple through the flimsy fabric, bringing it to a very prominent nub.

She found the courage to speak as he held his eyes closed

with a mild shudder. "Okay, so we have no choice but to go on from here. As much as I believe in pouring out my feelings, I am at such a disadvantage now. A little making out on the porch swing and suddenly, zap, you know I'm falling in love with you."

Charles let the pleasure of it all sink in. Rosy's love. It sounded so damn good. So damn right. "Don't you think I felt like a goof at the ball field?" he returned. "Pearce batting like the Babe and stepping in to play big daddy? There I was, standing around like a fifth wheel."

His insecurities gave her solace, a welcome feeling of leverage. "You did fine. You showed the boys how to field. But that whole scenario was separate from the man-woman tango. You were there for Lucas."

"Don't forget that Pearce brought the romantic angle into it because he was there for the express purpose of impressing you."

Her porcelain forehead creased in concern. "We're *pretty* sure that's true. Still, I like to be fair always…"

"C'mon, Rose!" His hand fell between them with a saberlike slice. "Don't backpedal on that important issue!"

"I'll always wonder if he thought of Lucas a little," she insisted.

"Go ahead. He didn't, but go ahead."

"Gee, it's nothing to explode over."

"You're right. It isn't like me. But his invasion of my territory here just steams me."

"Your 'territory'? You take so much more for granted now that you know…about me!"

He touched her cheek. "All things considered, don't you think it's high time we went on a real date? Just the two of us? How about tonight?"

She smiled pensively, picking up the laundry basket. "That would be nice. Where shall we go, the city?"

"No!"

Startled by his vehement reaction, she nearly lost her balance. Charles caught her by the basket. He didn't mean to sound so emphatic, but with his luck he'd run into some-one who knew his true identity. "Hey, steady. I was just thinking it would be fun to get to know your area better."

She smiled, accepting his logic. "Okay. I'll try to think of someplace nice. But there isn't much in walking distance."

"How about borrowing the aunts' flower power machine?"

"You want to use the van, then you'll have to do the asking."

"I saw Violet in the kitchen making up some stir-fry concoction. I'll just venture in and—"

"The van technically belongs to Daisy," she told him.

He deflated. "Maybe we can walk, after all."

She reached up to wipe a dot of shaving cream off his earlobe. "Go ask her, Charles. She's harmless, really."

"I wonder where she is. Probably in my room, snipping back doors into my jockey shorts or something."

"Not on a Saturday afternoon," she denied blandly. "She's always up in her studio before dinner."

"Great! The passion pit. If you don't hear from me, come looking." He was surprised when she drew a worried frown. "That was a joke."

"You just reminded me that she has been acting rather odd about the studio."

"How can you tell the difference between odd and odder?"

"Funny," she said sarcastically. "But ever since Osgood criticized her oils, she's gotten so secretive, carrying brown wrapped packages from the art supply store straight up to the attic, keeping mum about her work, asking not to be disturbed."

"If she's that preoccupied, let's take the van first and ask questions later."

"I'm only suggesting you knock first. It'll save your skin for later."

"Whatever you do, don't talk about my skin in the same sentence with Daisy!"

"It's all an act, I promise." Swinging the light basket, she waltzed her way toward the house.

CHARLES DID KNOCK on the studio door as Rose suggested, several times in fact, before he got a response. To some surprise he could've sworn he heard bolts sliding on the other side before the doorknob jiggled. Bolts that weren't there during his first and only visit.

"Oh, it's you, Charles." Daisy looked a little surprised to see him, but fine just the same, all businesslike with a bandanna over her head, garbed in one of her paint-speckled smocks. So why all the covert precautions? Such a trap was way too dangerous in an old tinderbox of an attic like this one.

"What do you intend to do in case of fire?" he greeted gruffly.

"Turn on the hose?"

"I mean, all those bolts you installed on the inside of this door." He rapped the wood with his knuckles, then tried to push his way inside. But she was prepared for his weight and steadfastly held the door open at the six-inch mark.

"You're the security nut around here," she reasoned cheerily. "I thought you'd commend me."

"What if you fainted from fumes or something? We'd have to break in with an ax!"

Spots of indignant color splashed her cheeks. "Fainting is for wimps. Besides, I have good ventilation in here."

His eyes crinkled, as though inviting a confidence. "C'mon give, why all the extra locks?"

"Because I want to be alone."

"You don't leave anybody else alone," he said silkily.

"It's my house and I make the rules."

His expression hardened. "I'm buying an ax at the hardware store at the first opportunity."

"Waste of good money. We already have one."

"Where?"

"In here. I use it as a prop for my models."

"Won't do me any good in there if I need it out here."

"Tough cheese. Now if you don't mind…"

Charles flattened his palm on the door as it began to close again. "You don't even know why I've come. Seems tacky that you're only interested in me when I'm half naked."

Her shallow cheeks filled with a suppressed hoot. "You were naked by more than half today."

Charles laughed in spite of himself. "You're incorrigible. But not without potential," he added as she leaned on the door again. "Your eyes haven't left my face once."

"You have a very nice looking face, boy. Now get to the point."

"I want to borrow your van."

"For what?"

"To take Rose out."

"Oh." She savored the idea. "Where are you going?"

"I don't know yet. Someplace for dinner."

"Very well, help yourself. The keys are on a Peg-Board in the kitchen near the back door."

"Thank you very much, Daisy. I'll take good care of her."

"Just don't ply her with a lot of heavy meat."

"That's your sum total of caution?"

"Rose is a grown woman."

He beamed. "Oh, yes, I did notice in passing."

"Huh. You're so gone on her, I almost feel sorry for you." With a noisy cackle she shoved the door and the locks back in place.

Chapter Twelve

"I am not exaggerating, Charles. It's always hard to get into The Old Spaghetti House on a Saturday night." Rose was awestruck as she scooted into one of the prized booths in the rear. "Without a reservation, it's usually impossible! Do you have connections here in Scarsdale?"

"Nope. Guess I'm just handy in all kinds of houses." Charles eased his long body along the banquette seat opposite hers, appreciating the high stained-wood walls enclosing them. Cheap fun really, for the twenty dollars he'd slyly passed the hostess. The freestanding tables positioned up front under the glare of brassy light fixtures were fine for hungry people intent on a few laughs. But he wanted this first meal alone with Rose to be special, memorable, romantic.

Rose looked especially memorable herself tonight. Charles centered the red candle jar between them, using it as an excuse to admire her at leisure. The cornflower shade of her sundress brought an intriguing vividness to her eyes, and its molded bodice uplifted her small breasts enticingly. Her hair was fluffed in loose curls on her bare shoulders, and gleamed in the flickering candlelight with her every move.

Cornflower eyes. Cornsilk hair. There was something so refreshing about the woman that made Charles want to take her to some grassy spot and make long and slow love to her.

"Hungry?"

Her amused query brought him back to reality. "How'd you guess?"

"You look ready to ravish something."

Ah, a woman who understood him.

The waitress appeared with a basket of bread, glasses of water and menus. She lingered to suggest several wines, including a popular merlot. With Rose's approval, Charles ordered a bottle.

Alone once again, Charles bared his teeth. "What were you saying? Something about ravishment?"

"I was speaking of food."

He chuckled when she added a saucy wink. "Guess I really am starved. It has been a long day, especially the ball shagging part."

"Lucas has a way of keeping all of us on our toes. He sure did a fine job on the field today, didn't he?"

"Excellent job. The other boys took him right in once they saw he could play."

"He's so proud to have you at his side."

"He sure wanted to come along to dinner, didn't he?" Charles retorted.

Rose picked up her menu, unperturbed as she scanned it. "He gives every cause a shot. But I think it best he see some lines drawn between the children and grown-ups."

And how. Charles had kept his relief over their escape in check this long and didn't want to risk overdoing it now. It didn't stop him from voicing a concern, however. "Does he have foot-stomping fits like tonight's often?"

"He's doing them less since you arrived," Rose said evenly. "It's as if he's sensed you won't tolerate it."

"I suppose in the heat of the moment, he fell into the old pattern."

"Calmly telling him tantrums aren't a guy thing was perfect."

The desperate risk of a rookie parent, Charles mused, sipping some water. But he had to do something to discourage that kind of behavior. Charles could see the aunts were just twitching to step in and humor him, but that wasn't a wise pattern to get started. Lucas was a Fraser, after all, and would eventually have many responsibilities to carry. Surrendering over little things at this point would only lead to a very spoiled and very rich manipulator. With the Fraser family wealth and privileges, he'd soon be out of control.

The waitress brought the wine, then took their orders.

Rose stared at her glass and the bottle with uncertainty. Charles fingered the stem of his, politely waiting for her to drink. "Is something the matter?" he finally asked.

"No, no." Her voice dropped a notch and she leaned over the table. "Let's go Dutch treat tonight. How about that?"

Guilt, shame and a sense of impatience rocked him. He could buy this whole damn place—as she could if she accepted her rightful legacy—and she was fretting over the cost of dinner. "Rose, Rose." He reached over, tugged up her chin with his hooked finger and stared deeply and affectionately into her eyes.

She tipped her head back with a defensive retort. "What? Student and shop clerk split the bill. Big deal."

"I wouldn't dream of allowing any lady to pick up a tab."

"But—but—but—"

He pressed a finger to her lips, finding them soft, moist and inviting. "You sound like a tugboat." *And feel like heaven.* The temptation to skim his tongue over those lips was giving him an ache that seared through all the social politics of their relationship. He smoldered openly and deliberately.

"Hey, you must really have a thing for tugboats."

"I have a thing for you, honey, and I very badly want to kiss you."

"That, at least, is free of charge."

"Forget all about prices, and checks and tips," he ordered gruffly. "I wouldn't be taking you out if I couldn't swing it."

"Honestly?"

"Absolutely. I'm not a pauper just because I'm a student. I've worked hard over the years and I've invested shrewdly."

"All right, then." She relaxed, graciously taking a sip of her wine.

Charles's tension lingered as possible consequences for his lies gnawed at him. She'd feel so foolish later on when she looked back on financial duels like this one. Hopefully by the time his cover blew she'd be his in body and spirit, so hypnotized by his devotion that she wouldn't have the stamina to rebel.

"I want to ask you a personal question, Charles."

"Okay. Go ahead and shoot, I guess." He tried not to flinch as though faced with a real gun barrel.

"Why exactly did you decide to show up for Lucas's practice? I know you don't want to discuss it, but I can't seem to let it go."

"Isn't it most important that I wised up?"

She shook her head, taking another sip of merlot. "With your impeccable references, I'd have expected you to fully understand right off."

He drained his wine, then stalled by refilling their glasses. How badly he wanted to answer honestly. "Let's just say I realized that Lucas needed to play more than I did today. Understand?"

"But you have background with youngsters."

"I have worked with children before," he said candidly, thinking of his interaction with young models and actors at the agency. "But I'm learning to relate on new levels with Lucas, digging deeper to do the best job."

She was watching him keenly, still unsatisfied. "But what could've possibly happened overnight?"

My father acted like a jerk and reminded me what it's like to be on the receiving end of such selfishness. "I thought to put myself in the boy's place," he blurted out in a surrendering rush, as though revealing a top secret code to the enemy. "I sometimes forget what it's like to be that young and dependent. I suddenly remembered, that's all, end of story."

Their salads arrived then. Rose dropped the subject, making a project out of slicing up her tomato wedges. But her thoughts were racing as the pieces of Charles Johnson fell more clearly into place. Such a proud man, picking up tabs, trying to reach into the mind of a child without fanfare. His blooper still seemed mighty big for a father figure, but he'd spun around hard and fast to correct it. That was the most even a real father could do.

She was the first to break the silence between them. "You know, I think I owe you a bit of an apology."

Taken by surprise, he swallowed hard, forcing lettuce down his contracting throat. "You? Why?"

"Because I'm stuck with a fault of my own, that my vision of a father figure became too customized, too perfected. Real fathers, like mothers, stumble without meaning to, and they aren't always expected to come up with detailed explanations." She reached across the table and stroked his hand. "If it's any consolation, I think you've left such a distinct impression of strength on the household, that I've come to take you for granted and expect way too much."

Charles stared at her dumbly, turning his hand as she gently massaged it. This kind of candor coming from one of his more aggressive lady friends would've seemed natural. But from the subtle and gentle Rosy, it was like a parting of seas, a scattering of clouds. She was making a major effort to understand him, accept him. *Seduce him.* He doubted she was aware of the tantalizing path she was clearing. A lonely young widow seeing hope of a new relationship, tempting him with kisses, jest and cozy small talk.

"For all I know," she went on haltingly, "you may have all sorts of commitments that can upset the balance of our…life together as we know it."

Charles gazed deeply into her eyes, his voice hoarse and certain. "There is no other woman, Rose. Not for me."

She became flustered. "You know how I feel already, of course."

He grinned like a sated daddy bear. "It would've taken you forever to tell me directly, so I see my eavesdropping as a delightful shortcut."

"Not true. I only hoped to have a conversation something like this one first."

"Well, it isn't the only topsy-turvy thing going on back at the ranch."

"All in all, I think you like our life very much."

"I do."

She gave his hand a final squeeze and released it.

He wiggled his fingers with a forlorn look. "All over?"

"I have to keep you wanting more."

Charles settled back on the seat and finished the bottle of merlot. Escaping into the yellow henhouse, sliding in the dead bolts, and losing himself inside Rosy would still leave him forever wanting more. The power she held over him was a little frightening. If only he could secure that sort of power over her. Before it was too late.

PEOPLE IN THE restaurant parking lot stared at them as they climbed back into the Weldons' psychedelically painted Volkswagen van. Charles quickly assisted Rose up into the passenger seat, and moved in behind the wheel. The chugging sputter of the ancient engine made him mourn his separation from his sleek black Viper with its purry V-10 under the hood.

Rose told him she had a spot to take him to back in White Plains, and she insisted it would be a surprise. She then went on to relate a story about when she and Dean were dating and using the van. Seemed Daisy had accumulated some parking tickets and cops pulled them over, forcing them to do some fast talking to get off the hook.

Charles chuckled, thinking how Dean could talk his way out of anything with anybody. Almost. He couldn't sell Rose to Hilton and that must have floored him.

Charles wore a grin all the way back home, in fact, the slow ride seemed special, driving fifteen miles an hour less than most of the cars to spare their sputtery engine. Amazingly he'd come to enjoy this more relaxed, carefree lifestyle in a lot of ways. But he also missed his privileges around the busy city, spending cash without qualms, being recognized and respected for his social status and position in the family firm. If only both worlds could merge.

Once back in White Plains, Rose directed Charles to a public park of rolling green hills and dense clusters of trees. It was nearly nine, so traces of night had settled in with shades of gray. Rose took him on a car tour of all the winding lanes and secluded nooks, which appeared shadowy and surreal under the faint glow of the old-fashioned lamps.

"What do you have in mind, honey?"

His deep roguish tone sent an electric quiver down her spine. "You'll see," she said saucily, pointing to the ribbon of blacktop veering left.

It took plenty to surprise Charles, but she'd gotten him again. The road led to a parking lot fronting a small circular lake. A quaint pavilion with a red-tiled roof loomed across the water, alive with light and music.

"This is really something!" Charles impetuously climbed out of the van and stood in the small lot with hands planted on his hips.

She joined him, pleased by his delight. "We may not have our own Spaghetti House, but we do have Regent's Park."

"This is a nice way to end the evening."

"It isn't over yet."

"No? What would you like to do?"

"Take a walk around the lake to the pavilion."

He held out his hand to her, "Perfect."

Rose slipped her hand in his, skipping a little to keep up with him on the hiking path. There were a few joggers, many walkers, and other couples like themselves, all enjoying the music echoing across the water. She noticed that women of all ages admired Charles with an automatic once-over. Feeling unusually territorial, she gripped his hand tighter.

Was she dreaming here? Could she hope to hang on to a city guy, most likely destined for great things after graduate school? How long would he be willing to hang around once summer was over? True, the season hadn't begun and she was already fretting. So much would depend on—so much!

So much would depend upon whether they had a rock-solid commitment between them.

For the first time since Dean's death, Rose was thinking of tying the knot again. Six years of comfortable solitude blown to smithereens in mere days by whirlwind Charles. There'd been something so basic between them from the start, something fateful, something valuable.

If only she could reach inside him, turn out all his secrets, his fears. It might take years to peel back his protective layers. How convenient that she happened to have years on her hands.

They soon reached their destination. Charles inspected the grand old pavilion with admiration. The front of the structure where they stood was skirted by another parking lot, and banked with a steep concrete staircase. The open air hall in the rear facing the water where the concert was in progress was visible from a side angle. There was a nice crowd in attendance, applauding as the music died away. Charles thought for sure Rose would take the concrete bank of steps around back, but instead she guided him through the front entrance.

Charles stepped inside the small café area and gaped at her. "You want to eat again?"

"I want to rent a bike." She gestured to a sign over the counter.

"I thought we were going to include Lucas on this kind of outing."

Rose eyed him shrewdly, her motherly instincts in high gear. "The trouble is, even if it doesn't work out, he'll still want a bike of his own."

"I hadn't thought of that," he admitted.

"One opportunity and he'll really insist."

Charles figured she had a valid point, but couldn't resist ribbing her just the same. He folded his arms across his chest, surveying her dolefully. "I think you mostly don't want him to see you wobble around."

"That, too. I'm bound to be awful at it."

He stared out one of the windows overlooking the lake path, sobering. "It's getting darker, Rose—"

"I know," she said gleefully. "This way, no one will see me too clearly. And the bikes do have lights."

Charles sighed, curving an arm around her shoulders. "All right."

Rose dragged him along, bright and animated. "Get only one."

"But I can afford—"

She pinched his muscular arm through the knit of his polo shirt. "Oh, shush. I'm thinking you'll need to have your hands free."

"I will?"

"To hold me up."

"Oh, that." He rolled his eyes, but was secretly pleased over her faith in him, and in being needed in these small matters.

A short time later, they were back on the path, Rose standing on tiptoe with a black three-speed bike beneath her, testing her bottom on the seat. "This feels good. Real good."

"You'll be ready for a Harley in no time."

She curled her lower lip. "Ha, ha. How are you going to help me?"

Charles clamped one hand to the handlebar and the other to the seat, bracing the bike with his body. "Put your feet on the pedals."

"I'll be helpless."

He struck a Herculean pose. "Not with me here, baby."

She carefully released contact with the ground, feeling as light as an astronaut in orbit. "Now what?"

"We begin to move."

"Do you know how much trust this takes?"

Or how much protective fuss? Moving his hand around the seat, he tried to tuck the flared hem of her dress between her thigh and the saddle. "Maybe we should get the boy a go-cart."

"No, no." She sucked in air between clenched teeth. "Though I wish I had a helmet."

"I'll cushion any falls."

"In that case, *you* should have the helmet."

"Pedal, woman, before the clock strikes twelve!"

She took the gruff order to heart and launched off with a mighty pump. Charles was glad he wore comfortable shoes, because he needed them to keep up with her. And in turn she needed him to keep the bike up. What she had in speed didn't compensate for her lack of balance. The bike snaked and wobbled under her shaky control. Pedestrians along the path watched her headlight bob and swerve, a warning beacon to leap out of her way.

Charles was huffing mightily when he finally slowed her down, guiding her to a wrought iron bench between some elms.

"That was..." She breathed heavily, untangling her legs from the machine. "Hard."

Charles took hold of the bike, leaning it against the bench. "Most little girls start off with training wheels."

"Yes, but at my age, that would look ridiculous."

As they sank together on the bench, Charles self-consciously acknowledged their audience and his lack of dignity. All these people were bound to go home and tell their families about the crazy couple with the bike. Amazingly, he instantly saw the fun in it. How wonderful and strange to laugh at one's self in such a delightful, un-Fraserlike way.

Charles couldn't help thinking how much better off Hilton would be if he could chuckle over the small things, before they mushroomed out of reason. Naturally, the aunts were on Charles's mind. If only Hilton could just see them as harmless hippies, eccentric relics full of love and charm.

"Penny for your thoughts," she lilted breathlessly, patting his knee.

He shifted on the seat and curved an arm around her shoulders. "I'll show you for a nickel." Hauling her up against his chest, he pressed a kiss to her glistening temple, her fragile jawline, ultimately coming to rest his mouth on hers, exploring lazily, conversantly, as though they'd been mates for ages.

For a long heated moment they were the only two people on earth, lost in their senses, the simplicity of the spring night. They soon came to realize their audience was growing, as the concert had ended. Charles released her with a wink, raking a hand through his tousled hair.

She smoothed her hair and bodice, feeling refreshed, aroused. "Guess we better get the bike back before the pavilion closes."

"You aren't up for another ride though, are you?"

She fluffed her skirt and climbed over the center bar. "Of course, I am." She leveled a finger at him. "You have a lot to learn about getting your money's worth out of things, Mr. Johnson."

Charles looked round the path, then self-consciously

rolled his shoulders. *He* was Johnson! Though, in his own defense, he rarely heard the name used. "Who me?" he teased, hoping to cover his blooper.

But Rose wasn't really listening as she launched off on the path with her own unique snaky wobble. He trotted after her, realizing he'd gotten off the hook fairly easy.

It was around eleven o'clock when Charles steered the van down Rose's familiar street. They'd stopped for an ice-cream cone at the pavilion and strolled around the grounds, generally reluctant to put an end to the glorious evening. Charles felt his heart sink a little as he guided the van into the garage and shut off the engine.

"Thanks for a lovely time." Rose leaned over and kissed his jaw.

Charles touched the spot, committing it to memory. "It was the best."

The only light in the garage was the bulb on the door opener, but his profile was easy enough for Rose to read, giving rise to some doubt. "You all right with everything? I hope you didn't feel too pressured by my questions. If I get to be too much—about parenting," she added shyly "—you say so."

He turned to her, grazing a knuckle along her chin before pressing the car keys into her hand. "You are too much about everything every hour of the day," he said huskily. "A very likable quality."

"That's sweet." She impulsively snuggled closer, nuzzling his throat.

It took monumental willpower on his part to hold her at bay as she tried to crawl into his lap. "I, ah, can't tell you how much I'd like to do this," he claimed in apology.

She stared up in dismay. "There's a problem?"

How to put it into delicate terms. "Rose, if I thought I could take you halfway, I'd have made a move in the park."

She searched his face, computing his message. "Half-way?"

"*Only* halfway. Understand?"

"Oh!" She slipped back some inches, anxiously, solicitously, as though allowing a wheezing man air.

"The more we touch, the closer we get...things are bound to escalate."

Her resigned sigh filled the cab. "I guess things can get out of hand easily at our age, with knowledge and practice to sweeten the stakes."

"And how." He gripped the door handle, staring out at the rakes and shovels hanging on the garage wall, thinking how unaware Rose was of her beauty and sensuality. The guys were ogling her quite openly in the park and she'd seemed oblivious to it. Sure, they were a little less interested in her on wheels, but she looked like a nut then. He impetuously wished he could keep her on the wobble just for himself, permanently fend off competition with the inference that she was a kook with no sense of balance.

"I guess this is good night then, Charles."

So wrapped up in his musings, he didn't realize she'd exited the passenger side and was now hovering by the open garage door. He quickly climbed out from behind the wheel. "Uh, Rose."

She stopped on a button, her pale blue dress floating around her slender legs as she twirled back. "Yes?"

Blood pounded in his head to a tribal mating beat. She was so lovely standing there in the pale moonlight, shy, eager, mysterious. He felt an achy swelling below the belt. How humbling it was to find himself so lost, fearing he'd shatter if he breathed. But he had to do something to reassure her.

"There will be plenty of other nights," he ventured huskily. "Other walks in the park."

"Of course."

What did she want him to do? To say? She centered her sights on the house again, preparing to leave him stranded with his straining manhood and pent-up desires. He barely recognized his husky voice as he called after her. "If you…you know, were to ever…want me, really want me, I'd deem it the honor of my life."

"That's incredibly sweet of you to say." She turned her body in a provocative twist, moving off like a smug blond kitten with a mug full of cream.

In no hurry to sleep, Charles lingered in the garage, then in the kitchen, removing his shoes and socks, pouring himself a glass of milk, snacking on mixed fruit in a plastic container. Analyzing their encounter, he decided Rose meant to force those wrenching admissions out of him. She hadn't been about to traipse inside in any all-fire hurry. She'd hemmed and hawed until he'd laid the big one on her, admitted he'd like nothing better than to make love to her—at her convenience no less! Why did she do it?

He eventually turned off the lights and trudged up the stairs, heading straight to the bathroom to brush his teeth. He glared at his reflection, his brain still wild with activity. How would she treat him tomorrow? Like a whipped pup? No, not Rosy. She wouldn't… Would she?

He tiptoed quietly down the hallway, past bedroom doors. Rose's was pitch-black already. Most likely she was dreaming of her next purry move. His door was closed, just as he'd left it. He eased inside, locking himself in. Moonbeams spilled through the windows overlooking the street to make the overhead light fixture unnecessary.

Suddenly he realized he wasn't alone. Rose was standing near the foot of the bed, bathed in silvery rays. He said her name in a rough gasp. "What is it? What's going on?"

"About your generous invitation. I'm here to collect."

Chapter Thirteen

He stumbled closer, jamming his toe on the footboard. "You want me. You want me *now?*"

She scanned his length. "Are you too busy?"

"No!"

"You told me to tell you when, so I am."

He had to be sleepwalking. Wordlessly, he raised her hand, turned it palm up and kissed her wrist. Her skin was soft, her pulse rapid. She was real. She was his. So the night would live on after all.

Rose stood motionless, centering on the pressure of his lips, the heat of his breath. It was his turn to tease. He was showing her what one featherlight kiss could do, and that he, too, knew how to stretch an encounter into sweet delicious torture.

Keeping hold of her wrist, he drew her close in a tango's embrace, burying his face in her hair, inhaling the fruity scent of her shampoo. Rose was feeling a deeper sense of urgency in this risky home setting, having been denied the joys of consummation for such a very long time. She stood on tiptoe, braced his cheeks and eagerly pressed her mouth to his.

Charles swallowed liquid lightning as her tongue grazed his. His plans of leisurely lovemaking incinerated as he stroked her back, tugging at the zipper resting along her spine. The dress fell away with a rustle. He kept right on responding to her kiss in a dizzy state of arousal, vaguely aware of her moving hands loosening his belt, his chinos, his shorts.

When they were stripped of all but her pink panties and his polo shirt, Charles took over. He clutched her silken bottom and pressed their bodies flush.

The hardness of him made her gasp, and she suddenly felt trapped in her lingerie. She couldn't help but release a sigh of relief as he reached down to strip the binding silk away from her skin. Another more impatient tug and he had his shirt off as well, added to the heap of clothing at their bare feet. As though lifting a delicate flower in his hands, Charles carried Rose the two short steps to the turned-down bed.

"You thought of everything," he crooned, gliding his body alongside hers on the tight bottom sheet.

"How?"

His hand slid over her hip to the sheet. "By pulling back the covers."

"But I didn't."

It took monumental effort, but Charles raised himself to a seated position and took inventory of the bed. "I smell something."

"Peanut butter!" they chorused.

Flipping back the pillows, Charles found an unwrapped peanut butter and jelly sandwich, slightly crushed, resting on a plate.

Rose began to giggle. "Lucas's favorite, right after hamburgers."

"So it is."

With a wince, Charles transferred the plate to the nightstand.

"You understand, don't you? His capacity for giving is so limited at his age. Homemade gifts are big in kindergarten."

"I appreciate the sentiment, but he did bite off a corner."

"Not a bad showing for Lucas. You could've done

worse. I found a pickle under my pillow once, and Aunt Violet a worm.''

He stared at the plate with new respect. ''Mmm, real good sandwich.''

With a merry laugh, Rose laid flat on her back. Charles placed his hand on her belly, caressing her satiny skin with long strokes, skimming over her pale triangle of hair, tickling his palm with the springy nest. She enjoyed the play with laughing eyes.

She made a huskier sound as he moved his hand between her thighs, rubbing her most sensitive places. Her breath came in hard shallow bursts as his fingers entered her, sliding in and out with fevered method. At the same time he was cupping her breast, bringing her nipple to erection with the flick of his tongue. Pinned in place, unable to move, she managed to guide her knee between his legs, part them and glide her thigh over his arousal with a steady rub.

Charles kept control, keeping up the same pace for the longest time, drawing her through waves of heat with his invasive massage. She finally clenched around his fingers, her entire body tightening with mounting pressure. Then he fit his hips to hers and drove deep inside her.

Her satiny legs wrapped around him like ribbons, and Charles picked up a precise, centered rhythm. Only when he sensed she was nearly ready to shatter did he let go of his own fevered desires, driving them on to a wondrous, explosive climax.

Rose arched into him with a soft cry, then sank onto the pillows. He followed her down in a shuddering heap.

She eventually half rose and grazed his brow. ''That was a...wonderful way to end the evening.''

He cracked one eye open. ''I dunno, it could be improved upon.''

''How?'' She rose on her knees, ready to strike.

He stared up at her boyishly. ''Can Lucas have his bike? Please?''

"What! Why you sneak." She collapsed on top of him in surrender. "I suppose it'll be all right."

Charles nodded, floating on a new level of smugness. "Great!"

They lay together for a while longer, cuddling together amidst the mingled scents of their lovemaking and Skippy extra chunky.

As she technically was the guest, Charles figured the first move should be hers. She eventually made it, swinging her legs over the side of the bed with a mild yawn. She rose and padded across the floor to pick up her dress without modesty.

Propped up against the headboard, with arms folded above his head, Charles watched the show. "No coy scurrying around behind a pillow or sheet," he remarked in tender appreciation. "Maybe I should've considered widows a long time ago."

She stepped into the rumpled sundress, tugging it up to her waist, drawing her arms into the thin straps. "So am I your first?"

He winked. "My very first. Come closer and I'll zip you."

"Not necessary. I live close by." She picked up her panties and stared over at him lovingly. "Your gentleness and sensitivity were appreciated."

He unfolded his arms and edged off the bed. "You make me a better man every day," he said huskily, sauntering to her.

She quivered as he approached, so large, so beautiful, so male. Even in the shadows she could read the true complete story in his eyes, the caring, the sincerity, the affection. For the first time she was glimpsing his very soul, the unsure bungler who made time for a bike pitch while making time with her.

Pulling her close, he gently pressed into her with his erection. "You could stay a little while longer."

"I can't, really. It's after three."

With surprise he glanced at the clock radio on the dresser.

"The aunts would bring us breakfast in bed," she said, "but Lucas…"

"We don't want to confuse or upset him," he agreed.

"So, see you in the morning then." She moved to the door, popping the knob's push-button lock with a turn.

"What's on for tomorrow?"

She hesitated. "Lucas has another practice."

"Already!"

"Beevee called earlier. There was an opening for a field and he snatched it up, figuring the boys could use the extra drill."

"Why didn't you say anything before?"

"I was afraid you'd get all grumpy for our dinner." She smiled at her freshly wounded warrior. "It won't be as bad as you think. Osgood has a showing at the gallery tomorrow and couldn't dare break away."

"That's something!"

"I won't be able to break away from work, either," she said regretfully. "Night."

"That leaves me on my own—" The protest died on his lips as the door thumped shut. He tramped back to bed, wishing he was the all-star player they needed and not the bat-shy chump he was.

CHARLES WAS THE LAST to rise the next morning. He descended the staircase in gray sweats to find Lucas glued to the television set in the living room and the ladies dressed in springy shorts and tops, clustered around the dining room table reading the Sunday paper.

"Morning, all." He sank down in an open chair, rubbing his face as they all offered their greetings.

"Hope this breakfast is all right," Violet said over her teacup. "Last week's spread was sort of a welcome feast."

Thank heavens for that! He for one wouldn't miss that sort of veggie fry, though the raisin buns and tea set out on the table weren't enough to keep him going, either. What he'd do for some coffee right now. Sunday papers without coffee just didn't seem natural. "This is fine, really," he said politely.

Rose peered over the top of the Classified Ads section. "You sure look like you could use a pick-me-up."

"Any ideas?" he asked beguilingly.

"It so happens I went down to 7-Eleven to get a couple of different newspapers and—"

Charles leapt up like a panther. Clamping his hands to her cheeks, he asked, "Did you bring me real roasted coffee? Tell me it's true."

Rose nodded, overwhelmed by his gratitude. "It was Lucas's idea. He was along and thought it would taste good after your midnight sandwich."

Lucas charged across the foyer at the mention of his name, barreling into Charles's arms. "Hey, man!"

Charles hoisted the boy into his lap, tugging at his dinosaur print shirt. "Thanks for the coffee—and the late-night snack."

"Oh, Charlie!" Lucas's huge eyes glistened as he hugged him fiercely. "Mommy told me all about my new bike! Thanks for talking her into it."

Charles gave his back a pat. "Did you thank your mom, too?"

His cherub face sobered. "Sure I did. For six minutes."

Rose lowered the newspaper, intent on contributing. "I want you to understand, Lucas, that your bike won't be brand-new."

He slipped to the hardwood floor with a splat of bare feet. "I know that! You *told* me. One hundred times."

"I just don't want you to expect too much. I've been thumbing through the ads here, and even the used ones—with training wheels—aren't cheap."

"Okay!" With arms flapping he darted off.

"Rose," Charles interceded firmly, reaching over to keep her paper lowered. "I will get the bike."

"You, Charles!"

Her brisk reaction startled him, but he kept his features even. "I can best hunt for it, make sure it's in good shape."

"Oh, thanks." She blushed, sorry she'd jumped on him. But she felt so funny about him paying for things. She'd given him her body, her affection, gladly, freely. But her stolid sense of independence would be the last to compromise. For some inexplicable reason, her intuition was prodding her to hold on tight for the time being.

The aunts had begun to make background sounds, clinking teacups on saucers, Daisy's silver-blond head tipping toward Violet's cotton-top one as they shared murmurs of dismay. Rose addressed them impatiently. "I know how you feel about bikes, but I tried riding one and think, with some precautionary measures, Lucas can catch on and do well."

"When did you ever ride a bicycle, Rose?" Daisy grilled, crumpling the Arts section.

Rose kept her chin high. "Last night, at the park—with Charles."

Violet pressed plump fingers to her mouth. "Did you wear a helmet?"

"No. But Lucas will. All the children around here do."

Daisy surveyed Charles keenly from across the table. "I'm sure you know we'd have rather seen you make love to our niece than saddle her up *that* way."

Charles mustered the shock he thought appropriate to the rash statement. "Really, Daisy! The things you say."

"Daisy, this isn't a choice between love and war!" Rose cried.

"To Vi and me, it is. All rough-and-tumble activities are small wars, so to speak." Daisy preened at Charles. "Think love first and you can't go wrong."

He winked conspiratorially. "I'll keep that in mind for our next date. Now, if you'll excuse me, I think I'll hunt down that coffee." Grabbing two pastries from the platter, he made his exit.

Rose refolded her section of paper, feeling a twinge of remorse over her aunts' disapproval. "Please don't be upset."

"Everything is happening so fast," Violet lamented. "Baseballs and bicycles. We always tried so hard to keep you from harm, Rose, showed you the best example. How can you let loose this way?"

For however long she wanted to do so for Lucas's sake!

Daisy leaned across the table, her faded eyes keen. "I hope you're not going along with all of Charles's crazy ideas because you're attracted to him."

Rose peered mischievously over her teacup. "Why, no, Daisy. I happen to think I'm attracted to him *because* of all his crazy ideas. Now if you'll excuse me, too, I have to get ready for work."

"Are you letting Charles handle the T-ball today?" Violet wondered.

"Yes, of course."

"I suppose Osgood won't like missing a practice," Daisy said with a tsk.

"He won't even know he has unless somebody squeals." Rose's threatening air made such a breach sound like a mighty serious offense.

"Fine and well," Daisy conceded. "Your own decision to make concerning the men. But someone from our fold should be in representation."

"You hate ball games."

Daisy shrugged. "We could never hate anything Lucas might achieve."

Violet dabbed the corners of her mouth with fretful motion. "A strange quandary indeed. Hating ball, loving Lucas. Hating bikes, loving Lucas."

"You'll get it all sorted out in your minds," Rose said breezily.

Charles didn't expect to run into Rose on the stairs moments later, but there she was, skipping up as he was tramping down.

"Charles! I thought you were in the kitchen."

"Took a detour to the bedroom. Fun place, don't you think?"

"Sometimes..." She lingered on his step, gripping the railing, feeling the heat of his survey. "Feeling especially fine this morning?"

As fine as a man could be with a cell phone wedged in the waistband of his sweatpants. He grimaced at the antenna lodged in his navel.

She skimmed his whiskered jaw with a filed nail. "You aren't feeling any doubt, are you?"

"About the ball practice?"

She rolled her eyes. "No! About last night."

He nipped at her finger. "You've got to be kidding, my little she-cat."

"To think practice leapt to your mind." She smiled wryly. "I swear, you are becoming obsessed with Lucas's happiness."

"I leave that obsession to your aunts."

She hesitated. "Speaking of them..."

He raised a hand in self-defense. "Don't tell me, they want bikes, too."

"Nothing that scary. They want to go with you this afternoon." She winced under his dark look.

"That's even worse! I can see them now, cooing at Lucas, throwing their bodies in front of flying balls."

Rose glanced down to the foyer, afraid they'd overhear. "They won't."

"Did you tell them not to?" he demanded incredulously.

"I didn't have time." She stood on tiptoe to kiss his nose. "Anyway, it seems like a job for the coach."

"You can't hang that on Beevee!"

She jabbed a finger at his chest. "I mean you."

With a head full of steam, Charles charged down the last stairs, through the foyer, pausing in the dining room doorway. "You can come," he blurted out, "but you have to stay put in the bleachers and keep out of the action." The old women stared mutely at him. "Okay? Okay!" He dared them to rebel, but they gleefully trumped him.

"I like a masterful man," Violet said with a dreamy sigh.

"I happen to like a man I can master," Daisy countered. "Still, it is tough to imagine Osgood Pearce, gallery and all, looking so scrumptiously virile."

In a fit of frustration, Charles marched away. The aunts couldn't see the tiny delighted smirk that danced across his face.

"HELLO, CHARLES. Calling from the black hole? A Vulcan space station?"

Charles gave the swing beneath him a gentle push, a steaming insulated cup in one hand and his red cell phone in the other. He'd decided to take his breakfast in privacy and Lucas's old play set was as far from the house as he could manage. "Marcia, Marcia, you don't sound thrilled with my interruption."

"I would've preferred last Sunday, but it's always good to hear from you."

"Spoken like a trusted personal secretary."

"I suppose you're calling about the Calhoon account."

"Partly," he said, deciding not to confide yet that he'd handed the reins back to Hilton.

"The test audience is due at nine tomorrow."

"Good. Better give Dad a buzz today and let him know."

"Will do. Was there something else you need, boss? Something to aid and abet your secret adventure perhaps?"

"I do have a personal favor to ask. It's a little out of line."

"Sock it to me anyway."

Charles planted his feet on the dirt gully worn into the grass beneath him, bracing himself. "I need a bicycle."

"Did I hear you right?"

He held the squawking phone away from his ear. "Yes.

A twenty-inch boy's bike. Not just any bike, either," he went on.

"Don't worry, I'll get the very best."

"No, the medium best."

"Care to explain that?"

"I want a good, sturdy midpriced bike," he stated slowly. "Nothing FAO Schwarz fancy with a lot of bells or whistles. Understand?"

"As you wish."

He took a sip of coffee for stamina. "Now here's the tricky part."

"There's more?"

"I want you to ride it around."

"C'mon, boss!"

"You're short enough, I think."

"Why would you want me to do that? Is this some sort of gag? Are you going to have a film crew following me around?"

"No, I'm miles away."

"Exactly how many?"

"Trust me, I don't have the time to tail you. What I'm after here is a bike that looks a little used, like a store return resold on discount."

"Really? Is this on the level?"

"I swear. And there'll be a bonus in it for you." He pumped the swing again, staring into the pines, straining for the ultimate carrot. "Like…a long weekend at that spa in the Hamptons that you like so much."

"Okay, let's get this straight. You want me to buy a medium-priced bike, sturdy and plain. I imagine we're talking about, oh, a $150 item."

"Yes, I suppose that's about the going rate."

"I'm to scuff it up a bit."

"Right."

"In return, you will treat me to a $3,000 weekend of pampering."

"Nothing dense about you, Marcia."

"I reserve the return compliment for now, Mr. Fraser. Anything else?"

"Oh, yes, get training wheels, too."

"I can't ride around with those."

"Yes, you can—"

"Hey, Charlie!"

Lucas! Pressing the receiver to his chest, Charles twisted round to find the child romping across the lawn with the fluffy white Beast on his heels. He quickly pressed the phone to his face again, speaking in rapid fire executive English. "Look, I have to go. Work it all out your own way. Just have that thing scuffed and ready at the office by tomorrow. Bye!"

Lucas climbed into the swing beside him. "You talking on the phone?"

Charles drained his coffee, setting the empty cup and cell phone in the grass. "Uh, yes."

"You gotta better friend than me?" he wondered anxiously.

Charles's throat tightened. How deeply his nephew had grown to care for him. "No way, man. You're the best."

"You're the best, too, man." Satisfied, Lucas curled his fingers around the swing's supportive chains, pumping his little legs. "Let's have a race to see who can go the highest. Hurry, hurry. I'll beat you."

Charles was sure child psychologists would advise against him taking a dive in the contest, but he did anyway. After all, didn't Rose, mother extraordinaire, say that even real parents could only aspire to perfection? With every passing day, Charles felt more equipped to join the rank of real parents. Having a real ready-made family waiting in the wings made the dream seem all that more attainable.

ROSE TRIED TO CONCEAL her nervousness at the gallery that afternoon, but Osgood Pearce had known her too long to be fooled. Though his place was brimming with serious art patrons boasting healthy bank accounts, he worried over her distress, making small overtures to get to the bottom of things. She'd gone to great lengths during the past two hours to avoid a deep conversation. All because of that hired hand, he fumed in speculation.

Hearing that Charles Johnson had taken another misstep that he could capitalize on would be music to his ears. Pearce was a civilized man, but his patience was thinning. He'd known Rose first! She should've seen his attributes more clearly a whole lot sooner. To find himself stooping to chasing her was appalling. Of course, the boy's existence was a liability that had dampened his enthusiasm all along, but now faced with competition, he was willing to make bigger concessions. And there were always boarding schools for pesky little lads. Pearce wasn't terribly wealthy, but he could afford that investment. It was high time he put a ring on Rose's finger and removed her from that fun house.

With renewed determination, he wended through his guests with a plastic smile, finding Rose seated at the desk in back writing up an order. "I would've expected Daisy to show up this afternoon," he said abruptly.

Rose looked all business in her coral suit with cream blouse, a perfect match to her on-floor manner. She stared up at him, not welcoming the personal question. "You know she isn't particularly interested in pottery."

"But she is interested in hanging about, mingling with the crowd."

"She had another priority." Rose went back to her order, tapping her finger on the calculator at her elbow. "Watching over Lucas."

"Oh, yes, her other great passion." With effort he kept his aplomb. "And Lucas? He's well today under Daisy's tutelage?"

"Yes."

"By the way, I'm afraid I won't be able to make my usual Monday night dinner tomorrow. A charity function in the city will be tying me up. Would it be possible for me to cash my weekly invitation in advance?''

"You mean for tonight? For dinner?"

"Yes, of course that's what I mean."

"No, Osgood, I don't expect there will much of a meal tonight. Life is sort of crazy for us today."

He stroked his goatee, a look of disappointment crossing his face. "I do hope nothing is really wrong at home. You wouldn't try to spare me bad news, just because I'm already under so much pressure here?"

It was Rose's turn at control. Spare him? How could a man be so self-serving every minute of the day? She'd always tried to find humor in Osgood's self-centeredness, but it was getting a whole lot tougher with Charles on hand in refreshing counterpoint. Not a quarter of an hour went by without her reliving a snatch of their date last night. The lovemaking had been so spectacular, so spontaneous. Heat settled between her thighs, making her fidget a little on the chair.

"Really, Rose," Pearce huffed. "I swear you're drifting in and out today like an overseas radio frequency. A fine way to treat a devoted suitor."

She bit her lip, sliding her pen through her slender fingers. How she wished Charles were here right now to fend off Osgood's advances. It probably wasn't smart to rely on him so much, but it seemed so natural, a comfortable fit. Osgood was hunched over the desk now, his knuckles on the teak surface, his expression wolfish. She would have to tell him something. Suddenly the ball practice seemed the quickest way to divert his attention. "I do have a lot on my mind, I suppose. You see, Beevee called an extra practice today—"

"Oh, really!"

"I knew you were overwhelmed here, so I didn't want to trouble you." She dipped her hand to her lap and crossed her fingers. Rose hated lies of any kind, but when one was trapped so tightly in a corner...

"What time? What time is that practice?"

She stared down at her watch. "Right about now. Threeish."

He pressed a finger to his dove gray jacket sleeve to reveal a silver watch and did some calculating. "Another hour and we should be ready to button up the gallery."

"Close early? That's unnecessary, Osgood. Lucas has enough support as it is. With Charles in charge, the aunts decided to attend."

"The aunts gave in? On a war game?"

Even though he had a right to be shocked, Rose felt her defensive hackles rise. "They only want the best for Lucas."

"So do I," he intoned. "It makes me wonder if Charles is up for the coaching job. Did he recover from yesterday's trouncing on the field?"

"You didn't even let him bat!"

"He didn't want to after I knocked out my share." He adjusted his stiff pinstriped shirt collar with a cocky tilt of his head. "Can't blame him for feeling inferior, being that I was a college star."

"A college star, eh?" Rose was more annoyed than impressed, again thinking that he could've volunteered at the rec center a whole lot sooner, or taken Lucas last year when he had no one. How true blue Charles was in comparison. It took all her self-control to behave cordially.

Unfortunately there would be no stopping him from charging over to the playground. All she could do was hope that Charles had won all of them over by now and made them forget that Osgood existed.

Chapter Fourteen

"Hey, Charlie, you sure you don't want to whack out a few?"

Mr. Beevee's bellow rang out in the warm spring air. Charles was standing in the outfield between Lucas in the right field and Johnny Whittier in the center, demonstrating how to dig a glove into the grass to stop a ground ball. He felt some sympathy for the head coach, for Beevee's face was getting a little red, looking a bit like a large pinkened potato. But Charles couldn't bring himself to take on that bat. He would be inexperienced and nervous, an embarrassment to Lucas.

Charles pretended to adjust the mitt on his left hand, taking a quick glance at the watch on his wrist. Ten minutes past three. So far he'd managed to evade home plate for over an hour, making himself useful in the outfield. Would this practice ever end?

Shielding his eyes from the sun, he gazed at the bleachers just right of the backstop. There were more spectators in attendance today, including the aunts, who'd shown up midway through in large-brimmed straw hats, knee-length shorts and baggy Woodstock T-shirts. It was hard to tell what was happening under those huge hats, but the brims jiggled a lot and Daisy seemed to be jotting something down on a sketch pad. Probably a full report in disfavor to Charles and the game.

"Let the boys bat around one more time," Charles called back. "Be good for—" His voice broke in astonishment as he saw a well-dressed couple step up behind the tall chain-link backstop. Rose—with that reptile Pearce! He coughed, hoping to conceal his dismay.

Beevee sent him a high sign of agreement then, presumably hailed by the newcomers, turned around to address them.

Lucas tugged at his shirt. "Hey, Charlie, Mom's here."

"Yes, isn't that great?"

"Wonder if Mr. Pearce will bat to us again?" Johnny asked excitedly.

"Gee, I don't know." Charles adjusted his sunglasses, glad his lenses were reflective so as to disguise the panic sure to be in his eyes. Suddenly the black sweatpants hacked to the thigh and the sleeveless red T-shirt emblazoned with the name of his gym that had seemed so appropriate now came off as tacky. Pearce and Rose were counterpoint chic, he in his gray linen, she in her complementing coral. They looked a little too right together for comfort. But that was only from a distance, Charles decided. A sham, a front, a mirage tormenting a sun-drenched man.

Rose belonged to him, Charles Johnson-Fraser. By any name, it all shook out the same. She purred to sensuous life in his arms, gave herself over to him with feline abandon. It was difficult, still so fresh from lovemaking, to see her hovering so dutifully close to Pearce—when a whisk of his pen could make her wealthy, free her of all commitments.

As wonderful as their lovemaking had been, it left Charles with a very uncomfortable longing in the pit of his belly to make Rose his own—under absolute honest conditions.

Pearce had started going through the motions of peeling off his suit jacket. But Beevee raised a huge hand in protest. Charles released a sigh of relief as the coach set the rubber tee back on home plate and called in Johnny from right field to start off the batting.

Lucas was second at bat, and went scampering in, waving to his kin. The aunts appeared to be prepared to charge the field, until Rose climbed into the bleachers to join them instead.

Lucas made a decent showing, swinging wildly but managing to connect with the ball on his third try. It went as far as the pitcher's mound, giving him time to make it to first base.

Despite his own shortcomings, Charles couldn't have been prouder of his nephew. He couldn't help but notice how excited the aunts were, too. It took them awhile to relax, but once they saw how slow the children moved, they were cheering with joy, immersing themselves in the action.

Once the team batted around, Beevee called it quits. Getting the boys into a cluster, he handed out a printed schedule of games, announcing that the first game was this Thursday. Encouraging the boys to hit, catch and throw as much as possible on their own time, he dismissed them.

Lucas and Charles were quickly surrounded by their personal entourage. The aunts gushed over Lucas, replaying near every move he made, declaring him the most agile of players.

During this lovefest, Charles's reflective lenses quickly locked with Pearce's grannyish black ones. Like any reptile, Osgood Pearce sensed Charles was acutely uncomfortable.

"How did things go today, Lucas?" Osgood inquired jovially.

"Super-duper, Mr. Rogue."

Pearce's mouth thinned in distaste at the reference, still he gave the boy's capped head a playful pat. "Your buddy here do any slugging today?"

"Nope." Lucas tipped his round face up to his mentor's. "You were too busy, weren't ya, Charlie?"

Charles pinched his cheek. "Right, man."

"Right," Pearce mocked. "Best to leave it to the children."

Charles balled his fists, his entire body cording in a menacing way. Rose had been admiring his dense, powerful limbs for her own pleasure and caught the danger signal on the rise. If Charles got his hands on Osgood, he'd crack the art dealer in two.

"It's time to go home," Rose said brightly. "It's almost dinnertime—" One look at Osgood and she clammed up, realizing she gave him his opening.

"If I might impose," he said to the aunts, "I'd like to trade my Monday night invite for one tonight."

The women exchanged an amused look under their awning-size straw brims. "Are you trying to invite yourself to dinner tonight?" Violet asked.

"That's the size of it, yes."

The aunts yielded to Rose, making her the center of attention. She could feel Charles's eyes roving her, claiming her. Understandably so, after last night. If only they could ditch Osgood, go home and relax as a family.

"Surely a glass of lemonade would hit the spot?" Pearce wheedled. "That freshly squeezed stuff of yours, Violet, is perfection."

"We better get goin'," Lucas pleaded, stroking Rose's sleeve. "The Beast is by himself."

Charles watched them all make a move to leave, with Pearce mingling in the center, impossible to shake. He spoke up then, sure he didn't have the stomach for both Violet's sweet citrus drink and the pill of an art dealer. "I believe I'll stay behind and help Mr. Beevee with his equipment." He gestured to the head coach, lumbering along the chalk line picking up bases. The look of disappointment on Rose's face both tore him in two and gave him a lift. He would be missed. Hopefully she'd never lose that feeling.

"LUCAS, HONEY, it's time for that outer space show you like so much."

Rose peered through the front screen door to find him sitting on the front porch, his bottom planted on the top canary yellow step, his chin planted in his hand. She went out to join him, nudging her hip against his.

"Where is he, Mommy?" he wailed. "Where's our Charlie?"

"I don't know exactly...."

Lucas shook his head in mournful bewilderment. "He just disappeared off the earth. What if aliens stole him?"

Rose was shaken by her son's distress, growing angrier with Charles by the second. Didn't he realize Lucas would be worried?

A tiny inner voice rose in a scolding reminder then, that she was the one who'd blundered biggest, first bringing Osgood to the field, then to the house for a snack. It was clear that Charles was fed up with him, that Osgood was anxious to make Charles look second-rate. But faced with Osgood's come-on at the gallery, her natural instincts had been to run to Charles for support and protection. She should've taken into account that he was already busy trying to father her son, and perhaps was struggling with a game that he'd been uncomfortable with from the start.

"Charles is safe and sound," she said with conviction. "He just got busy with Mr. Beevee, I suppose."

Lucas stomped his foot on the wood plank in a fit of anger. "Oh, no, he didn't. I called up the drugstore."

"You did?"

"Aunt Daisy's got that number taped right to the cupboard. For all her homogenized stuff."

Gentle humor touched her features. "For her homeopathic deliveries."

"I thought maybe Mr. Beevee could deliver Charlie in his truck, too." He threw his hands in the air. "But nobody was there, except the answering machine."

"Did Charlie seem upset today, before Osgood and I came?"

Lucas gazed thoughtfully into the dusky street. "Sorta."

"Because the boys wanted Osgood?"

"Yeah. Charlie said he had to work. Then he smiled fake like this." Lucas bared his teeth, making his mother giggle.

"You kind of look like your Charlie when you do that."

"Oh, boy! I like the way he looks, don't you, Mommy?"

"I certainly do." Rose angled an arm around his shoulders and pulled him close.

"Did Charlie ever bat today?"

"Nope. Mr. Beevee asked him two times and he said no."

"Do you think maybe he doesn't know how to bat?"

The boy popped up like a rocket. "My Charlie can do anything!"

Rose grabbed him round the waist so he wouldn't topple over. "Nobody's perfect, hon. I've just been trying to figure all this out. Could be Charlie just doesn't know much about baseball. It would explain why he wasn't so interested at first, why he doesn't bat."

Lucas's frown deepened. "But he should try. He makes me try stuff."

"Life gets touchier as a guy gets older," Rose said slowly, trying to keep Charles's image as sterling as possible. "After Osgood did such a good job, it would be tough for him to look, well...like a beginner."

"Oh."

"And Charles doesn't want to let you down, Lucas. He wouldn't want to embarrass you in front of your friends."

"Poor old Charlie!" Burying his face in his hands, he began to cry.

Rose stood up, and pressed him close, her voice quavering. "Come on now, dry those eyes. I think I may have an idea of where Charlie is."

"Can you get him back, please?"

"Will you come with me?"

He sniffed, standing up straighter. "Course."

Rose fished a tissue out of the pocket of her cuffed white shorts and held it to his nose. "Dry your eyes and blow your nose. Can't have your Charlie feeling worse 'cause he worried you."

Lucas stuffed the tissue into the pocket of his denims. "He's *our* Charlie, Mommy. And you better wipe your eyes, too."

They made it to the playground in record time, scurrying along the residential sidewalks. Rose came to a halt on the sloping grass, keeping a firm hold on her anxious son.

There was Charles, just as she predicted, two hundred feet away, under the lights, a lone figure in a cage, slamming the balls bulleting from an automatic pitching machine.

"He can hit, Mommy," Lucas said in a stage whisper.

He could now, anyway, with a wide, level swing full of strength and dexterity, and she feared, a fair amount of rage.

Lucas lost his patience. He wrenched free of Rose and went barreling down the incline. "Charlie, oh, Charlie!"

Charles froze in recognition. Dammit. He gritted his teeth, whirling around to find mother and child closing in at their respective paces. Lucas tore at the latch on the chain-link pen and rushed through the tall narrow gate, charging at his mentor like a miniature linebacker.

"You were so lost, Charlie!" Lucas sobbed into Charles's red T-shirt.

"I haven't, I—" Charles gripped the bat in astonishment, staring down at the trembling child clamped to his waist. He hadn't expected this kind of fuss. He was so wrapped up in his shortcomings, he hadn't expected anything. He stared up at Rose as she waltzed inside, reading her expression full of smug accusation and bare relief. "I am so sorry," he croaked. "I lost track of the time."

"Mommy don't believe that s'cuse."

"I didn't stop long enough to think I'd be missed." He

stared dazedly at Rose. "Though I still can't believe I'm missed quite this much."

"You have a lot to learn, our Charlie." Rose's reprimand was velvet, surprising even her with its depth.

Our Charlie. His heart squeezed with dazzled wonder. "I suppose I do have lots to learn." Charles was shaking as they exited the cage, guiding Lucas like a third leg, carrying the bat in his free hand. Remorse and helplessness overwhelmed him as he gently rubbed the boy's back in a circular motion. "Hey, man, I didn't mean to make you cry."

Lucas loosened his grip a little. "Why'd you stay here?" he asked, peering up at him with huge blue eyes.

"Because I needed extra practice."

"Why?"

"Can't you just let it go and forgive me?"

"How'd you like it if I made you cry?"

Charles chuckled hoarsely then, his throat nearly swollen shut. "Not much."

"I don't care if you're no good at baseball," Lucas proclaimed bravely. "I don't care if you're no good at anything!"

"Well, thanks," Charlie said dryly.

"I think Mommy needs a hug, too," Lucas said in a loud whisper. "She's been all worried and sniffly."

Charles felt a bigger fool by the minute. How could he leave Rose standing there? His only excuse was that his system had nearly shut down with the emotional trauma of the moment. "C'mere, Mommy." He dropped the bat to the ground with a thud, opening his free arm in welcome. They huddled together for a long intense moment. Charles sought Rose's mouth and kissed her tenderly.

"Hey, we better get this back to the rec center!" Lucas exclaimed suddenly, breaking free to pick up the bat. "Coach Beevee says we gotta return all equipment..." He rambled on with fresh enthusiasm.

"Was this your first time?" Rose asked gently, looping

her arms around his shoulders. "I can identify a novice, you know. My bike ride..."

"First time someone's cared about my whereabouts," he admitted, not daring to get too specific.

"Oh, Charlie, the life you've led, with no one to miss you, to get you on a ball team. Tell me, did you drop out of the sky into some lone nest?"

"Did ya, Charlie, did ya?" Lucas chimed in, swinging the bat in the air from a safe distance.

Charles kissed the tip of Rose's pert nose. "If I tell you, will you keep calling me Charlie forever and ever?"

"Ever and ever," she wheedled mischievously.

Slipping an arm around her shoulders, he steered her toward the center. "All right then, I did land in a nest. In a huge Central Park oak tree. I was raised by the mounted police—"

"Didn't you have a bedtime?" Lucas called back.

"Same time as yours." Charles glanced at the darkening sky. "Which must be past, man. Isn't this a school night?"

"School's over!" Lucas huffed in disgust. "Don't you know anything?"

Charles reached over and ruffled the boy's fair head. "I am beginning to wonder, man."

CHARLES HAD TRIED to get in the habit of saying goodnight to Lucas on the main floor of the house, so fearful that he'd reveal something when confronted with Dean's mural in the boy's bedroom. But tonight was an exception. Lucas refused to go to bed unless Charles spent time in his room. Charles complied, settling back in the sturdy maple rocker, leaning sideways to peruse the boy's bookshelf.

Lucas scampered in from a trip to the bathroom, ready for sleep in his green pajamas. He climbed into Charles's lap, wiggling until he was comfortable.

"So what'll it be, Lucas? An adventure on the high seas? A caravan through the desert? A teddy bear's picnic?"

"Let's talk, you and me. The men."

Charles shifted in the chair, trying to relax. Lucas was rubbing Charles's whiskered face in a gentle massaging motion that was almost hypnotic.

"What do you want to talk about?"

"You get scared, Charlie?"

"Sometimes. Why?"

Lucas's eyes traveled around, as though looking for a new landing. "Mr. Rogue said you were scared to hit the ball."

"He did, did he!" Charles knew better than to let that jerk Pearce get under his skin, but the emotions he'd tamed his whole life were rebelling big time as this duel for position escalated. He was evolving into a volatile cave man straight out of the dark ages, whacking, scrambling, fighting for territory. The fact that he barely recognized himself made it tough to land with sure footing.

"You scared, Charlie?"

He only hesitated a second. "Yes. I was afraid I'd let you and your mother down because I couldn't coach well enough."

"I told Mr. Rogue he was wrong!"

"Thanks for defending me, but I've discovered there's no shame in being scared once in a while. Life is full of challenges. If a guy is willing to try something he's scared of, it seems like he can get over it."

"You scared to get married?"

"What!"

Lucas beamed helpfully. "Maybe you should try that, too."

Charles chuckled heartily. "Maybe."

Lucas twisted sideways, wrapping his skinny arms around Charles's neck. "Are you done with school, too?"

"No, I'm afraid I'll be going to summer school."

Lucas rested his head on Charles's chest with a sigh. "When can we play?"

"We play a lot." Charles rocked Lucas gently as he noticed his gold lashes were drooping. "And you have your friends from the team now. Your mom can call their moms, and you can get together.''

"They all ride bikes. I don't got mine yet. Mommy's still looking in the newspaper.''

"Tell you what, Lucas, you get a good night's sleep and I promise you'll get a surprise tomorrow.''

He cracked an eye open. "Are you staying home?''

"No, that's not the surprise. Though I may be able to take Tuesday off.''

"Ask your teacher. Say you got a tummy ache.''

Charles arched his dark brows. "You ever try that?''

"No way. Aunt Daisy would make me take too much gunk.''

"I don't want that gunk, either!''

Charles rocked on, listening to the child's breathing as it slowed and evened. His mission, his charade were forced into the blurred edges of his unconscious as he focused on the moment, reveled in his new and prized position in the household. He was the man. He was the father figure. He was the lover Rose had taken into her bed and confidence.

Big responsibilities all. Charles stared at his brother's smiling image, feeling the weight of his new role, wanting to make good, wanting to make it permanent. But would Rose want him after the sly way he'd stationed himself here?

Oh, Dean, he thought, *you always did approach things just a bit smarter than I.*

CHARLES ENTERED his suite of offices at Fraser Advertising early Monday morning, bringing a look of surprise to Marcia Haines's cheery face.

"Good morning!'' she said briskly, efficiently trailing after him with a mug of steaming coffee and her steno book full of notes.

"Yes, I believe it is.'' He sat down in his tall leather chair and wheeled it close to the edge of the desk.

She scanned his handsome figure, dressed in a spotless

navy gabardine suit, white shirt and silver tie. "Glad you're here. You'll have plenty of time to go over the Guant Oven Cleaner proposal before their vice president gets here. And the test audience is set to preview the Calhoon Soup commercials. Mr. Calhoon hasn't checked in with us at all, by the way."

Charles shook his head in disgust. "Jed Calhoon's more interested in playing with Hilton than he is in his own advertising. Life should be a serious business from nine to five if you ask me."

"Strictly business. That's my chief." Marcia studied him as though reacquainting herself with a long lost pal, then sat down in a guest chair opposite the desk, flipping open her notebook. "First of all, I have several inquiries concerning active accounts to discuss—"

"Sure." Charles waved a pen through the air. "But about that bike."

Marcia leaned closer, clearing her ear of red curls. "The bike?"

"Yes. You know the one—"

"Naturally I know. Just thrown by your timing, oh nine-to-five taskmaster."

His eyes narrowed. "Timing is of the essence here."

"The bike is ready," she assured. "Stored in the security office downstairs. The delivery service across the street is on alert, just waiting for an address. Shall I—"

"No!" He shoved a scratch pad across the desk. "Give me their number and I'll make the arrangements."

Marcia flipped through her notebook and reached over the desk to jot the number on the pad.

Charles sympathetically acknowledged that she was accustomed to sharing most of his secrets and ignored the rude click of her tongue. He was about to say business would soon be back to normal when Hilton appeared in the connecting doorway. Marcia took her cue to leave, closing father and son in.

"I'll be with you in a minute, Dad." Charles raised his

index finger in greeting then punched in the number of the delivery service. He outlined his instructions for the bike, reciting the Weldons' address. "Yes, that's it. Set it on the porch. No sign-off necessary." He disconnected that call, dialed the security office in order to release the bike, then finally hung up with a sense of accomplishment.

"My namesake didn't even have a bike!" Hilton thundered. He reached into the inner pocket of his black silk jacket and produced his pen and notepad, as well as his reading glasses, which he swung open and planted on his nose.

"You aren't writing that down, Dad!"

"I am."

"It's so insignificant."

"As most of your reports have been." Hilton glared over the tops of his half lenses. "It'll take a shrewd orator to build an airtight case against Rose with the scraps you've given me. I expected lots more from you."

"I can only report what I see."

Hilton grunted disapprovingly. "How's the boy doing in general?"

"Wonderful. He's home for summer now. Excited about getting a bike, excelling at T-ball."

"So how's the ball team working out?"

"He's every bit as good as the other boys."

"I mean with you as a coach."

"I haven't beaten anybody silly, if that's what you mean."

Hilton winced a little at his snapback. "They win a game yet?"

"They haven't *played* one yet."

"The boy must like you."

Charles smiled gently. "Yes, I think he's growing quite fond—"

"Good. It'll make the transition to my life easier."

Rage expanded Charles's chest to button straining proportions. After all he'd done to pave a path inside the Weldon camp, Hilton was still viewing him as a mere stepping stone to his goal! He sought control with slow breaths. No matter how many regrets he had over their plan, he was in too deep to break off from Hilton. Hilton would toss him out on his ear and charge the Weldons with a tank. Such a move might scar Lucas for life, might destroy the child's faith in him.

Charles hung his head in remorse. No one understood better than he the desire to please one's father figure, to win him over, to bask in his love and approval. Nor how unattainable it all could be. He wanted better for Lucas. He wanted a star his nephew could reach, by standing on his shoulders.

If only he could manage to convince Rose that he was sincere. That would be the key. Charles's entire body began to tremble as he envisioned her rejection, falling into another man's arms, allowing him to love her.

Hilton obviously understood Charles was mulling under dark colors. He immediately made moves to leave. "Did Marica tell you the test audience is set to view the soup commercials?"

"I'm up to speed. So how's your returned client doing?"

"You didn't mean the things you said Friday. You were blitzed."

Charles smiled tightly. "You were the drunk one, Dad."

Hilton reared. "I'm only entertaining Jed because you've been busy."

"Sure, Dad."

"See you in the screening room then."

"No, I'll be tied up with the Guant account."

"Guant, eh? You haven't briefed me at all on that one."

"I know. It's brand-new and all mine."

Charles lost track of time as he conferred with clients, tried to clear his desk of paperwork. Marcia was at his side with some contracts to sign when the small red cell phone in his briefcase began to ring.

Marcia faded back to a file cabinet as Charles scrambled to answer it. "Hello. Hi. You still there?"

"Hey, man, the bike came! In a big white truck!"

"Oh, good."

"Is that my surprise? All mine?"

"Of course. Unless you'd rather have a new leash or something."

Marcia straightened, her eyes gleaming with intrigue.

"No way, the Beast has plenty of leashes. Can't wait to go for a ride."

"You wait until I get back, okay? I want to be in on it."

"Did you hold Mommy's seat? She said you did."

"Girls need more help with their seats."

"Yeah, I'll need just a little help."

"Right."

"Guess what, Charlie."

"You're always way too far ahead of me."

The small voice grew feather soft. "I love you more than my dog."

Charles tipped his head back with a satisfied croon. "No kidding. You love me that much?"

"Yeah."

"I love you, too. Just as much." The sentiment spilled easily from his mouth, bypassing every internal filter Charles possessed. And it felt so good.

"Please come home."

"I can't come yet."

"Pretty soon?"

"After noon sometime. I've decided to take tomorrow off, too."

Marcia hovered over his desk, making a sound between a gasp and a snort. It didn't waver the dreamy look on her boss's face.

"That's when we'll really do some riding," Charles promised.

"Okay, man! Oh, Beast wants to say hello."

"Just make it quick. And no licking the phone." Charles

listened to the commotion on the other end. He hung up moments later, assuming Marcia had bailed during the crazy conversation.

"Yes!" he hissed triumphantly under his breath, pounding the arm of his chair. "Loves me more than the dog!" He swiveled around, shocked to find Marcia was still in the room, sagged against the files. "I thought you'd gone," he said tersely.

"I don't mean to pry," she said haltingly, "except out of concern."

"Nothing to be concerned about." He slipped the phone back in his briefcase, along with some other papers.

"Is that important to you, Charles?" she ventured nervously. "Being loved more than a dog?"

"In this particular case, it's everything," he enthused.

"Are you feeling well? I mean, your work is sliding, you're short tempered and distracted. I only want to help."

"I'm perfectly fine. Never better."

"It would be natural to crack a little under your father's rule. Maybe fall for a—a party girl of some kind."

"You have the wrong idea," he insisted. "You'll laugh about it all soon enough, I promise."

She laughed then, in a forced tinny way. "Can't wait."

He closed his case with twin clicks and rose to his feet. "Well, I'm off to meet with Guant. You can reach me in Room B until noon. After that, I'll be incognito until Wednesday morning."

She boldly blocked his path. "Please give me your cell phone number. Just in case. Please."

He sidestepped her in amusement. "No, I'll check in."

"Make sure you do, Charles. One short person on a bike can't be all that important."

"You'd be surprised, Marcia." With a nod, he was gone.

Chapter Fifteen

"Is something wrong, Rose?"

Rose tore her attention from the Rogue's Gallery's front windowpane to Mr. Witherspoon standing opposite her at the customer service counter, examining his new framed nature print. "Everything's fine. I thought I just spotted my son running by in a bicycle helmet."

The dapper man teetered on his shiny shoes. "Is that so unusual?"

"It is, considering that he has no bike."

He shrugged. "All the children look alike in those things."

"Yes." Perplexity marred her forehead, but she applied herself to business again. "As you can see, this burgundy frame worked out extremely well, complementing the reddish hues of the tree trunks."

"And the cream matting is just right." Mr. Witherspoon beamed at her. "You have such a talent for framing. A real artistic eye."

Rose basked in his praise, adjusting the belt of her smart jade shantung dress. "Guess it runs in the family."

"Ah, yes. How are the aunts doing?"

"Very well."

"I knew them in the old days, you know, back in a wilder Greenwich Village. That Daisy...such a minx."

"Were you one of her models?" she asked coyly.

"I was," he proclaimed. "Don't look so shocked. I was a good bit leaner then, a proud buck." He leaned closer for a confidence. "I was one of the smarter ones, bought every oil and sketch of me she did. So I feel free to speak of the adventure, knowing I can shade the facts to my liking."

Rose laughed in pure delight, tearing his bill from the book. Mr. Witherspoon exchanged it for a check to the gallery and one made out to her personally. "You don't owe *me* anything."

"Such diligence deserves a bonus, for that gallery nest egg of yours."

Rose went through the motions of wrapping his purchase in brown paper, wondering if it had been wrong to confide to patrons that she one day hoped for a place of her own. But it hadn't been a calculated bid for future customers, simply small talk. "This town can't possibly hold two galleries of this caliber," she demurred.

Mr. Witherspoon craned his neck for any sign of Osgood Pearce.

"He's in the city today," she reported.

His pudgy face settled into contentment. "Then I can freely say that you could run him out of business in no time."

"He has spoken of relocating in Manhattan, but not recently...." Not since Charles arrived on the scene, distracting him. "And it would take more money than I could possibly raise."

"Don't be too sure, m'dear. It's a safe bet that investors would appear."

"Really?"

"Absolutely." He took his package and set his felt hat on his head. "Have a fine afternoon."

Rose was so immersed in entrepreneurial dreams on the walk down her home street of Chestnut that she never saw the four-wheeler clattering up the old uneven sidewalk—or the father figure and son making it go.

It wasn't until she heard a sharp warning jingle that she made contact with a mile-high jump onto the boulevard.

"Hey, Mommy! It's me!" Lucas rose slightly off the bike seat to apply his brakes with drama.

"Hey, boys." Rose readjusted her heels on the sidewalk, folding her arms across her chest in a wary stance.

"I wasn't gonna run you over," Lucas assured soberly.

"I don't think you can pedal that fast yet, man," Charles teased, moving his hand from the bike seat to the child's shoulder.

"Where did this bike come from?" Rose circled it with a keen eye.

"Charlie found 'er in the city," Lucas exploded in a babble. "Two men came in a big white truck."

"It looks brand-new." She centered an accusing look upon Charles, causing him to nervously push his sunglasses farther up his nose.

"That's 'cause I washed it three times," Lucas reported matter-of-factly. "It was a real mess."

"A real mess," Charles confirmed.

"How do you know? I washed it two times before you got home."

Charles grimaced. The boy had so much to learn about male teamwork. "I know because it was a mess in the city." Or so guaranteed by his secretary. Charles reached over and tweaked Rose's nose. "It's nothing fancy. A mid-priced return at a lower east side dealer. I got it for a song."

"I'll reimburse you," she proclaimed. *Somehow.*

They made the trip back home, Lucas rolling along in the lead. Charles couldn't resist laying an arm over her shoulders. "How was your day?"

"Very nice. Osgood was away."

"Would've stopped had we known!"

Rose took a closer look at her son's helmet. "So that was Lucas at the shopping center today."

"Dropped by the hardware store for the headgear. Lucas

insisted upon wearing it home even though we were on foot."

"So much has gone on behind my back," she lamented.

And how! "It can be kind of fun to run right into a windfall," he suggested playfully. "Big or small."

Her profile hardened. "I disagree. Dean and I didn't operate that way. Up front and honest is my policy."

"You had to figure I'd try to help."

She gave him a softer, sidelong glance. "Guess it did cross my mind. Just didn't expect such quick and efficient action."

"I happened upon this deal last minute," he said in lying earnest. "I wasn't sure it would work out, so I kept it to myself." He mentally crossed his fingers, hoping the boy wouldn't catch on and mention that Charles had promised him a surprise last night. Luckily, Lucas was in his own little hot-rod world, singing under his breath.

She grew thoughtful. "It's tough to argue with a dream come true. Still I would've liked to have had a say— Oh, never mind. Accept my thanks."

"Which cancels any payback," he was quick to bargain.

"We'll see," she said sweetly. Noting his chagrin she added, "After all, it can be fun to run right into a windfall. Big or small."

ROSE CAME TO HIM again that night, rapping lightly on the door, testing the knob. He'd left it open ever since their tryst, hoping upon hope that she'd hunger for more one night soon. How he longed for the time when he'd feel free to seduce her anyplace, at any hour. But for now, it was her call.

She took one look at him, stretched out under the sheet, his broad bare chest propped against the headboard, and melted. "Am I disturbing you?"

"Oh, yes, you little windfall." He growled in appreciation, patting the mattress beside him. "Come closer and really work me over."

She leaned against the door, reaching around to close it, secure the lock. "I must warn you, I want something."

How fortuitous then, that he was her willing slave. He tipped his head back against the headboard, surveying her shape, a feminine delight in white gauze shorts and a cotton blouse knotted at the waist.

He crooked a finger and a naughty smile. "So do I..."

She advanced, the gentle pat of her bare feet on the wood flooring was suddenly the most provocative tattoo imaginable. She oozed onto the bed, crawling against his chest, fitting her body close to his. Peeking under the sheet, she said, "You like lounging around in your underwear, don't you?"

"Take it off if it bothers you."

She laughed gently, knowingly, kissing his jaw. "I can't talk with your hand in the elastic of my shorts."

He shifted over her, freeing his other hand to play with the buttons of her blouse. "So we won't talk."

She lightly swatted him off. "Lucas mentioned that you were taking tomorrow off."

He dragged his finger along her throat. "I'm thinking about it."

"You can't do that!"

"I'm barely touching you, Rose."

She dipped over and bit his roving finger. "No, I mean, it's not fair to lead Lucas on if you're not sure."

He came to a new alertness. "You're right. I'll definitely stay home."

"No classes to attend?"

"Nothing I can't make up."

She stared up at him in wonder. "You are such a dedicated student, Charlie, the hours you put in."

Try as he might to fight it, he always felt especially like a heel when touching upon his aspirations. She respected him in part because of his studies, his interest in social behavior. The only time he ever felt completely free was when they were making love, lost in fevered desire. Again

he touched her blouse, this time working at the knot
cinched at her waist. She raised no protest this time, stroking the slope of his lean hip.

"How I wish I could play hooky, too."

He kissed her pouty lower lip. "Just do it, honey. We
could make a day of it. Go on a picnic or something. Bring
the aunties if you want!"

"It's tempting, but I have an insane workload. This
whole week is sure to be hectic. As for the aunts, they
already have ideas of their own. When they got wind of
your plans, they decided to visit a wellness convention."

His chest heaved. "Well, it's just the guys then, I
guess."

"But in the meantime…" Her fingers danced across his
hair-dusted rib cage, over his sensitive nipples, causing him
to shiver.

Having loosened the tail of her shirt, he'd gone on to
swiftly unbutton it. He pushed the cotton fabric aside now
with a lusty groan. Holding her in the crook of his arm he
skimmed his hand over her creamy breasts, fondling them,
measuring their weight in his palm. When he dipped his
mouth to suckle her sweetness, she sank into glorious,
mindless space.

IT WAS A LONG WHILE later when Rose rose from the bed,
hunting down her clothing. Finding her departures as sexy
as her come-ons, Charles raised himself up on an elbow,
boldly watching her every move.

She eased into her panties. "Almost forgot, I have something for you."

He roused himself a little, sleepy and boyish. "Something more?"

Reaching for her shorts, she extracted Mr. Witherspoon's
bonus check from the slitted side pocket and handed it to
him. "Here." She spoke in a nervous spurt. "I endorsed
it, to square us with the bike."

"I don't want this!" he thundered in shock.

"I insist. Is it enough? Be honest."

He was tempted to be damn honest, to insist she swallow her pride, stand tall as a Fraser and fight for her rightful fortune. "That should go in your gallery fund," he finally said.

She wrapped her blouse around her ivory torso, fumbling with the buttons. She spoke in a mumble, with her chin on her chest. "This is more important."

He jumped up like a bare panther to assist her, carefully pushing the plastic pearls through their tiny holes. He shuddered when she leaned against him, knowing she'd find his heart hammering out of control. Sure enough, she did ultimately lift her gaze to study him with suspicion. "The bike was twice this price, wasn't it? A couple of hundred?"

"Forget it, dammit."

"Can't you see, I need to work this out for my own peace of mind? You had to know I wouldn't have scoped out such a nice bike."

"He deserves it!"

"I know that! But I can't—"

"Shut up and enjoy it." Cupping her cheeks, he kissed her once more, recapturing one last taste of intimacy. "You have to know I'm dead serious about you, Rose. What's mine is yours, for always. I love you!" With that he dropped the check in her shirt. The tail left unknotted, the slip of paper dropped clear through to the floor.

Her hands fluttered to his corded neck. "I love you, too. I just have a terrible time letting go of my independence."

"A bit of spunk is sexy." He raised a finger to her nose. "But you're stompin' on my pride here."

"So let's compromise. Show me the sales slip and we'll go Dutch."

"I don't do Dutch! Now pick up that check and scram."

She stepped back to inspect his powerful bare form. "I'd rather watch you pick it up, sexy."

"Either way you are taking it back." With that he scooped it up.

She used the diversion to whisk out of the room. Moments later he stuck his head through the doorjamb with a dangerous glower. "Rose..."

"Models are referred to the third floor, sir." Blowing him a kiss, she ducked into her own bedroom.

CHARLES HAD NEVER been in the center of a female tornado before, but Tuesday morning proved to be his initiation. He and a trembling Beast sat together at the kitchen table while perfumed energy swirled round them.

"I can't find my silk scarf!" Rose raced on the scene in a squeal, tearing through a laundry basket near the basement door.

"I wore it on my head to the grocery store last week," Violet sang out in confession as she dashed to the fridge to throw together a semblance of breakfast. She paused at the open refrigerator door, a hand on her ample hip. "Hard to believe you can drape that bitty thing around your waist like a belt."

"You know I save it for this mauve dress," Rose scolded. "Now I'm going to be late for work. Osgood is expecting me early...."

Charles groaned at the mention of the art dealer, sure that the white powder puff dog on his lap made a whiny sound of protest, too.

Daisy appeared, amazingly proving to be a calming force. "You'll be right on time, if we drop you off on our way out of town."

Rose unearthed the wrinkled scarf with a cry. "It's hopeless!"

Daisy raised Rose off her knees. "Wear a nice gold chain belt instead. Meet you in the van. Have a nice day, Charles. Come on, Violet."

Charles sighed deeply once the door slammed for the last time, grateful for the peck on the cheek Rose had paused to give him. "Remember my advice, don't let Lucas take you over completely the way I always do."

"Huh?" he called out as she flew out the back screen door.

Lucas groggily shuffled in then. "What's going on? An earthquake?"

"Worse. Girls' day out."

Lucas kissed his jaw close to the imprint of lipstick left by his mother. "I'm hungry."

"Me, too." Charles scanned the jug of guava juice and crumbling leftover muffins left by Violet with a dissatisfied grunt. "Go get dressed, man. We'll go out for a real breakfast."

Lucas clapped his hands. "Like for coffee and bacon and stuff?"

"Exactly."

"Will we be ridin'?"

"No, partner, the bike will have to stay behind with Beast."

Charles smiled as the boy dashed off with his trusty pooch in tow. He was already dressed for a trip to Rose's bank, so why not make it a real outing? He'd felt a little odd, digging through the household papers in the sitting room desk this morning in search of her bank book, but how else could he deposit that bonus in her account? He burned every time he thought of falling for her ruse, stooping for the check to allow her escape. Very sneaky, especially with that crack about the studio for studs upstairs. He should really show her up and drop about ten grand in that wimpy account of hers.

His angled features softened at the thought of lavishing her with everything, making her his queen. It would all come true, given time.

THE FELLAS WERE finishing up a grand meal at the Pancake Palace an hour and a half later when Charles decided to check in at the office via his red cell phone. Seemed the perfect opportunity, as Lucas was busy at the cash register two feet away, picking some candy out of the glass display case with the help of their obliging waitress.

"Charles! Thank God you called!"

The toothpick between his teeth dropped into the pool of syrup on his plate. "Why, Marcia? What's up?"

"It's all hitting the fans here. The test results for the Calhoon Soup commercials are back. The news is bad."

In a rush of family loyalty, Charles quickly forgot that he'd quit the account for good. "The audience hated them?"

"Let's say no one raved about either one."

Charles felt a sharpness in his chest. It was impossible to judge this crisis without seeing those commercials. He'd been a proud fool to let his father take over his concepts in the final hour. What if they lost Jed Calhoon's account altogether? "I should've gone to the screening yesterday."

"Well, your father's been pretty difficult."

Charles examined plans of action and their consequences. "I'll have to come in pronto for a look at the damages."

"Shall I schedule something with Calhoon and Hilton?"

"No, I think I'll slip into the building unnoticed."

"So you have space to think," she assumed.

"Something like that." Space to hide a pint-size heir was more like it, of course. He couldn't explain Lucas to his employees or vice versa. Hilton himself was the biggest threat: as much as he already loved Lucas in theory, he might break down with personal contact, giving away the whole show.

"In an ironic twist, Calhoon has finally tired of the big man's company," Marcia whispered over the line, no doubt watching her back in the office. "Guess he's looking back on his deluxe week of play and wondering if Hilton should've been strictly tending to business after all."

Charles grew smug as he reached into the back pocket of his tan chinos for his wallet. "Are you inferring that I am looking better to our dude client?"

"Yards better. He's been asking for you. Falling back on the technicality that you are in charge of his account."

Charles was gleeful and fretful all at once. Times were tough, but he was back in the saddle with the soup king. "I'll be there ASAP."

"Shall I send a limo?"

"No, I'll grab a taxi. In the meantime, put the tapes of those commercials in my private lounge. Then stay put at your desk until I call."

"You don't want me there, either?"

"I need you to hold down the office," he claimed lamely. "And it is my day off. I plan to duck back out without a fuss."

"In an emergency like this? Where are your priorities?"

Charles glanced in automatic response to the young carbon copy of Dean, dressed in tiny jeans and a royal blue T-shirt, stuffing gumdrops into his mouth on top of a man-size serving of eggs and bacon. How quickly his priorities had changed shape and substance, stretching the limits of his self-centeredness to include a canary-colored house full of kin. Marcia would sooner swallow a real canary than gulp down the cause of his remarkable transformation.

"My priorities are right where they should be, don't you worry."

"Don't do anything to fan the flames," she said awkwardly.

"Like what?"

"Like sneak your wild new girlfriend into the lounge for the show. Hilton wouldn't handle the sight of her very well at all right now."

Charles signed off, then drained his coffee cup. Funny how Marcia had stumbled upon that indisputable truth about Rose with all her probing and guessing. The day would come when Hilton got a blast of his son's new reality and he wouldn't take it well. He put on a smile as Lucas ambled back to the table with change from their check. Charles set the crumpled bills out by the salt shaker for the tip. They were a little sticky from the boy's sugarcoated hands, but it wouldn't alter their value.

Charles pulled Lucas close. "How'd you like to go to the city with me?"

His mouth sagged, revealing candy-speckled teeth. "No kidding?"

"We have to ask your mom first, though."

Lucas pointed to the shopping center across the street. "Let's go over to Rogue's and do it. Hurry!"

Charles grabbed his arm before he could scoot. "Let's call her instead. That way, Mr. Rogue can't poke his nose into our business."

Lucas squinted in agreement. "Okay. I know all the numbers."

Charles punched in the digits as Lucas rattled them off. Charles exhaled in pleasure and relief when she answered. "Hello there, is this Fong Yong's Chinese Takeout?"

"Very funny, mister."

"What gave me away?" Charles asked woundedly.

"Lucas has a very distinctive giggle."

"Oh, so it's his fault."

"What are you guys up to?"

"We're across the street for breakfast."

"That was nice of you, Charles. Lucas must be thrilled."

"He's great company." Charles cleared his throat, getting serious to make his pitch. "I would like to take Lucas to the city for a while if you don't mind. I spoke to one of my professors just now and one of the behavioral videos we're making...for class, didn't turn out well. I'd like to go see it."

"Oh, Charles, I don't know. On the subway and all..."

"We'll take a cab," he bargained, hating to admit the luxury, but knowing it would ease her mind. "I'll take good care of him."

"I'm sure you would, but—"

"Oh, Mommy, pleazzze," Lucas pleaded in a shout.

"Well... Did you leave food and water for Beast?"

"We did, Mom." Charles answered, glancing at his watch over Lucas's shoulder. "And we'll be back by three. I promise."

"Okay," she relented. "Have fun."

"What'd she say? What'd she say?"

Charles set Lucas on his feet and gave him a high five. "We're off!"

THE TAXI DROPPED THEM off on West 40th Street in front of the Capshaw Building housing Fraser Advertising. Charles leaned over the front seat, nervously peeled bills out of his wallet for the driver, then steered Lucas out of the car and onto the bustling sidewalk. He'd been lost in a sea of troubles the entire trip, bouncing from his floundering ad campaign to how he'd smuggle Lucas in and out without notice. Lucas himself was a loaded weapon as well, with his ability to read on some basic level. Charles would have to be careful about exposure. If only he could blindfold everybody.

Lucas tugged his hand. "Is this where you go to school, Charlie?"

"Yup. Look across the street. See the library? Great place to study."

Giving the curious boy no time to absorb incriminating details, Charles took him to a side entrance to a less-traveled bank of elevators. Whisking him into an empty car, he pushed the button marked forty-three. They made it to the top with only a couple of companions, strangers who made no eye contact as they whisked in and out the gliding doors. Hilton had deliberately positioned their adjoining lounges in a far-off corner of the Fraser suites, accessible from a private rear door. As Charles fit his key into that door, he figured he'd never made better use of the perk.

Lucas stepped into the hushed gray carpeted corridor, clearly dubious. "This is a funny school, Charlie. Where's all the teachers?"

"College is different from kindergarten, man." Looking

around like a thief, Charles inserted another key in the door bearing his name. He hustled Lucas inside before he could get a look at the telltale plaque.

Lucas bounced on the plush burgundy sofa. "Everybody get keys?"

Charles almost offered a dismissive yes, then thought how it would sound to Rose and the aunts. "Uh, no, my professor gave them to me, so we could use his office."

"Cool."

Charles raided the portable refrigerator for two cans of cola. "Thirsty?"

"Sure, Charlie. We can have a burp contest."

Charles chuckled, feeling some of the tension ease between his shoulder blades as he popped open the cans and handed one to Lucas. He turned on the television and VCR, and fed the test tape to the machine.

"Is it a movie? Like *Star Wars*?"

"Not really." Charles set his untasted can down on the small wet bar against the wall, then sat down in a chair closer to the screen. "It's sort of a video experiment, a study of people."

Music rose and the Calhoon's trademark model family came to life on the screen, father, mother and two small boys putting together a hearty meal centering around the new line of hearty stewlike soups, tossing plates, dancing around. The mother took her skillet and tossed it in the trash bin, declaring that some soup and bread is enough of a meal with these heartier varieties, even making dessert an impossibility.

Charles fell into a pensive funk. The spot was lively, appealing, warm. Lucas made a sighing sound from the sofa, spaced between belches, but Charles paid him little mind. He watched the ad again, then went on to the second spot, highlighting the beef burgundy soup, with the plump mama pretending to add ingredients as family members came into the kitchen warning her not to tamper with perfection. Charles had to admit that this one, too, looked more pleasing at the storyboard stage. Was it the setting, the actors? He definitely needed time to think.

"I'm hungry, Charlie."

Charles wasn't sure how long he'd been seated with his chin propped in his hand when Lucas called to him, but both cans of soda were now on the oval table flanking the sofa. "Let's see what we can come up with." He stood, stretched and wandered over to the wall cupboard behind the wet bar. There was a package of mint cookies and some crackers. He opened the packages and set them out on the table. He was so engrossed in playing host, he didn't hear the lock trip the door, or notice that they had company.

"Charles!"

"Da—" Charles spun around to find Hilton hovering beside him. "Da *Professor!*" he said significantly, slanting his eyes to the sofa.

Hilton stared down at the blond child, swinging his spindly legs from off the cushion, stuffing cookies into his cola-stained mouth. Lucas was openly frightened by the large, forceful man in a pinstripe suit. Amazingly, the man was even more off balance.

Charles couldn't remember ever seeing his father reduced to such a quivering mass. Ever so slowly, as though trying not to spook his quarry, Hilton extended his hand to the boy. "Pleased to meet you."

Lucas offered his small hand tentatively, as though fearing he'd lose it.

Charles had already learned a good deal about children through his nephew and understood how well they could read people on a gut level. If only Hilton would simmer down, resist the temptation to seize Lucas in a smothering bear hug. That would be a whole lot harder to explain than splurging on cab fare, or this plush classroom.

Hilton did keep his head on straight after all, offering a sage handshake with a quick release. But the old man didn't completely snap back, instead he stared down his grandson in bare awe, stricken with the intense emotion that the Fraser men generally suppressed. Charles understood the trip, having taken it himself recently. He firmly guided his father over to the bar and went through the motions of getting him a glass of mineral water.

"I have to pee, Charlie!" Lucas piped up, cringing when both men whirled on him.

"Two cans of cola will do that to a guy. Go right through there." Charles pointed to the door beside the bar. "There's some pine soap in there."

"Like a tree? We only got lilac soap at home." Lucas dashed by Hilton with a scramble of tennis shoes.

Once the boy was closed away, Hilton sagged against the bar. "What a shock!" He slid his glass around. "Sweeten this with some vodka."

Charles took inventory of the variety of bottles on the shelf below before producing the right one. He splashed some liquor in Hilton's glass, quickly removing the bottle from view again. "He's a lot like Dean."

Hilton's eyes hardened to ice chips as he slurped some drink. "You brought him here with no intention of calling me."

"I didn't know if you could manage to keep your cool."

"Proved you wrong!"

Yeah, sure. "There's no reason to be offended," he reasoned confidently. "It was risk enough bringing him on our turf at all. Marcia's Calhoon SOS gave me no option, however, being that I'm baby-sitting today."

"Well, seeing what a fine lad he is, I am all the more anxious to get this custody matter settled."

Charles smiled tightly. "How predictable of you."

"I want to speak to him a while longer."

"How predictable of you, too."

The bathroom swung open again. Lucas returned, sniffing his pine-scented hands. "We gotta shave sometime with all that neat cream, Charlie!"

"Sure, sure."

He tipped his head from side to side, dimpling. "Watcha doin' now?"

"Talking about the videos."

"I don't like 'em," Lucas confided, circling wide by the bar.

Hilton brightened, his curiosity piqued. "Why not, Lucas?"

"Let's play them again and you can tell us," Charles proposed. He picked up the remote and pushed the Rewind button. As the tape whirred, Charles watched his father make advances on Lucas, sitting with him on the sofa, a cushion apart. The child drummed the armrest, staring at the screen.

Charles wandered the room as the first commercial played again. He hit the Pause button as Lucas made a moaning sound.

"What's the matter?" Hilton rumbled.

Lucas pointed to the television. "Where's the poor little sister? She die? They don't want her no more?"

The men exchanged a significant look, then congregated at the bar.

Charles glanced back at Lucas, suggesting he have another cookie. "I felt that same loss, Dad."

"Make that a unanimous Fraser ruling," he whispered.

"The test audience pick up on it?"

Hilton grimaced. "Their reasoning was less clear. But due to the tabloids, the adults in that audience know that the bratty actress playing the sister was dumped because she was expensive and impossible. Thinking it a just firing, they might not be sure why they felt let down. But our Lucas, pure at heart, would view the commercial without that kind of tainting—like a pro!"

"Yes," Charles concurred with excitement. "He's missing the fictional sister, that's all he knows."

Hilton rolled his eyes. "It will cost a mint to get that girl back."

"The commercial isn't going to work without her."

Charles grew thoughtful. "Hash it out with Calhoon, see if he wants to stretch the budget."

"He wants you now," Hilton muttered childishly.

"He can't have me right now." Charles gestured to his charge. "I'm spoken for."

Hilton did a double take on both man and boy. "Could it be you're a little too involved in your second job?"

Charles tapped his father's lapel. "You courted Calhoon and got me this father gig. Now eat some humble pie and keep Jed on the string."

Hilton lumbered back to the sofa, a beaten man. Lucas felt more comfortable with this vulnerable side of him and scooted to the center cushion, nudging his leg. "It's okay, Professor."

Hilton blinked, giving the boy's head a pat. "Let's roll 'em again, Charles. Give this lad a chance at number two."

The trio watched the second offering with the parade of family members telling their wise and meek mama not to tamper with perfection. The adults focused on Lucas, as though he were about to part the Red Sea.

"That old man is mean to the lady cooking," he spouted.

"I found the husband is a little sharp-tongued, too," Charles conceded. "It might put off housewives."

"Who buy eighty percent of the soup!" Hilton bellowed in agreement. He reached over and shook Lucas's hand again. "Thanks for your help. You've given me much to think about."

Lucas sat awestruck. "Okay."

Charles aimed a finger at his charge. "Sit tight, man." He walked Hilton to the door, following him out to the corridor. His heart twisted in envy as Hilton beamed in parental pride.

"Wish I could stay, but I have a lunch date. Must say, the boy's got the Fraser savvy. A real natural for the business. To think I was afraid he might be a loony Weldon poet, a simpering Milquetoast. Not that I wouldn't have worked with him. But this discovery is such a joy!" He grasped Charles's shoulders. "Imagine a ready-made heir with razor instincts!"

"Calm down," Charles whispered. "You're still light-years from any claim."

"When will you feel comfortable blowing the lid off that nuthouse?"

"September?"

"That's three months away!"

Charles would've preferred light-years. A clear and eternal future with Rose and Lucas. If he thought they could run off then and there without Rose ever discovering his real identity, he'd be mighty tempted. But that was make-believe, like the commercials.

"Pack your bags and get your affairs in order," Hilton directed gruffly. "I'm siccing the lawyers on them soon. The sooner the better!"

Charles glared at him, his body vibrating with fury. "Not yet, Dad. Not until I'm good and ready."

They stood toe-to-toe, father and son, so alike physically, intellectually, so evenly matched. Charles was not surprised when Hilton backed down under the pressure. As much as Hilton ruled the roost, it was Charles who held the key to the Weldon door, the prized grandson in the palm of his hand.

"Very well," Hilton snapped. "But you call more often. I want to know about everything that kid does, down to every sneeze."

"If it makes waiting easier, think how much more the boy has now under my tutelage. A new bike, a place on the ball team."

"How's he getting on with those challenges?"

"Great. He's riding around the neighborhood with his new friends and his first ball game is Thursday night at the playground. I'd hate to see his summer upset by your lawsuit," he added.

"Don't pin any blame on me. I'm the grandfather denied.

I'm well within my rights.'' With that he stalked off to his lounge the next door down.

Charles lingered, envisioning how effective that spiel would sound in court. Hilton did have some rights, and he was bound to win sympathy as a grieving parent, a pining grandparent, a pillar of the community.

Rose would only hope to survive the attack long enough to kill him.

Chapter Sixteen

Charles continued the week with the subtle feeling he'd blundered somehow. The day in the city with Lucas had turned out well. Charles had used diversional tactics on him after the office, taking him to the public library, a museum, and ultimately a ferry to Ellis Island. An ingenious plan, as Lucas glossed over the 'school' visit with mention of snacks and videos. But ask him anything about the Statue of Liberty and get a report!

The T-ball game Thursday night proved to be a huge family event now that the aunts were over their biggest misgivings. Everyone was set to attend and gathered in the foyer for the walk over to the field.

Rose was all smiles as she descended the staircase in a green terry cloth sunsuit a shade brighter than their team jerseys. "Think I'll fit in?" She did a pirouette on the tiles.

Charles seesawed his brows. "Yay, team." He delighted in her quick hug round his waist. Ever since their love-making, Rose was growing more affectionate toward him in front of the family, preparing them, he hoped, for their union. If only he could hold Hilton off until they were bonded.

Daisy wanted to take the van to the playground, but Lucas was so mortified that she backed off. It was clear that she was hurt, but even Rose did not come to his rescue. This was her son's turf and he deserved to feel most comfortable. Rose found herself utterly contented. This was the kind of scene she'd imagined when pregnant with Lucas—a loving family centered around an active child. It was all thanks to Charles. Without him, none of this would've shaken out this way. Certainly no teenager could've held firm against the aunts on so many fronts, or put a sense of romance back in her life and given her hope for a second chance at happiness.

Charles rubbed his hands together, surveying the chattering crowd. "So, are we gabbin' or goin'?"

"Goin'!" Lucas shouted. Pulling his cap over his eyes, he stomped out the front door, his oversize shirt billowing.

The only flaw in the day was Osgood Pearce. Charles beat him to the field, took on a bat like a warrior with a sword, but it wasn't long before the other assistant coach appeared on the sidelines with a leer. Charles ignored him, tapping ball after ball to the boys in the field.

"May wonders never cease."

"Get stuffed, Pearce."

The tall pale man laughed in gulps. "You've surprised me here. I thought you'd never held a bat, but that's obviously not true."

"Mind your own business."

Pearce sidled closer, making Charles flinch. He didn't like anyone within swinging range. Suddenly his swing lost its smooth tempo. He chopped two and missed both. He finally stopped, digging the tip of the bat in the dirt, wishing it was Pearce's face.

"You're the one butting in," Pearce growled in his ear. "Rose is mine!"

"Hah! Any man who'd string Rose along the way you have doesn't deserve her." Charles stared up into the bleachers to find Rose and aunts busy conversing with some of the other spectators. The last thing he wanted was any interference here. This showdown was long overdue.

"Rose and I have had an understanding a long while," Pearce snorted.

Charles glowered at him. "A hundred percent to your benefit."

"I've treated her like the finest art piece."

"You've treated her like an indentured servant! Chicken feed pay, long hours, denial of her talents—talents you've cashed in on bigtime."

Pearce folded his arms across his shallow chest. "Who are you to challenge me? Some career student feeding off those females. Maybe you have forced my hand, but I'm geared up for war now. I'll be pursuing Rose with all my might and have much more to offer her. Once she settles back, stares beyond the beefcake, she'll see where her secure future lies."

Charles curled a fist, out of sight between them. "We'll see about that!"

Beevee lumbered over to break them up, suggesting Pearce get the bases out of the bag. He traded Charles the bat for the score book, directing him to take it over to the other team to exchange lineups. Charles edged through the crowd, only to be detained behind the backstop by a large familiar hand. "Dad!" he whispered fiercely. "What the hell? *What the hell!*"

"I couldn't stay away," he blustered, anxious, defiant.

Charles exhaled. This was the mistake niggling him. He'd told Hilton about the game. Lucas's brilliant mind and his own ineptitude with baseball had been too big a lure to resist.

"What in blazes are you doing here, son? Batting a ball around!"

"Don't grind that old song at me. I'm perfectly capable."

"Be extra careful," Hilton chastened. "Oh, also wanted to tell you that Calhoon's agreed to revamping the shots."

"Congratulations."

"To you, too. He doesn't know you ever quit and I'd like to keep it that way. If you relent, I promise to give you the reins."

"It's a deal." Charles scanned the area. "Now if you'll kindly leave—"

"I will not! I'm here for the game. No one will recognize me, son. Not in this getup." He had on a boater, gross plaid shorts and a pastel shirt.

Charles surveyed him mockingly. "Treasures from your closet?"

"Marcia got them for me someplace in Times Square."

"Why didn't you ask your own secretary?" he groused.

"And have Dorleen lose all respect for me?"

"Thanks loads." Charles noticed the other scorekeeper waiting for him. "If you won't leave, at least sit on those bleachers opposite."

Hilton was aghast. "With the enemy?"

"You really think you have any friends here, Dad? Now go."

The game progressed smoothly. Charles was so proud of the way Lucas blended right in with the other players, many of whom were on their second year of ball.

The score climbed higher and higher into the twenties as was common with T-ball. Osgood Pearce did more than his share of mooning into the stands where Rose sat, Charles noted. To his satisfaction, however, she and the aunts ultimately ignored him as the game grew exciting with hit after hit. Charles was doubly grateful for the action, as it detracted from Hilton's presence, too.

If only the whole game would end and Charles could spirit his group back home. Tensions hit a new unexpected peak however, as the game went into an extra inning over a tie. Charles paced by the players' bench, wondering if there'd be no end to the stressful setup. He slanted a look to Hilton, frowning under the bill of his cap. The workaholic suddenly seemed to have all the free time in the world. Why now of all times!

Because Lucas would be Hilton's priority forevermore. Charles would simply have to get used to the idea, not allow it to tinge his own love for the boy. The last thing he wanted was to lose him the way he lost Dean.

So absorbed in his own musings, Charles nearly missed Lucas at bat. The crowd was cheering madly. There were two outs against the green team, one home run would break the tie. A glance to the stands showed all the Frasers and Weldons were braced against the pressure.

Then it happened. The bat cracked hard against the ball, sending it flying through the air. Lucas was on the run, something he did exceptionally well. The ball sailed to the right field, plopping between two outfielders. Children scrambled everyplace, screaming, flailing. Lucas ran on from base to base, second, third, then home. The ball was making its way at the same time, first to the pitcher, then to the catcher.

It ultimately smacked Lucas squarely on the upper arm as he slid into home plate. He rolled over in the dirt with an agonizing cry. The footsteps rattling the aluminum benches sounded like thunder. Beevee and Charles were kneeling with the injured child, examining his bruise as Hilton pried his way close.

"Let me through!" he barked. "Is he hurt badly? Call an ambulance!"

"That doesn't seem necessary," Beevee boomed evenly, ruffling Lucas's hair as the boy sagged against Charles. "He's more startled than hurt. Wasn't much power behind the toss."

"You sure?" Hilton lowered to his haunches. "Tell me yourself, son."

Lucas blinked his dewy lashes, recognition in his eyes. "I'm okay. Did we win?" Beevee confirmed it, sending Hilton and Lucas into whoops.

Charles found himself caught between the two generations of uncontrollable Frasers. "Simmer down, Dad!" he hissed. Slowly rising to his feet, he found himself backed up against a soft, familiar form and whirled to find Rose and her fretting aunts. "Lucas is fine. Don't panic, ladies."

Daisy and Violet ignored him and converged on their great-nephew.

"Charles? Your father came?" The smile on Rose's face faded as Hilton rose as well, peeling off his boater. "You!" she seethed, pointing a shaky finger.

Charles backed her away from the cheering players, close to the pitcher's mound. "Don't spoil Lucas's victory, please."

"Hilton Fraser." She gaped at the older man some feet away, then at Charles, the enormity of the situation flooring her. "This makes you—"

"Yes, Rose, I'm—"

"One sorry son of a bitch!" she whispered furiously. "If we were alone I'd slap you senseless!"

The curse and the threat were foreign to her gentility, Charles knew, but she had to be feeling threatened, hopelessly betrayed. For once Charles was mighty glad they weren't alone!

She scrunched some jersey and chest hairs in her fingers, drawing him close. "What are you doing here, Fraser? What are you trying to accomplish?"

"He's been acting on my behalf," Hilton snapped. "This is my show."

She released Charles with a toss of her blond head, centering a lethal eye on Hilton. "Is that so? Exactly what are *you* after?"

"My grandson," Hilton announced silkily. "I intend to take him over, Rose, through the legal system."

She pressed a hand to her chest, the wind knocked out of her. "You can't hope to gain control of my child!"

"Calm down, honey," Charles whispered, grasping her shoulders.

She twisted free. "Don't 'honey' me, you spy…you traitor! How dare you go so far! Even make love to me!" she added in a anguished hush.

"I didn't tell him to do that," Hilton drolled.

Rose propped a fist on her hip, a mocking smile forming

as she relived past spars with Hilton. "Ah, so Charlie had one idea of his own, did he? Dean would be so proud."

Charles hardened. "Don't get ugly, Rose. Not about us. Don't do it."

"What could be uglier than this rich man's trick!"

"Please, give me a chance to explain my own personal side," Charles demanded. "This picture is so much bigger—"

She stepped back with her palms up. "Do not touch me again. Ever!"

Charles grimaced as Osgood Pearce advanced, finally realizing something was afoul. With some degree of relief, he watched Rose brush off her boss, too. Hilton made a move to follow his ex-daughter-in-law back to the cluster of players, but Charles detained him. "Leave it be."

Hilton frowned, then nodded. "Suppose there's nothing more to be gained here. Though I would like to say goodbye to Lucas."

"We'll have to settle for a wave, unless you want to wrestle the aunts."

"My car's parked in the lot," he babbled. "C'mon, let's go home."

Home? Charles fondly saluted his hero nephew from afar, suspecting he'd never again be welcome in the only genuine home he'd ever known.

ROSE EXPECTED to be plied with every remedy known to the aunts and sipped as much sweet tea and sympathy as she could hold. Feeling like a waterlogged dupe, she sank deeper into the living room's biggest recliner. "All this time, he was a Fraser," she repeated between sips. "Hilton's hatchet man. To think how many times I almost called that old tyrant to see if he'd changed any since Dean's death."

"My dear." Violet tsked, sinking onto the sofa to massage her limp wrist.

"I was sure right not to. Hilton is incapable of any inflexibility." Violet lifted her gaze to Daisy for a significant exchange, but Rose barely skipped a beat. "It's all too horrible to comprehend, a Fraser plot to take away my baby, that my Charles is *that* Charles." She choked back a sob, jiggling her cup on its saucer.

Daisy deftly removed the china from her hand, setting it on an end table. "Surely you can't write Charles off completely. I believe he was sincere in many of his efforts. Some things can't be faked—"

"But some things can! You know full well that men can...they can rise to most any occasion, especially when they're the exceptionally virile kind."

"What makes you think I was referring to sex?" Daisy huffed.

"Weren't you?" Rose squinted up at her towering aunt.

"No, I was remembering other things, dead bolts and rocking chairs and fond glances." She sighed wistfully, her aged face showing weary strain.

"I have to be the dumbest woman in the world, giving that family entrée to this house, opening everything wide!" Another sob bubbled up Rose's throat. She buried her face in her hands and rode it through.

"You'll have to get ahold of yourself," Daisy said. "The team's ice-cream party can't last forever. Mr. Beevee will be dropping Lucas off soon."

"That's true," Violet agreed, her plump hand stroking Rose's hair. "Which means it's high time for us to get everything out in the open, eh, Daisy?"

Rose sat up straight, dropping her hands from her face with interest.

Daisy cleared her throat, sitting beside her sister. "The truth is, Rosy, I had some help in this blunder. I sent your ad—the clipping—to Hilton in the first place. I started the whole thing."

"What!"

"I hoped to shame him into caring, dear. I thought news of a grandson without a father figure would do the trick.

Seems disgraceful for you to be living on a shoestring when Lucas's relatives are sitting atop an empire."

Rose balked. "Have I ever complained?"

"Why, no," Daisy admitted. "But Lucas is entitled to his inheritance."

"For all Hilton's bluster, he does want to share," Violet peeped.

Rose leapt up from her chair. "Not with us! Don't you see, we may lose Lucas completely. Hilton wants custody."

"On what grounds?" Violet wondered dubiously.

The answer sliced through Rose's heart. "Whatever grounds Charles managed to scrape up, I guess. It's clear he came to spy." To her surprise, Daisy laughed. "This isn't funny. He intends to take me to court!"

Daisy shook her ponytailed head. "He won't win."

"Really?" Rose lectured sternly. "Does that deduction come from the same font of wisdom that lured Charles here in the first place? Which brings up another question, how long have you known Charles's true identity? You were expecting some action from the Frasers, so you must have suspected."

"We knew at first sight," Daisy confessed. "Right name, right age. Right other things…"

Rose thought she'd explode. "No wonder you were pushing so hard for me to take him on! Didn't it occur to you that he might mean us harm?"

"He seemed such a nice young man," Violet replied defensively.

"You were annoyed with him at first."

"The initial adjustment did seem insurmountable." Daisy shrugged. "Then we found him asleep upstairs, all tender and vulnerable with Lucas in his arms and were completely sold."

"He does look mighty innocent asleep," Rose admitted. "But that's no excuse for all your secrets, and no excuse for his lies, either."

The doorbell interrupted them. Rose, already on her feet,

headed for the foyer. She swung open the door to find Charles on the porch, still dressed in his jersey and jeans. Her heart tugged painfully. He looked like her Charlie, but that man really never existed. "What do you want now? The Beast?"

Figuring he'd receive no welcome, Charles barged inside. Then he froze in the entryway like a trapped animal. Her pain filled the air, filled him.

"Lucas isn't here."

"I know that," he said quietly. "Beevee invited me to the celebration just as I was leaving. He said they'd be out until eight."

"So he'll be back soon, Charles, and I don't want you here then."

Daisy and Violet appeared in the doorway, stern with betrayal. "Here's your fan club!" Rose raged with a sweeping arm. "They've known your identity all along. By gosh, Daisy even sent Hilton my clipping."

"Really?" Charles was clearly puzzled. "Why?"

Daisy advanced with a swish of her lounging pajamas. "Unlike Rose, we trusted you because of who you really are—Dean's brother, Lucas's uncle, a decent man a bit nervous around children. Never did we suspect that you'd come to do us damage. We expected a reunion, a mending of old wounds."

"Of course you would," he acquiesced, hanging his head. "Because that's the kind of open-minded ladies you are. As for me, I did try to fulfill the fatherly requirements, and at the same time assure Hilton that Lucas was well cared for."

"But he didn't want to hear that, did he?" Rose mocked.

"No, he didn't. But can't you see I found myself caught in the middle? My father on one side, you and the boy on the other?"

"You had to know you'd be busted sooner or later."

"I hoped for later. Hoped for a chance to make you mine first."

Rose hooted. "Naturally, that sounds pretty trite right now."

"Nothing's left but to pack up my things, then." He abruptly snagged her by the arm. "And make you understand exactly who I am. C'mon."

Charles had to half carry her up the stairs. To her disgust, her meddling aunts did nothing to intervene. Fine time to cut her off cold turkey! He ushered her into her old bedroom and flicked on the light. She thought of escaping, but his powerful gaze pinned her in place.

"Well?" she prompted, moving to the closet for his duffel bags, then roughly tossing them on the chenille bedspread.

"For starters, you should know that I am sorry for who I am."

"I'm sure you didn't mean that the way it sounded."

"Oh, but I do." He began to empty the dresser, torn with anguish. "My situation is a unique struggle. Sure, I have wealth and all the privileges—something you'll look back upon with anger, I imagine."

"A trip already in progress," she said icily. "But do get to the point."

"But I suffer other slights, especially in the nepotism department. Dad's never paid much attention to me. Dean was always his only pride and joy."

"Until I came along and took him away," she deduced.

"Precisely. After that, Dad had no pride and joy." She lurched in surprise and interest. "You see, that kind of devotion doesn't automatically pass to the next in line. In this case, it jumped a generation. To Lucas."

She packed his socks. "That's what Hilton's up to? Trying to replace Dean with Lucas?"

"Yes. Did so sight unseen, on the basis of a two-inch news clipping."

The torment in Charles's face singed her deep inside, but she held firm to her stoic front. One crack in her armor and she'd be his all over again, blind to the dangers ahead.

"Still, you've been so kind to my child," she challenged. "He's your rival, and you've shown him nothing but affection."

His featured softened. "Partly because he is an innocent child. And my nephew as well! I truly love Lucas, Rose. He can't help being related to Hilton, nor can I."

"But you could've leveled with me long ago. How could you seduce me amidst all the lies, Charles?"

He seized her close. "That part wasn't a lie!"

"How do I know that?" she wailed helplessly.

"Because I'm telling you so."

She broke free for the closet, peeling shirts off hangers with rubbery fingers. "Surely you can see my dilemma, the liar claiming to tell the truth."

He batted the air in concession. "Yes, yes, I can see it. All I know is what we have is real. Look back and feel, Rose."

"When I think back on our talks of Dean, our going Dutch treat—" She broke off in an embarrassed peep. "I feel like a poor dopey relation."

"You and Lucas deserve a slice of the Fraser pie, Rose. Don't you understand by now that I want to help you out and protect your family?"

She unceremoniously stuffed the shirts in a duffel. "You must have been first prepared to help Hilton, though."

"Not in any big battle, not unless you had proven as unfit as he hoped." She turned her slender back to him wiping away the tears springing to her eyes. He trapped her close to the box spring and turned her round. "Honey, one day here and I knew you were capable. Why, one minute here and I knew you were an angel."

"So you didn't give Hilton anything to use against us?"

"I tried to appease him with dumb little things, like the locks, the rickety swing set, the vegetarian meals."

She sniffed hopefully. "Hardly sins, I'd say."

"Of course not. Had I given him absolutely nothing, walked off, he'd have hired a private eye to come in. I managed this the best I could, trying to protect you. I didn't mean for it to end this way. I thought I could string him along a while longer, until you and I were an unshakable team.''

"That might have happened, Charles,'' she admitted sweetly. "If you weren't such a low-down sneak.''

"I am not! Not usually, anyway.''

She worried her lip. "So you think Hilton's got no case?''

He hesitated. "I'm afraid his fancy attorney will make a case.''

"But you said—''

"I can't keep him from the courts. My last-ditch effort just failed.''

"Great! He's impossible to stop.''

"Unless…''

"What, Charles, what?'' She touched him for the first time, her fingers roving his chest. "You got a plan?''

"I was thinking we could get married, Rose. That'd stop him cold.''

"That's your rescue idea? A quickie wedding?'' She paused, torn between suspicion and hope. If he was tricking her again, she'd really be sunk, legally tethered to the family again, Lucas so bonded to Charles. "Is this another of Hilton's ploys?''

Charles flushed, this time wishing she had slapped him instead. "No, my dear,'' he snapped curtly, zipping his bags shut. "The last thing Hilton would do is hand over to you a second son, even a second-rate one like me.'' With that he hoisted his gear over his shoulders and marched out the door.

CHARLES KEPT HIS RED cell phone close that night as he rested in his apartment bed, hoping upon hope that he'd hear some news from Lucas. Leaving him in his finest hour there on the field had been incredibly tough. To his delight, the phone did ring shortly before ten.

"Where are you, Charlie? You go 'cause Mr. Rogue's here?"

Pearce was already hand holding. The jerk had the instincts of a snake. "No way, man."

"Mommy said you got called off."

His version was accurate but unlikely. "You mean called away?"

"Oh, yeah."

"She's right. So, how's the arm?"

"Okay. I shouldn't have cried like a baby about it."

"Everybody cries sometimes, man."

"Even you?"

"Sure."

"You cryin' now?"

Charles blinked moist lashes. "Naw. Hey, about that game today. You did great."

"Yeah… Oh, hi, Mommy. Mommy's here, Charlie. Says I gotta go."

"Take care of yourself," he said quickly.

"When will I see you?"

"Soon, I hope. Bye." Charles broke down then, crying like a baby himself.

CHARLES HAD TO hand it to his father. Hilton managed to rope Calhoon faithfully back into the fold, butt into the Guant account and hurry along a preliminary custody hearing with speed and efficiency. Charles found himself trudging into the downtown courthouse on a gray drizzly Thursday afternoon in mid-June, wishing he were anyplace else on the planet. Rose was standing in the hallway near the courtroom, huddled together with Osgood Pearce and the hotshot lawyer he'd arranged. Though absent from the nest, Charles had been keeping close tabs on its inhabitants, a painful, but necessary responsibility in his mind.

It took forever, but Rose finally broke free to use the water fountain. Charles closed in on her then, blocking her path. "Rose, I'm so sorry things have come this far."

She stared at the floor. "Sure."

"How's Lucas?"

"Fine. In the dark about this. But that luxury won't last much longer." She raised her tired eyes to his. "I'd hoped you wouldn't be here, Charles."

"I'm not here to harm you! I couldn't—"

"Are you sitting with us then?"

"You can ask that," he protested, "when you're cuddled up to Pearce?"

"He's found us a good lawyer who'll accept timed payments."

Some kind of hero. "I hope you don't settle for him on the rebound."

"Certainly none of your business anymore." With that she rushed into court.

The judge seated on the bench was a no-nonsense matron. She listened intently to the Fraser attorney outlining the reasons for the suit, mentioning charges it hoped to prove through its very reliable witness, Charles Fraser. Charles sank a little in his chair, only to feel Hilton's elbow in his ribs, but it didn't rouse him as the lawyer droned on about arrests, unkempt quarters, lax security, poor nutrition. The only thing not covered was Rose's lack of a brassiere. Surely withheld as a surprise barn burner.

Rose's attorney returned with tell of the Fraser's nasty sting operation and gross exaggeration of minor incidents in the Weldon household.

Both sides longed to get ahold of the star witness under oath.

Another court date was set for the following Thursday. Charles was trembling under his charcoal suit as he exited several paces behind the Fraser team. The hall was crowded with opposing relatives. He tried to keep to the wall, intent on the nearest stairs. Despite his evasive tactics, he ran into Daisy, sporting a macramé shawl over a purple frock. Her cagey smile confused him. "If you have a dagger in that stringy sack, use it now."

"I make love not war, remember? So, do you love our girl, or not?"

"I do, dammit. But even a proposal of marriage didn't sway her."

"Well, she's humiliated and confused. Partly my fault too, of course."

Charles arched his brows. "You should know your lawyer's frowning upon our chat."

"The greedy wimp. If this drags on, I'll have to sell the house to pay him."

He touched her hand. "Send me the bill."

"Your generosity reaffirms my faith," she said. "As it is, I have a better way to nip this joke in the bud, if you're game."

He perked right up. "Count me in."

"Meet me at the Four Seasons in thirty minutes and we'll dish."

He affected a scowl. "Daisy Weldon, are you trying to lure me into modeling again?"

"Only trying to prove there really is a free lunch in this world. Ta-ta."

ROSE RETURNED HOME from work the following Monday morning a mere thirty minutes after she left. She joined her aunts in the kitchen where they were piecing together remnants for a quilt. She joined them at the table, drumming her fingers on swatches of fabric. "The nuttiest thing has happened." Daisy and Violet peered at her over their drugstore reading glasses. "Pearce has sold out to somebody. Just like that! Over the weekend."

"Must've been an offer he couldn't refuse," Daisy surmised.

"Definitely. He was ecstatic, packing up, babbling on about a better studio in the city." She propped her chin in her hand. "Funny he didn't call in advance to share the news."

Violet sighed absently. "I suppose he'll be moving to Manhattan."

"Yes, immediately." Rose was openly baffled. "I knew this was his dream, but I didn't think it would happen so abruptly, in the midst of my trial."

"He didn't invite you along or propose or anything?" Daisy queried.

Rose hesitated, her pride taking a direct hit. "Earlier on I thought he'd suggest we join forces to fend off Hilton...."

"But in the end he's just tucked tail and run," Violet observed blandly.

"He did the next best thing to committing though," Daisy protested snidely, "finding us a high-priced shark to drain us dry."

"Okay," Rose cried. "So Osgood hasn't turned out to be heroic material."

"Something you really sensed all the while, dear," Daisy chided gently. "The reason why you didn't encourage him sooner."

Violet shook her curly head. "You just lost your head here at the end and finally accepted him. Sadly, faced with the realities of the burden of a wife and stepson, it seems Osgood grabbed at the first available out."

Rose squinted. "You two don't seem surprised enough by all this."

The aunts shared one of their cryptic stares. "We heard of his closing, but didn't want you to rush over there in a panic and feed his enormous ego."

"I am out of a job! A little panicking should be expected."

"It's my understanding through Beevee that it will remain a gallery."

"So I can reapply there," Rose realized hopefully.

Daisy nodded encouragingly. "Apparently there's some kind of opening this Wednesday night already."

Rose popped up, a new woman. "We must attend, Daisy. Maybe I can save my job, maybe you can chum up to the new owner yourself and finally get the exhibition of your dreams.''

Daisy smacked the table. ''You know I may just join you!''

ROSE KNEW there was something fishy about the new gallery the moment they stepped through the entrance. There was no sign in front advertising a showing, no refreshments, no music, no patrons on the floor. By all appearances the place was closed. That didn't stop Daisy from locking them inside or turning on the overhead fixtures.

Light poured over the showroom, revealing a circle of easels covered with dust sheets. ''Anybody home?'' Daisy sang out.

Charles entered from the stockroom, with an irate Hilton in tow. ''Good evening, ladies.''

Rose squealed in affront, shaking clenched fists. ''This is outrageous!''

''Ditto,'' Hilton snapped. ''Someone better talk fast or I'm leaving!''

''It's in your interest to stay, Dad. Daisy is about to give us a preview of her art.''

''I don't give a damn!''

''You will.'' Charles strode to the first easel, sweeping off the cover. Rose and Hilton gasped at the sight of a beautiful sketch of Lucas and Charles out on the ball field. Charles flicked off cover after cover to expose other sketches and watercolors of man and boy at play with the bike, the Beast. The last was the best, a watercolor of Charles and Lucas, asleep in the rocking chair, with Dean's old lamp in the background.

Hilton's mouth pruned, his eyes moistened. ''So, what does this mean?''

''It means that we'll stomp you in court, Hilton,'' Daisy proclaimed. ''As hard as you might try to disgrace us, these pictures, along with Charles's honest testimony, will tell the true story.''

Rose was dumbfounded. "This is the new vein your art has taken?"

"Yes. Of course I didn't expect them to be so useful, but no showing Osgood could've supplied me would be more satisfying than this one."

Rose threw her arms around her aunt. "You did it! You saved us!"

"And without that overpriced attorney," she retorted proudly.

"Hang on to your peace sign just a minute," Hilton barked. "Do you really think this is enough to slap me down, with that brilliant, adorable child's future at stake?"

Daisy grinned. "No, Hilton, a mule like you naturally needs more." She approached the final easel, whisking off the cover. There was a golden-framed oil underneath, of a very proud man in naked splendor.

"You got Charles to pose after all!" Rose clamped a hand to her mouth. "Daisy, you can't hope to humiliate him in court with this."

"I wouldn't," she crowed. "It's Hilton I hope to humiliate. It's *him*."

"No way." Rose advanced on the easel with teenage eagerness, studying the proud, sinewy model. "No shortage of magenta oil back then."

Daisy sauntered closer. "Had a bigger budget, more guts, too. It wasn't easy, but I tracked this down to a dear friend back in the village. How fortunate that she kept it."

"Will you females quit staring at me that way!" Hilton bellowed.

They inspected the older, fully clothed, in-person version, then shifted back to the portrait again.

He shook a bony finger. "How dare you, Daisy. How dare you—?"

"Remember you, Hilly, from the wild Greenwich Village days?"

He hung his peppered head. "I was so sure you'd forgotten. You never said a word when Dean courted Rose."

"I've always felt the past was done. The sixties were swinging for everyone. If some wished to forget, I understood. But you stretched even my elastic ethics, Hilly, with this atrocious excuse for grandparenting."

This last portrait was even a surprise to Charles. "Dad, I don't believe this! You knew Daisy before Dean knew Rose? No wonder you were so set in your opinions on the Weldon sisters. They held your racy past in their memory banks."

Hilton ignored his son, speaking to Daisy in a grumble. "What are your terms?"

"Let's start with my *point*. It's only human to have some flaws. You've got a nerve trying to exploit ours for gain. You know full well Violet and I are decent women who enjoy a liberal stand. Just because you chose to abandon your bohemian ways, reshape your image into a boring old poop, doesn't mean we're suddenly wrong."

Charles marveled. "I can't believe you weren't always a boring old poop."

"I worked a summer in a jazz club, experimented a little. So what!"

Daisy hooted. "You did a lot more than that! Admit that Charles is right. We Weldons make you nervous because we can blow your cover."

"I never did let go—not like you—not with you!"

Daisy fluttered her silver lashes prettily, but her voice held steel. "I have a remarkable memory. Shall I do a sketch of one of our sessions, during a heat wave, when I wore only a painting smock?"

"No!" He harshly brushed her off. "Just tell me what you want. But don't think of cutting me off from Lucas. I couldn't stand it."

"The idea of losing him completely is horrible, isn't it?" Rose taunted.

Daisy confronted Hilton, her heels bringing them nose to nose. "Here's the deal, back off the custody case and agree to normal visits. And accept that Lucas is perfectly fine where he lives. Should be easy enough with your own son attributing to the fact."

"Very well, you have a deal. But what about that mealy-looking Pearce? Rose can't be serious about him."

Charles swiftly responded. "Don't worry, Dad, Pearce is gone."

Rose gasped. "You bought him out, Charles, didn't you?"

"Yes," he admitted solemnly.

Rose shook her head in awe. "He let you win, just like that?"

"He has no idea I'm the real buyer. Would've charged me double had he known."

"Or not left me at all!"

Charles closed in on her. "I'm sorry, but he jumped at the chance to leave town. Guess the pressure of commitment proved too much."

"And who made it too much? You Frasers!"

His patience snapped like a dry twig. "Like you ever cared for him! You think I'd buy this place for you and Daisy if I thought you did!"

"For us?" She distanced herself a few paces. "I'm not taking this place."

"Speak for yourself," Daisy crowed, looking around with approval.

Hilton glanced at his watch. "Let's cut bait and go, Charles. You've made the biggest fool out of yourself, rescuing these hippies, making a joke out of my lawsuit. Now we've ended up with nothing!"

"Nothing?" Daisy seethed. "Hilly, you were blessed with two fine sons and a grandson—with room for expansion!" She gestured to Charles and Rose. "Why destroy this union when Lucas turned out so well? Would it really be so bad if these two kept our bloodlines mixed?"

"Enough!" Rose cried. "I'm sick of this manipulation, the fake father, the bought-off boss, the gift of this gallery—and now matchmaking? I've always taken pride in running my own life, and I want that feeling back.''

"But half this place is yours," Daisy said, following her to the door. "I insist you take it."

"Do you?" Rose frowned ferociously. "Then I believe I'll open a rib joint on my side!" Assured that Daisy was appalled, she flounced out.

Charles was in pursuit, his temper boiling, too. He grabbed her arm, detaining her on the sidewalk. "You're not walking home alone in the dark."

"Woe to anybody who dares harass me tonight. Now buzz off."

"I left something behind at your place and I'd just as soon collect it."

She sagged a little. "Oh, very well. But don't you dare touch me!"

Violet was on the porch swing when they arrived, walking in sync at arm's length. "He's forgotten something, that's all," Rose was quick to report.

"I said I *left* something here," he gently corrected, following her up the steps.

With a nod of encouragement to Charles, Violet slipped into the house.

"There's a difference?" Rose challenged, tapping her foot on the porch flooring.

He anxiously searched her face. "All my happiness, my dreams of a future family. Lost items, not forgotten ones."

"You Frasers are so high-handed, Charles, spying on me, then buying out the gallery to get rid of Osgood."

"I've only been trying to undo the damage that I have done. I figured I drove you into Pearce's arms, and I felt it my duty to rectify that mistake."

"You had no right! Over and over, you had no right."

At the end of his rope, his voice shook with raw emotion. "Do you think I could live with the knowledge that he had you? Do you think I could live without you under any terms, for that matter?"

"Oh, Charlie," she sobbed, swiping her eyes. "Quit getting to me all over again."

He hooked her chin with his thumb, eyeing her keenly. "You do still love me, don't you?"

"I love the man I thought I knew."

"I am that man. Only a change of last name and career are necessary."

"How will we ever explain this fiasco to people?" she lamented.

Violet hovered behind the screen. "Since when do Weldons explain?"

Charles made approving sounds. "I'm seriously thinking of becoming a Weldon. Adopt me, Violet, streamline the process."

"You're already in, dear. We voted."

Rose gasped in dismay. "I didn't vote!"

"You were outnumbered in any case," Violet chuckled.

Charles grasped her shoulders in a last-ditch rush. "I'm a desperate, sorrowful man who's suffered enough. Just think, for instance, of having to live down that garish nude oil. Which you mistook for me," he suddenly recalled with irritation.

"Only for a moment," she consoled. "You are, shall we say, better endowed?"

"Say it all you like." Spotting a twinkle in her eye he dipped down to kiss her.

She nuzzled in his shirt. "I do love you so, Charlie. I can't help myself."

"Mmm, I could go on like this for...six minutes."

Carefree laughter spouted from Rose. "That's all I need, two guys using the six-minute line."

"Hey, Charlie, thought I heard ya." Lucas bounced out the screen door in his pajamas. "Glad you're back. Very, very."

Charles scooped him up to his chest. "You should be asleep."

"What you guys doin'?"

246 **Father Figure**

"Well, I was about to check with Mom here and see if she's ready to marry me." He met her gaze tenderly. "The pressure's off, thanks to Daisy. And any doubts should be gone too, thanks to my fast talkin'."

"What do you say, Mommy?"

Rose looked from man to boy, noting how well their dimples matched. "I have to say yes. How can we possibly break up this family?"

Charles's mouth curved sensuously. "A family due for expansion."

Rose opened the door for Charles and her son. "I'd like to see a ring first, if you please."

"Heck," he squawked. "I just gave you a whole half gallery."

She let go of the screen door and it booted him in the rear.

"Don't worry, Dad," Lucas said with a conspiratory grin as he threw his arms around Charles's neck. "We'll work on her."

Head Down Under for twelve tales of heated romance in beautiful and untamed Australia!

Here's a sneak preview of the first novel in THE AUSTRALIANS

Outback Heat by Emma Darcy
available July 1998

'HAVE I DONE something wrong?' Angie persisted, wishing Taylor would emit a sense of camaraderie instead of holding an impenetrable reserve.

'Not at all,' he assured her. 'I would say a lot of things right. You seem to be fitting into our little Outback community very well. I've heard only good things about you.'

'They're nice people,' she said sincerely. Only the Maguire family kept her shut out of their hearts.

'Yes,' he agreed. 'Though I appreciate it's taken considerable effort from you. It is a world away from what you're used to.'

The control Angie had been exerting over her feelings snapped. He wasn't as blatant as his aunt in his prejudice against her but she'd felt it coming through every word he'd spoken and she didn't deserve any of it.

'Don't judge me by your wife!'

His jaw jerked. A flicker of some dark emotion destroyed the steady power of his probing gaze.

'No two people are the same. If you don't know that, you're a man of very limited vision. So I come from the city as your wife did! That doesn't stop me from being an individual in my own right.'

She straightened up, proudly defiant, furiously angry with the situation. 'I'm *me*. Angie Cordell. And it's time you took the blinkers off your eyes, Taylor Maguire.'

Then she whirled away from him, too agitated by the explosive expulsion of her emotion to keep facing him.

The storm outside hadn't yet eased. There was nowhere to go. She stopped at the window, staring blindly at the torrential rain. The thundering on the roof was almost deafening but it wasn't as loud as the silence behind her.

'You want me to go, don't you? You've given me a month's respite and now you want me to leave and channel my energies somewhere else.'

'I didn't say that, Angie.'

'You were working your way around to it.' Bitterness at his tactics spewed the suspicion. 'Do you have your first choice of governess waiting in the wings?'

'No. I said I'd give you a chance.'

'Have you?' She swung around to face him. 'Have you really, Taylor?'

He hadn't moved. He didn't move now except to make a gesture of appeasement. 'Angie, I was merely trying to ascertain how you felt.'

'Then let me tell you your cynicism was shining through every word.'

He frowned, shook his head. 'I didn't mean to hurt you.' The blue eyes fastened on hers with devastating sincerity. 'I truly did not come in here to take you down or suggest you leave.'

Her heart jiggled painfully. He might be speaking the truth but the judgements were still there, the judgements that ruled his attitude towards her, that kept her shut out of his life, denied any real sharing with him, denied his confidence and trust. She didn't know why it meant so much to her but it did. It did. And the need to fight for justice from him was as much a raging torrent inside her as the rain outside.

Take 2 bestselling love stories FREE

Plus get a FREE surprise gift!

THE BRIDES

HARLEQUIN®

AMERICAN ♦ ROMANCE®

There's nothing like a white wedding
bash to have the most eligible
bachelors running for cover—
especially in the Wild West
town of Grazer's Corners!

For a rolicking good time, don't miss
THE BRIDES OF GRAZER'S CORNERS

July 1998
THE COWBOY & THE SHOTGUN BRIDE
by Jacqueline Diamond (#734)

August 1998
A BACHELOR FOR THE BRIDE
by Mindy Neff (#739)

September 1998
THE HOG-TIED GROOM
by Charlotte Maclay (#743)

Available at your favorite retail outlet.

HARLEQUIN®
*M*akes any time special ™

OF GRAZER'S CORNERS

Don't miss these Harlequin favorites by some of our bestselling authors!

HT#25721	THE ONLY MAN IN WYOMING	$3.50 U.S.	☐
	by Kristine Rolofson	$3.99 CAN.	☐
HP#11869	WICKED CAPRICE	$3.50 U.S.	☐
	by Anne Mather	$3.99 CAN.	☐
HR#03438	ACCIDENTAL WIFE	$3.25 U.S.	☐
	by Day Leclaire	$3.75 CAN.	☐
HS#70737	STRANGERS WHEN WE MEET	$3.99 U.S.	☐
	by Rebecca Winters	$4.50 CAN.	☐
HI#22405	HERO FOR HIRE	$3.75 U.S.	☐
	by Laura Kenner	$4.25 CAN.	☐
HAR#16673	ONE HOT COWBOY	$3.75 U.S.	☐
	by Cathy Gillen Thacker	$4.25 CAN.	☐
HH#28952	JADE	$4.99 U.S.	☐
	by Ruth Langan	$5.50 CAN.	☐
LL#44005	STUCK WITH YOU	$3.50 U.S.	☐
	by Vicki Lewis Thompson	$3.99 CAN.	☐

(limited quantities available on certain titles)

AMOUNT	$ _____
POSTAGE & HANDLING	$ _____
($1.00 for one book, 50¢ for each additional)	
APPLICABLE TAXES*	$ _____
TOTAL PAYABLE	$ _____

(check or money order—please do not send cash)

To order, complete this form and send it, along with a check or money order for the total above, payable to Harlequin Books, to: **In the U.S.:** 3010 Walden Avenue, P.O. Box 9047, Buffalo, NY 14269-9047; **In Canada:** P.O. Box 613, Fort Erie, Ontario, L2A 5X3.

Name: _____

Address: _____ City: _____

State/Prov.: _____ Zip/Postal Code: _____

Account Number (if applicable): _____

*New York residents remit applicable sales taxes.
Canadian residents remit applicable GST and provincial taxes.

Look us up on-line at: http://www.romance.net

HBLAJ98

DEBBIE MACOMBER

invites you to the

HEART OF TEXAS

Join Debbie Macomber as she brings you the lives and loves of the folks in the ranching community of Promise, Texas.

If you loved Midnight Sons—don't miss Heart of Texas! A brand-new six-book series from Debbie Macomber.

Available in February 1998 at your favorite retail store.

Heart of Texas by Debbie Macomber

Lonesome Cowboy	February '98
Texas Two-Step	March '98
Caroline's Child	April '98
Dr. Texas	May '98
Nell's Cowboy	June '98
Lone Star Baby	July '98

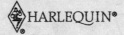

HARLEQUIN®

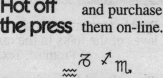

COMING NEXT MONTH

#733 AKA: MARRIAGE by Jule McBride
Big Apple Babies
When Shane Holiday offered marriage to Lillian Smith so she could adopt a baby, he did it to get close to the woman he'd tracked for seven years. But what started as marriage with an agenda suddenly had Shane thinking he was a husband and daddy for real!

#734 THE COWBOY & THE SHOTGUN BRIDE by Jacqueline Diamond
The Brides of Grazer's Corners
One minute Kate Bingham was about to say "I do," the next she was swept off her feet by sexy fugitive Mitch Connery. Although Mitch was innocent, Kate's newly awakened desires were not!

#735 MY DADDY THE DUKE by Judy Christenberry
When her grandmother, the Dowager Duchess, put out an APB on her dad as the World's Most Eligible Bachelor traveling in the U.S. to find a wife, little Penelope Morris went along with her father's disguise as typical Americans. As long as he stayed close to Sydney Thomas, who Pen handpicked to be her new mommy!

#736 DADDY 101 by Jo Leigh
Along with the fortune he had inherited, Alex Bradlee got a set of rules for love. They'd served him well...until he met Dr. Dani Jacobson, who had some rules of her own, the first of which was "Run—don't walk—away." But her daughter had other ideas....

AVAILABLE THIS MONTH:

#729 WANTED: DADDY
Mollie Molay

#731 HUSBAND 101
Jo Leigh

**#730 THE BRIDE TO BE...
OR NOT TO BE?**
Debbi Rawlins

#732 FATHER FIGURE
Leandra Logan

Look us up on-line at: http://www.romance.net